David Crackanthorpe was born at Newbiggin in the county of Westmoreland, where his family had lived for some eight hundred years. His antecedents include Richard Crackanthorpe, the 16th-century logician mentioned by Sterne in *Tristram Shandy*, William and Dorothy Wordsworth and the notorious Daniel E. Sickles, a general in the American Civil War. He studied law at Oxford University and practised as a barrister in London, where he married the Irish actress Helena Hughes, now deceased. He has written a biography of Hubert Crackanthorpe, a young writer of the 1890s associated with the *Yellow Book*. He lives in France where he has worked as a forester, gardener and cultivator of olive trees.

David Crackanthorpe

THE
RAVENGLASS
LINE

review

First published in 2001
by Review

An imprint of Headline Book Publishing

10 9 8 7 6 5 4 3 2 1

British Library Cataloguing in Publication Data

Crackanthorpe, David
The ravenglass line
I.Title
823.9'14[F]

ISBN 0 7472 7045 7

Typeset by
Letterpart Limited, Reigate, Surrey

Printed and bound in Great Britain by
Clays Ltd, St Ives plc.

Headline Book Publishing
A division of Hodder Headline
338 Euston Road
London NW1 3BH

www.reviewbooks.co.uk
www.hodderheadline.com

For Jennifer Lowther

In token

Part One

Chapter One

'RICARDO. ON YOUR feet.' Jason lowered them into his trainers and stood. You don't overdress in an oven and with four of them in here the stink rose, but didn't set, with the sun. 'Get a shirt on.'

They say if you've done time in a cash-down boarding school, prison afterwards comes as no great shock. Well, Jason had only walked, or been thrown, out from a couple and he was not hardened. He'd found sixteen weeks banged up in the Baumettes on the outskirts of Marseille long and painful. Every time there was a clicking of keys on the far side of the door, vague hopes rose.

'Bring your stuff.' He was being moved again. He must be a subversive element. Or they'd decided to share him round because he was known to still have a bit of cash about him.

'Where are we going?'

'In a British prison you ask such questions? Like a club? Not here.' There were two of them and they marched him along a corridor and upstairs. From a narrow window he saw the blue water and the islands out there for the first time since he came in. Desert mirage through bars. They entered the assistant governor's office.

'Ricardo, the examining magistrate orders your release,' the assistant governor said without looking up.

'I'm acquitted?'

'In no way. You leave these gates on conditions and provisionally.' The assistant governor detailed the conditions but Jason hardly listened. The sea was there and the SS *Kendal*, his ship, was in the docks. A tramp steamer can slip away without a lot of trouble because these days everyone's pleased to see the old tub go. Anyway, the docks were mostly deserted. Trade had died out. Just car ferries to Corsica and cruises for the retired. 'Did this man have a weapon when he was brought in?'

'*Non, Monsieur.* He seems a peaceful type.'

'No fights?'

'He can look after himself.' They all stared at Jason, up and down. 'The men are careful of him now.'

'Give him his pay and papers and put him on the street. Not the passport. That goes to the judge.'

'Thank you,' Jason said.

'We'll see you again,' the assistant governor said, and looked at his watch. 'Make sure it isn't on a new charge. You'd go out of circulation for a long time. The judges don't like Englishmen who play about with the trade in *stupéfiants*.' It was midday.

On the pavement, Jason totted up. He was down to his last five hundred or so francs. A taxi to the docks, a look round the *Kendal* to see what was left, then a promenade on the Vieux Port, note who was about, what the chances were. Five hundred would soon go. There was always Alex. Alex often had something on the back burner. But he could be tricky, especially if he thought you thought he was under some obligation. Also, he was up there in Paris.

No need to search for that taxi. There was one waiting the

other side of the road in the roasting sun, and standing beside it, looking this way, was Hugh, the one good thing in what had lately been a decidedly crappy world. A letter every week throughout the four months. Jason ran over and they put their arms round each other like Mediterranean brothers. As they were, fifty per cent; their father was off these shores even if it wasn't known for sure which one, and it was too late to ask. Jason put his money on Malta.

'You need a drink and a square meal,' Hugh said. Jason stepped back to have a look at him. White linen suit, razor sharp, oval shades, Italian shoes. He blended perfectly. Good-looking too, in a neat way. Jason knew he was more clumsily put together than Hugh, and less buttoned-up. Hugh had the Mediterranean physique and he had the temperament – fugitive and fickle, so it went.

'How did you know they were kicking me out today?' Jason asked. Like school, when Hugh had never been kicked out of anywhere. Now they were both laughing on the pavement, Hugh holding the car door.

'I fixed it,' he said. 'Get in.' The driver seemed to know where to go. They took the Avenue du Prado and turned along the Corniche towards the Vieux Port. Jason watched the sea open and close and open again as the taxi rounded the steep bends. He ought to say something to Hugh, thank him, for example.

'Where are we making for?' he said.

'I have to explain a few things, Jason,' Hugh said as the masts in the port came into view at the end of a high narrow street. 'Bring you up to date.'

'What on?'

'The bottom line.'

He must mean the Ravenglass profit and loss, his chief

concern in life. *I.e.* mostly loss on unviable tramp steaming. *I.e.* the *Kendal*. Hugh was sweating heavily; it was coming through the linen of his sharp suit. 'Let's stop and pour a bit of drink in us,' Jason said. 'And before we go down to the bottom line, remember I need the *Kendal*. She's about all I've got.'

The golden days of shipping when everyone knew who ruled the waves and even a small affair like Ravenglass made easy money – they were a thing of the past. Now the few remaining tramp steamers slunk about the seas under a Maltese flag while the company, waiting for planned diversification into road haulage to get going, fed off its reserves of fat. Not helped by the private activities of its owner Mrs May Ricardo. May left the management of the business in Hugh's hands and concentrated her energy on pleasures, emotions, and philanthropy – expensive tastes, the lot of them.

Hugh was never her preferred son; he was steady and stealthy, a north country Ravenglass. Now Jason, the elder, that was different. Hugh had watched May's reaction reading Jason's latest scribbled note from the Baumettes. He could see she took vicarious pleasure in the excitements of Jason's life and obviously respected him for paying up like a man. Not that Jason had any choice: he'd got caught, but that made no difference to May. She had her own system. Jason might be fickle and on the run like his father, of whom Hugh had never heard her speak a good word in his life, but she still liked him best. Hugh didn't resent the favouritism and never had. It somehow seemed Jason's right. Anyway, he got his hands on a lot more money than Jason ever did. And over there, still behind bars, Jason must be brought pretty low.

Today, two items of awkward news on family matters took Hugh's mind off the worrying bottom line. He had a meeting with the Ravenglass legal adviser, Deakin of Deakin & Deakin, under the trees of the Victoria Embankment where no one would overhear them, shaded from the terrific heat of the July sun and with an illusion of cool air rising off the Thanes.

'With due respect to Mrs Ricardo,' whispered Deakin & Deakin, 'I feel you ought to know that in my view she wants watching. Speaking as an old friend.'

'Watching at what? You know she lives a pretty free and active—'

'I believe so,' said the lawyer stiffly. 'And I was instructed in her divorce. That's not what I mean. I refer to the cause she has espoused.'

'You mean her refugees?'

'Yes, the refugees. And her friend—' he murmured the name close to Hugh's ear '—Mr Seker.'

'She isn't involved with Charlie Seker any more.'

'Not so closely perhaps. But I've reason to think there have been payments. Substantial ones. And recent.'

'It's her own money.'

'Ravenglass isn't a limited company. There's no thin red line between your mother's account and the Ravenglass account. Even more serious, the payments are an index of something worse.' They'd reached Cleopatra's Needle and the legal adviser stood studying the hieroglyphs and then the sky. 'There's money these days in refugees. Sad but true. And what strikes me, as your company and family lawyer, is that while your mother in good faith puts money in, Mr Seker seems to be by way of getting it out. He and his associates, Miller and Emanuel Solicitors, well known to me by repute, are up on an application for legal aid franchise in refugee asylum cases.'

'Isn't that a good thing?'

'A good thing? I dare say. But for who?'

'I mean the refugees, to help out?'

'The procedure can run for years. Legal aid flows in and the asylum-seekers disappear. You just need to argue well-founded fear of persecution. There's plenty of that,' Deakin said above the roar of the buses.

'A racket?'

'Potentially, a terrific racket.'

'And my mother's in it?'

The lawyer looked shocked. 'Without a shadow of *mens rea*,' he breathed. 'But in need of watching. This is where I cross.'

'I can't watch over her,' Hugh said as they stood on the island in the middle of the traffic. 'She'd be suspicious. I keep the books. She doesn't exactly love having me hang round her at the best of times. I'm not the preferred son.'

'Rum lot,' Deakin muttered; then added more loudly, 'I was thinking rather of your prodigal, if he's the one she likes, for him to keep an eye open. Where is he?'

'Jason's in the Baumettes prison in Marseille, pending investigations.'

'On what charge?'

'He ferried some clandestine Moroccans over the Mediterranean in the SS *Kendal*—'

'One of yours?'

'One of the last. They were picked up on landing with a whole lot of drugs.'

'Soft?'

'Cocktails, they call them.'

'He's held as accessory?'

'That's all so far.'

'They could hold him for years without trial. The system over there . . . and five or six to a cell, I've heard. I'll see my partner who deals with French law. We might lift him on bail.'

'Your firm—?'

'No. You would go over. My partner can send you to the right people. You will have to offer sureties.'

'Sounds heavy. There are liquidity problems at Ravenglass right now.'

'Mrs Ricardo needs protection from her own generous impulses. And remember there's no thin red line. If she goes down – Ravenglass goes with her. Keep me posted. Any way I can help – as I say, your mother's an old friend.' By the way he said it, probably an old lover too.

Hugh crossed the river by Blackfriars Bridge and walked towards the Ravenglass office on the Southwark fringes. If he rescued Jason there would be a shift of the balance. Jason never was able to hang on to cash; very likely he had nothing left from the Moroccans, and Hugh would be giving him a mission and stipend. He would come back in range of market forces. The lawyer's idea had a lot to be said for it. Hugh felt warmly about getting Jason out. And it was good he'd written him those supportive letters. He'd meant them. Jason was a leading light and Hugh wasn't a man with a lot of friends. Come to think of it, Jason was about the only one.

The day's second item of news reached Hugh from the vehicle yard at the rear of the office building. Several of the new trucks that the future viability of the company depended on were lined up against the wall, shiny and sleek, with 'Ricardo' prominently on both sides and 'Ravenglass' rather smaller. These were container trucks – the name of the game nowadays. Not laboriously filling some old rust-bucket like the *Kendal* with flour, to be as laboriously unloaded the other side of the water. Containerisation, also known as ro-ro. Roll on, roll off.

'Not like your dream lover,' is what his wife Rosie had said

9

about that. 'Roll on roll off.' Hugh laughed but felt uneasy with the allusion. Jason always knew about taking his time in the love department. Hugh turned his attention to the line of trucks and saw one of the drivers crossing the yard towards him. These men were important and must be made to feel indispensable.

'Like a quick word, Mr Ricardo.'

'Any time.'

'A bit off the record.'

'Come on to my office.'

'Be better up in my cab.' They settled in among the pin-ups. 'You said to always keep a watch out on the competition, Mr Ricardo.'

'That's right.'

'Well, I can tell you something about those furniture vans your pal Seker's running under the Tunnel.'

'Seker isn't a pal of mine, specially.'

'I've seen him here in the office.'

'On business. I sold him the vans.'

'Well this is business all right. The funny kind. A mate of mine drives one of those vans. Goods for tax exiles, he says. And filling up for the return with different goods in Brussels. Goods is the word and that's what bothers my pal, and which is why he told me. In among the stuff from Brussels, there's people.'

'Refugees? No papers probably. People on the run. Seker fixes help for them over here – legal aid, moves like that.'

'These ones don't run anywhere. They're shut in crates. Legal aid isn't what they need most. It's food and water. Women and children, he says, though he's never seen them. He tells by the weight. And from the sound.'

'Where does he deliver them?'

'Another bloke takes over his waggon here in town. That's the last he sees of the crates.'

'Thanks for telling me. You've done the right thing. I'll remember it.'

'I won't forget, neither,' said the driver. 'Question is, what're you going to do about it?'

'Investigate on the quiet,' said Hugh. 'Leave it with me. No point your mate losing his job, not these days.'

So Seker was a wrong guy in more ways than one. Here was something Jason would have to find out, or hopefully not find out, for himself. Hugh didn't want Jason sidetracked by old-fashioned chivalrous impulses. Dodgy operations with females in crates, no concern of theirs, would take his mind off the essential task. His brief would just be to take a look at the dealings between May and Seker. That affair had lasted a long time but Hugh knew for sure that carnal relations were no longer on the agenda. And a good thing too. He thought his mother should lead a quieter life in every way.

'You ought to mind your own business,' Rosie'd said when he admitted to this.

'The Ravenglass Line is my business.'

'But not your mother's sex life.'

'I don't want her getting hurt.'

'I thought you knew her better,' Rosie said. 'Anyway, I think it's just oedipal prurience.' She sometimes produced ideas like this when she was tense. 'Hurt, she isn't going to get, believe me.'

'I'm thinking of her best interests,' Hugh said. 'Jason will too.'

'Sometimes I wonder if I'll ever meet this Jason of yours. If he exists.'

'You will, soon. And I want you to try and like him.'

11

'Bit of a hero for you isn't he?' Rosie raised a hand to his cheek; a brief, dry touch like setting something in place on a shelf. 'I'll see. No promises,' she said.

Whatever way it turned out, one advantage of the plan was that Jason would be off to Marseille when he'd done his stuff. No point in him hanging round London with no income. Bail would be provisional. While he looked out his passport for tomorrow Hugh went over it. Why should they ever disagree? They never had, confidence reigned; Jason chose the sea and he chose the office. Jason had the *Kendal* and he had Rosie. Gazing at his own photograph, Hugh had a brilliant idea. As general manager of the Ravenglass Line, he could offer the *Kendal* in surety for Jason's bail. That would cost nothing; the ship was Jason's only home and it wasn't going anywhere. No more gainful employment awaited it. It was a liability but Jason loved it, and when the time came he would give himself up rather than do a runner and see it forfeited. That much was sure. The idea was bombproof. And he'd soon be seeing Jason which was a lift and a warm feeling again. He could show off Rosie while they were still so obviously in love. It would probably make Jason feel quite old.

Chapter Two

JASON PAID FOR the drinks. It was his first free act and it felt good. Also there was an air-conditioner in this bar and Hugh looked cooler. Still a bit . . . shifty perhaps, like not perfectly on the level, but that could go with the suit. Local colouring. Hugh asked if he had reserves stashed away somewhere outside.

'Not a sou.'

'No bank account?'

'It's a while since I had a cheque book, Hugh. In fact not since I had a salary.'

'You're still getting pension rights.'

'Oh great.'

'Live on cash?' The inside pocket of the Armani jacket must be weighed down with credit cards.

'Nothing but.'

'Then you'll need some.'

'That's what the *Kendal*'s for. You don't send her out but I know a few who will. The sea's an open highway. It used to say so on the Ravenglass notepaper.'

Hugh didn't answer this straight away. Under the Maltese flag practices went on that no one at Lloyd's would like to hear about. 'We insure her,' he said. You bet. Over insure, probably. Jason only ever saw the certificate. 'But not for ever—'

'You sold the *Kendal* while I was banged up?' Jason wished they could have stopped this, like a lift going down, at the level of jokes and farces.

'Oh no. Who'd buy her? If she'd been saleable—'

'You'd have sold her long ago?'

'Just as well not, as it turns out. Let's grab another taxi.' Before he got in, Hugh directed it to the docks. 'La Joliette. Gate 3A.'

'That's not where I left her,' Jason said.

'I've got to explain some things,' Hugh said a second time as soon as they moved off into the traffic.

'No one's died? May never wrote.' If that had happened Jason would be really sorry. There was a question of identity in there.

Hugh laughed. 'Don't worry. We'll be coming round to her. The world's still her breakfast oyster. I mean about reality.' Jason knew that when people get on to reality it's best to wait and give them time to work something out. And reality had always been Hugh's thing. Too much. And getting it together, he was hot on that too. Those were the values that put you into Armani suits. 'Reality's taken the *Kendal*, is what I'm getting at.' Hugh edged away, watching. But he was the one who had the temper, not Jason. He would go white in the face and reach for the nearest sharp or heavy object. It happened about twice a year and was part of life. Rising to it would be impossible, against nature. You rose above.

'Is that right?' Jason said. 'How?'

'Didn't they tell you you're on bail? I put the *Kendal* up as surety. We get her back the day you give yourself up for trial.' Hugh touched his arm. 'The advocate's all lined up and paid.'

'Smart work, Hugh.' He meant it. It was a simple equation,

but it hamstrung him. There'd be no slipping out of La Joliette without lights on a moonless night. He was left with Hugh as a lifeline and that was what Hugh was holding back. The one good deed in a crappy world was beginning to look a bit curled up at the edges. 'Have they put the seals on her?'

'Not yet. The court bailiff's at the dock gates. I've said your belongings are on the ship, you'll need to fetch things. We have the okay for that, then they put the seals on.'

'I left three men in the *Kendal.*'

'Paid off. The ship's empty.'

There was no cash on board, but there was a spare passport when he left. 'Do I have to clock in? Weekly? Monthly? In this country trials wait for ever.'

Hugh wiped his brow and moved the other hand to indicate the driver's back. 'Later,' he said.

'What gate again? 3A?' the driver asked. Jason knew that 3A led to a fouled-up backwater for ships waiting to go out of commission; and further on, to the dry docks. Mostly used these days for breaking up. So the *Kendal* had been shifted for her last journey.

At the gate, the watchman on duty seemed to remember him. 'It's you. Well captain, the bosses and the lawyers, they're fucking your ship for you,' he said. 'I hear her creaking in the night like a used-up old whore.' He raised a fist and a blast of the day's red wine intake blew through the taxi window.

'Drive on to the quay,' Hugh ordered. So he still didn't care for talk like that between strangers. It was used to disarm and naturalise, but on him it had the opposite effect. In adolescence Hugh used to have a little snag with premature ejaculation. Jason never took it seriously. A tosser's problem, not a headache for a Ricardo. The reality Hugh went in for so hard must have got it sorted by now.

'Will they break her up?' he said.

'You mean if you disappear?'

'Can they?'

'I think so,' Hugh said. 'But if you give yourself up on the day, they can't do a thing.'

'You're keeping the insurance going?'

'Where now?' the driver asked. He had one arm hanging from the window and held the steering wheel between two fingers of the other hand, while the taxi lurched across the uneven surface of the quay. Out over the sea a thundercloud, black at the base, bore down on the coast with others behind it, swelling up from the horizon. It was the time of day when the July heat in town sapped interest in survival. This driver spoke with Mediterranean fatalism; if they said into the water, that's where he'd go. In the Baumettes Jason had learned more about despair and the Mediterranean temperament – Corsican, French, North African, his own – than he'd picked up in all his years of chasing around as a free man with Ravenglass privileges behind him.

'Môle D. Quai Wilson,' Hugh said. But the driver failed to understand him. Hugh's French was purposefully anglicised. Jason explained.

'Just out of the Baumettes?' the driver said, tapping the side of his nose. 'And is he your *papa-gâteau, l'Anglais?*'

'Meaning what?'

'Pederasts,' the driver explained. 'They fetch their little friends from there every day of the week. They meet inside.'

'This is my brother,' Jason said. Why? Who cared? Not the taxi driver. It was because there was something between brothers that had to be named, that was why he said it. Luckily for Hugh and him the watchword was trust. 'My younger brother.'

'He looks older. It must be like in Corsica. One elegant

16

brother, the other in the shit. Excuse me, I didn't mean to presume.' If they'd been Corsicans, apology wouldn't have wiped out presumption.

'There's my ship,' Jason said.

'A right old sieve.' The driver sounded much more cheerful now.

From the deck, you saw across the top of the breakwater built of grey-pink limestone quarried from the surrounding hills. The storm was already above the islands, flashes striking the water while the background darkness drew across the sea. In a few minutes the sky would split open on docks and town. Under his feet, Jason could feel the ship stir in the first swell. There were cockroaches on board, and probably rats, and no electricity or water. The inside of the ship stank of blocked latrine and oil and waste, and the sound of their steps rang on metal and echoed round deserted companionways. Infections everywhere. Plagues of a deserted hulk.

'Enough to send you up the wall. Fetch your gear and let's clear out,' Hugh said just as the first drops, hard as bullets, hit the carcase of the *Kendal.*

'When did you pay off the men?'

'When the ship was moved.'

'Before you gave her as surety, then.'

'She can't sail away without you Jason. They wanted wages.'

'Those men trusted me.' But there was no point going on. The men had left a bit sooner than they would have had to anyway, that was all. Trust was an idea with no salary attached.

'I've got a project for you,' Hugh said. 'Something in your line. We'll talk about it when we get away from this ghastly bloody boat and into a hotel with air-conditioning and another drink.' Hugh didn't match the surroundings now. He looked as if all the breath had been sucked out of him by the heat.

'You'd better get off and under cover. I'll join you,' Jason said.

He found his cabin rifled, which was no surprise. It was probably done when the famous trust ran out. There was nothing worth rescuing here; only, in a compartment behind a bulkhead, that spare passport obtained a couple of years back – through the good offices of a Maltese civil servant he'd been able to help with a sensitive problem of maritime carriage, religious art works, Jason believed, for clandestine export. But he hadn't opened the crate to find out. A far-sighted deal, and with his British passport in the hands of the examining judge, one that was going to pay dividends. He found a wrench and removed the plate hiding the compartment. Thank God the passport was still there, with the only scrawls he'd had from the one woman he ever regretted. She'd thrown him over to get married and have children. 'I can't wait for you any longer, you're a drifter, Jason,' she said, and went. That was all. He took the passport and chucked the letters out of the porthole to float till the next Mistral on the oily surface.

Down on the quayside Hugh waited in the open, letting the rain get to him. The storm had passed on to the mountains, and the horizon above the sea where the weather was coming from was already blue. In twenty minutes the heat would be back in force. July rain cooled nothing for long, but it could wash the sweat away. Beside Hugh was a pile of old truck tyres and behind, a smashed-up covered ramp leading to a hangar, smashed-up too. The smart new ferries to Corsica were visible half a kilometre away, under the exit from the autoroute. This was a prison-dock, a dead end where even fish wouldn't come in from the open sea. Jason didn't blame them. When he reached

Hugh, he saw that he was considering the *Kendal* with a careful eye.

'If ever this old banger went to the bottom—' Hugh said. 'You know, Jason, Ravenglass future's in containers.'

'Roll on roll off.'

'Oh you're on to that are you?' Jason was taking a last look at his ship and didn't answer. Odd, how you could get fond of a tub like that just because you'd floated around and milked some cash out of her. 'You've never met Rosie,' Hugh said.

'No. All honeymoon still and okay?'

'Overboard. Over the moon.'

'Why didn't you bring her?'

'Too much to do in a short time.'

Jason could raise no interest in any woman of Hugh's. It had always been like that – an inhibition of some kind, not abusing an advantage, imagined or real. They kept their catchment areas separate. 'We should have hung on to that taxi,' he said.

'We did. I told him to wait at the gates.'

'Let's hope he understood you. This isn't London. Drivers round here aren't first cab off the rank, intelligence-wise.'

'I didn't pay him,' Hugh said simply. He'd always understood better about economic leverage than Jason.

Hugh had a couple of rooms in a hotel high up in the town, with a garden and a view of the sea in the distance over roof tops. They sat in the shade of a big mulberry tree with a bottle of cold wine on the table between them. There was some movement of air and freshness from grass still damp after the storm. Silent insects rose from it to settle round your ankles.

'So those are about the only clothes you've got,' Hugh said, 'plus what's in your sack? Not exactly Hugo Boss.' There you go.

'That's it,' Jason said. 'It doesn't matter.' He really thought this. Clothes boiled down to money, and he'd always before now found ways to get his hands on enough of that to keep covered. Also, he knew Hugh had an idea at the back of his head. He was in no hurry to accept Hugh's idea, whatever it might be, just because he was short of clothes. Anyway, he had contacts among Moroccans and others in transit through this town and across the seas where clothes weren't what counted most, and money surfaced in unexpected places, like water from limestone. All you had to do was know the time of day and be around.

'It'll matter in London.'

'London?'

'Yes. Listen, Jason. You're not supposed to leave the jurisdiction but we need you over there.' Hugh peered about him among the palm trees. 'How, that's the only question. There's plenty of big English yachts around. Ravenglass could pull a string through some boatyard and get you quietly on board and away.'

'Don't bother. I've a Maltese passport in my pocket. I can go to London, if I want to go to London. I don't know if I do.'

'There's nothing to keep you here.'

'Since you gave my ship to the judge,' Jason said without rancour. He lifted his glass. He hadn't had that many cold drinks recently and Hugh was looking all right again. It was good sitting here with him opposite. A bit like a film, with those shades and shoes. 'Come to the point. I'll listen to anything.'

'May could be in trouble,' Hugh said.

'She's always in one kind or another. It shows she's alive. Who is it now?'

'I think you don't know Charlie Seker.'

20

'By name. Bad news, you said. Later you said the good news was it was finished.'

'It's finished and it isn't.'

'Is he the trouble?'

'I thought if you came over, you could find out. As he doesn't know you either.'

'You mean he wouldn't see me coming?'

'Yes.'

'Just what is it?' The idea of looking at his mother's private life in her own best interests wasn't specially repugnant to Jason. His feeling was protective. He understood her because they were alike. Or perhaps he understood her because she understood him. Which comes first? In any case, meetings could be rare because neither of them ever changed, even if she was getting older while he stayed roughly the same ideal age, slightly withered recently from lack of sunlight.

'Seker runs a refugee resettlement outfit. He started for love when it was fellow-Hungarians. Now it's more from the Balkans proper. And nothing done for love either.'

'Politicals on the run? I've carried one or two to Malta. They pay. Then they hop across to Libya. It's open arms there.'

'For God's sake.' Hugh looked again at the boles of the palm trees. 'No, not that sort, Seker's trade. And May's too interested in them – you know, lash out with the heart and cheque book. She subsidises Seker and Ravenglass picks up the tab. There could be more to it. Much more.'

Jason noticed how fast Hugh skidded from the subsidies to the more, left in the air. 'Well?'

'I'm told there's a scam in legal aid franchise and social security claims. An agency gets the cash and doesn't hand it on, or just a fraction. And there are an awful lot of these wandering people. I don't know about France but in the UK they flow across with every tide and settle down on whatever they can scrounge. That's what my paper says.'

'Which one's that?'

Hugh didn't answer the question. He was a subscriber, for sure, and Jason subscribed to nothing. 'I'm not accusing the refugees. The danger's if May's caught in it the day it surfaces at the Old Bailey.'

'Where did you get the information?'

'Solicitors. Strict confidence.'

This was looking different. Perhaps Hugh wasn't holding anything back after all. Perhaps prison left you paranoid. Jason made up his mind at once, as he liked to do. 'Okay. I'll come,' he said. 'We'll have a look at Charlie Seker and hope it's not too late. I'd need to get to see him without him knowing who I am.'

'That I can fix. We've a new lover in our family. Younger than you – or me. He worked for Seker till May picked him off the floor and carried him to bed. One Brian Foley. He doesn't like Seker either. You know, the big guy who left a stain in the mattress before him.' A mother for two sons – someone has to come off worst, left with the unwholesome curiosity. Too bad.

'If he and Seker haven't fallen out.'

'Brian doesn't fall out. In his situation you never know when you're for the chop. You need options.'

Jason felt restless now, with problems of the moment but stuck under this mulberry tree listening to the tone of Hugh's voice, leaving something in the air unsatisfied for both of them. The wine bottle was empty too. He stood up. 'I'm going for another of these.'

When he got back, Hugh had some papers in front of him on the table. One of them looked like a letter. He handed it over. 'Our advocate on the terms of your release. You're supposed to report once a month at the *Commissariat Central*. A formality, given the unusual value of the surety. He can see to it if you're still away in a month. As I think you will be.' Jason read the letter and returned it in silence. 'Look at this,' Hugh went on, holding out a postcard-sized photograph. 'Isn't she lovely? That's Rosie. We met at Cristabel's.' Jason didn't know about Cristabel's, probably a club – Hugh was shit-hot on the dance floor – and he didn't answer. After a moment, Hugh took the photograph back and put it in the inside pocket of his jacket hung over the chair, with the credit cards. 'We'll pack up here tomorrow morning. I fly to London but you'd better go somewhere else first. Like Malta – probably via Nice and Rome. Don't worry about cash. You look half starved to me.' Hugh leaned over and punched Jason lightly on the arm, his signal of solidarity. 'There's nothing more to do here except grab a good dinner. I was never in love with the place. I expect our dad passed through it too often.' It was odd hearing such a familiar term for someone almost unknown.

The photograph had reminded Jason strongly of something, a feeling more than a person, something rank you can't pin down, like a smell perhaps, a heady, fundamental smell. Except that authentic smell comes from outside. This was in the head. Hugh was wrong about there being no more to be done here. There was, and Jason knew a bar near the Opera House where he could get it seen to. Girls as unlike the woman in the photograph as possible. Mediterranean realism. 'Lend us a thousand, Hugh. Say three. Then I'll meet you where you like. They'll still be serving at ten.' If Hugh was running things, he must fork out for current expenses. Saying nothing, he did so. Jason touched him on the shoulder as he got up. 'Cheers. You know how it is. You should have brought Rosa.'

'Rosie.'

'Sorry.'

On the way down in the taxi Jason remembered that nothing had been said about Byland. May never went there any more: she claimed it made her too sad, too old. She'd outgrown it. Probably it was falling down by now, in that climate an unloved building soon decays. A picture formed in his head of Byland falling down, a heap of stone in the middle of a Pennine so-called forest. The picture was driven out again by one of what lay ahead in the bar near the Opera House. You never outgrew that however old you get – not May, not him.

Chapter Three

JASON DIDN'T FOLLOW Hugh's proposed itinerary. Any official seeing him try to pass himself off at the barriers, *in Malta*, with a Maltese passport would pounce. An Englishman to lock up. So instead, he took a train to Paris. He didn't ring Alex to warn him he was on the way. Alex Békassy, known as the *bécasse* for his dodgy and elusive skills. Otherwise, nothing less like a woodcock could be imagined. Alex was slow-moving and fat, so fat you could never know what, or whether, he was thinking. Any facial expression was stifled like an unwanted baby under a pillow. Jason waited patiently on the pavement after ringing Alex's doorbell, down in the steep sunless Montmartre street. Nothing would happen for a long time because the small apartment was on the top floor and this wasn't the kind of house with an entryphone. Pigalle was fifty yards down the road and the poor whores' customers had to be vetted, for safety, out in the open under the dim street lighting. He waited because Alex, to his way of thinking, owed him. Not a formal debt, just a binding obligation between gentlemen.

'So it's you,' the gravelly alto voice said as soon as the door was half open. Jason inserted a foot in the traditional way.

'Hallo, Alex. I've been out of circulation. I expect you know. I'd like to come in.'

Alex held out a hand, warm, dry and soft as the foot of a girl on a beach. 'It seems you are in. Glad to see you at large again. I often thought of you. How was the food? Come up. I'll go first, being slow.' Alex turned round and began lumbering ahead up the stairs, Jason following several steps below. Neither of them spoke till the door of the flat was shut behind them.

'Business good?' Jason asked. It was a general question because Alex had no one definite business but many. Languages were his speciality. He spoke and wrote a dozen of them with fluency as far as anyone could tell, and he'd managed to make himself the focus for cross-frontier transactions almost any-where, with Montmartre at the centre. Nothing big-time, but full of variety. Jason's Moroccans, also the Maltese civil servant who helped with the passport, and quite a few others had all come to him through Alex. There was a whisper of specialised videos too, made in Romania and available through some website, but Jason had never seen any of that. Some people believed he had enormous sums of money stashed away, for example in Switzerland, but there was never any outward sign. Probably a myth. Paris breeds them like rabbits. He lived on his top landing with several tired prostitutes long past their best as his neighbours, and looked after himself alone in the cramped and shabby spaces of the little flat.

'Middling,' he said. Alex must know that Jason had no interest in business except when there was some profitable mission, and that he wasn't here to listen to answers to polite questions. He was here for money, but there was something else as well.

'Haven't you got a cousin in London, Alex? A Hungarian cousin?'

'All my cousins everywhere are Hungarian. Sit down and have a glass of this.' Alex produced an open bottle of purplish red wine without a label. 'Even a few in America where you have to be American.'

'And stick together with other Hungarians, wherever they are?' Opposite Jason on the wall was the only picture in Alex's room, showing a country house of nineteenth-century French style in the landscape of the Great Hungarian Plain with a pond in the foreground. Alex's father, or his grandfather, had been expropriated by the Communists, so he said, leaving the Békassys to fend for themselves as they hadn't done for centuries. And if it meant incidental traffic in pornography, well those things were looked on more indulgently in Central Europe.

'Mercurial Hungarians coalesce like mercury, that's what they do,' Alex said. He sounded as if he really believed this, another article of myth. Jason wondered if he had any of those himself. He didn't think so. The sea, perhaps.

'That's what I thought. Well, there's one in London I'd like to know more about. Charlie Seker. Ever heard of him, at all?'

'It's a very common name.'

'Try harder.'

'He could be Jewish, with a name like that.'

'Yes?'

'There were some Sekers in Budapest . . . dealers, you know the sort of people.'

'You're a dealer yourself Alex.' Jason could see Alex playing for time while he decided what if anything to tell. 'Charlie Seker gives his life to helping refugees. He's a bit of a hero for them, I'm told.' Jason hadn't ever been told that but it seemed another possible myth. And if Alex had anything on Seker, a reputation of hero would bring it out. A hero has the weight problem licked and he gets the women.

'Yes, I've heard of him. A family of court painters.'

'Vienna?'

Alex shrugged. 'Where else?'

'I want to know anything you've got on Charlie now, the real Charlie.'

'You're an impatient man, Jason. You're just the same.'

'I'm not so chancy.'

'That's not what I mean. You're arrogant. If it's built-in, prison doesn't change it.'

'I didn't know,' Jason said sincerely.

'Oh yes?' Alex said. 'This Seker of yours, I think he's someone who's made out.' He was flipping through a card-index, skimming like someone who knows already.

'A credit to Hungarians?'

'I mean Seker has been received in society.'

'I don't think there's any society in England the way you mean, Alex. It's not the same as here.'

'He's been the recognised lover of a lady who rides about in a limousine – anyway, a Rover.'

'You're well informed. It was probably my mother.'

'Ah. I begin to understand. You want him assassinated. Quite normal. You disapprove. Nothing out of the ordinary.' Alex looked as if some expression was struggling through the layers. There was a shift behind his features which might have ended in a smile. That's the trouble with fat friends. You can never be sure of the buried signals. 'But leave me out of it. I don't help with murders. However, Seker is certainly an imperial shit. I don't blame you. Now if my grandmother—'

'It isn't that. They—' Jason cast about for the right word to say that his mother was no longer shagging with an imperial shit. 'I mean they discontinued. But there's still some link. And

28

it's his being on your card-index that I want to know about. What sort of a shit?'

Alex extended his right hand and rubbed thumb and index together. 'That sort.'

'Other people's money?'

'It says so here.'

'Small scale? More ambitious?'

'I think Seker's an ambitious man.'

'And always women?'

'That's what it says.'

Alex seemed to be leaning a bit heavily on the card-index for his answers. He was hiding something. 'I think you know him, Alex, don't you?'

'Our paths have crossed.'

'When?'

'When we were boys.'

'Where?'

'Here . . . all over the place. Charlie was in films, then.'

'A child actor?'

'In a way, yes.' Alex offered a chocolate and ate two himself in one go.

'Did you work as a child actor too, Alex?'

'Just a couple of times. I didn't have the right physique. Or the taste. Specialised, you see.'

'Yes, I see. But Seker had the taste all right?'

'The money was good. Charlie was pliable.'

'How about physique?'

'I'd forgotten, you've never seen him. When he was a boy he looked like the infant Jesus. There was a lot of demand for the infant Jesus here in Paris. What do you call it in England? Hot cakes.'

England seemed a long way off, a long time ago. 'They were

the kind of films circulating more in video these days?'

'Exactly,' Alex said, and put away the box with his card-index. His tone was final. Jason wasn't into the video side of his activities. 'Have another chocolate. More wine.'

'Just one thing – are you ever in touch with him at all now?'

'If it wasn't for your worries about your mother . . . Charlie's on a mailing list.'

'Little boys?'

'No, that was mercenary. It's little girls. You wouldn't like to see the product he orders. I'm used to it but I'm not so hardened.' Alex's bulk shuddered, a violent movement ran all through it. 'That's a dangerous breach of confidence. People like Charlie Seker have a long arm. But I know you came for information and money and as I can't give you any money, Jason, I've given you the information I can. For a favour. One-off, remember that.'

'I won't forget. Trust me.'

'I do. If you were a Frenchman, I wouldn't tell you anything at all.'

When Alex was excited, his English pronunciation sounded more French. So he was excited. But one thing was sure – there was no advance to be got out of him. That was a pity. It might be possible, of course, to lean, but Jason had seen too much leaning in the Baumettes. Even so there was something more here, he felt sure. What Alex said about those films in his boyhood dated from long ago, and videos were just a trade. 'I wonder if old Charlie still has the Jesus resemblance. It might explain my mother.'

'It explains a lot of women.'

'You mean he has?'

'Charlie has charm to multiply loaves and fishes just by regarding them. He pisses in the water, it turns to wine, that's what he thinks. With a beard, he'd be the man of Galilee himself. What an example—'

'Yes?'

'Mistaken identity, of course. Could a con-man aim higher? I told you he's ambitious. Women go for it.'

'Did Charlie once take one off you, Alex?' Jason asked in a low voice. The right answer mattered. Sympathy mattered. You may think ready tears come into the eyes of a fat man due to hormonal imbalance; but a scar can be painful as a wound.

'She was just a girl,' Alex said. 'Fifteen. But made how I am, the only one for me.'

Jason had never seen Alex with any girl. As far as he knew, Alex's female acquaintance began and ended with the tarts on the landing. 'What became of her?'

'Her school friend said she went with Charlie on his motor-bicycle into the forest of Fontainebleau. It was never proved. But she didn't come back. Charlie was much hairier than the infant Jesus by then but no one asked. You only had to look at him to know.'

So maybe that was when poor old Alex started getting fat. He guzzled for comfort. A bad happening all round, leaving an unsettled account between Charlie and Alex. Worth remembering. 'I'm sorry Alex. Really sorry.' And he was. It was an example of fixation and Jason had read about such things, while the SS *Kendal* rocked gently at the poor man's end of Mediterranean ports. They can leave you unable to get it up except for a memory. A truly tight corner. Still, it was not good of Alex refusing to fork out. Something else to remember, because Alex was a man with a conscience in his own way. He'd know he hadn't lived up to the image of a gentleman in this and he'd feel bad about it if his attention was drawn to it at the right time, when he had something to gain or lose. That's how it is, and if you're unrealistic and your clothes aren't Hugo Boss or Armani, it's an aspect of reality you get your head round in the end.

'You're a national of Malta, Mr Ricardo?' the official at Dover asked, passport in hand.

'Maltese citizen,' Jason said loudly as if any question of this could only be racist-based. 'Ricardo of Malta.' He tapped his tongue on the *r* sounds – about enough for an island within a few hours' sailing of Sicily.

'Okay, get along.'

'Thanks,' Jason said in his normal voice.

'Just a minute.'

'Yes?'

'There's no one else on here.'

'Right. No one.'

'No dependants?'

'Not known,' Jason muttered.

'Well that's a turn up,' the official said to the colleague next to him. 'No known dependants, this chap, and off a Catholic island. What does he do with it? I must warn you, Mr Ricardo,' he said formally, 'keep your Maltese passport safe. There's a lot of frontier games these days. Passports aren't what they were. Frontiers aren't what they should be. Ever heard of public money, Mr Ricardo?'

'I don't know about money,' Jason said. However boring, it was the truth.

'I'll watch out for your name on the screen,' the official said, motioning with his head towards the office behind him. 'In the handouts file. What's your whereabouts while in England?' Jason gave the address of his mother's flat in Pimlico that she'd had for years, since he and Hugh were boys, on the top floor in

St George's Square overlooking the Thames. 'Oh very up-market. Is this Mrs Ricardo Maltese too?'

'She's my mother. She's as English as you are.'

The man looked thoughtful for a moment, saying nothing. However fishy the whole set-up, the passport was genuine and so was the address. He wrote it down. 'We'll know where to look for you if we need to.'

'I'm not hiding,' Jason said. He found a telephone and rang Hugh at the Ravenglass office.

'I've made it to Dover,' he said.

'I'm tied up here till six at least. When you get to London go to my place. I'll ring Rosie to expect you.'

Jason felt strangely unwilling to do this. There was some inner obstacle, not clearly identified. Perhaps it was just that he was more or less straight out of prison and had never met Rosie. 'I'd rather wait till you're free and we arrive together.'

Hugh laughed. 'Is this something new? Where's the old confidence?' From the laugh, Jason could tell that Hugh wasn't too bothered. 'So what's it about?'

'I'll come to your office and wait.'

'No trouble with the passport?'

Jason hung up without answering. The white cliffs had altered his mood. The Mediterranean was a mythic world but made, like God, to fit man exactly until he grew out of it. Here, you had to think again. A man with an office and a wife called Rosie stood taller in London, obviously, than someone whose only home was a tramp steamer put in hock to get him out of the slammer. That didn't matter much in itself – Hugh was part of him. But it called for rethinking all round.

Jason did some of this rethinking in the train to Charing Cross. His first conclusion was not to go to the Ravenglass office after all. He must face up, go to Hugh's house in Fulham and be nice to plain Rosie till Hugh got back. Self-respect demanded it. The second was to get hold of some cash fast because until he did he was dependent on Hugh. This was more difficult. It was six years since he was last in London, and he had none of those fringe contacts which round the Mediterranean make one thing so soon lead to another. Also, there was the May/Seker project. He didn't have time to go and get himself into any more trouble. The May/Seker project was essentially a safe mission. The train was crawling through some thick woodland in the Weald of Kent where a lot of old trees had been blown down. Uncared-for woodland like at Byland. Byland-in-the-Forest was the postal address, or used to be. Apart from bent old oaks, the supposed forest was more an untamed hazel and hawthorn scrub like the one once covering all this part of England and still to be found, here and there, on northern hillsides. And an idea came at once. At Byland was something of his. May owned everything and sensibly didn't trust him with any of it. She gave official trust without love to Hugh because she had to. That was something Jason understood and disapproved of. Hugh had a right to better. But their father, before leaving never to return, had given Jason a small package to remember him by.

'Hang on to this, son,' he had said. 'It's worth some money to do you a good turn on what you English call a rainy day. And God knows, they should know what that is. It came from the bottom of the sea. Don't give it to your mother. In fact don't say anything about it. If you do she'll throw it out after me.' That was the last Jason saw or heard of his father, except one word with the final pat on the head. 'Be a drifter like me if you want, but don't run away like I always do.'

The object was about a foot long and wrapped in a bit of leather tied with string. Jason hid it unopened for a long time because he felt too angry. When he did have a look he found a metal figure, female. Metal like a bell. She stood there, defiant, trying to cover herself with her hands. The thought made him laugh now but then it was deadly provocative. The little bronze was expecting a rape, and for a long time after he would take her out of cover at private moments till the day he first got his hands on the real thing. He always felt bad about not showing her to Hugh, but he didn't. There was only one of these and Hugh would have to manage. Then at the end of the last holiday before the return to Pimlico Jason noticed that the figure was beginning to lose her force, she was a fetish on the decline. So not to abandon her for ever he hid her again. It was as good as certain she was still in the old ice-house beyond the kitchen yard. A rainy day, his father had said. He must get up to Byland and see what she was good for, the rape victim from the sea.

The taxi passed between ranks of fruit stalls in the North End Road before turning into a street of houses with front gardens. Strangely, everyone on and about the stalls was standing motionless while he went by, as if warned. In the side street you could see at a glance the houses were now inhabited by people much better off than those they were built for. There were gothic greenhouses and lacquered knockers on doors, and drive-in garages. Hugh had gone up in the world too, since Jason's last visit when he was living alone in a flat the other side of the river. Perhaps Rosie had money. Or the house belonged to Ravenglass on a mortgage. Jason lifted the knocker and banged twice. Hearing sounds behind him he turned to look. A big old-fashioned hearse followed by mourners of all ages was slowly passing down the street and into the North End Road for a last salute. On its side in silver lettering were the words,

'To Our Gran'. So there were still real people living and dying here. A kind of people unknown to Hugh and Rosie, for sure. The door of Hugh's house opened.

'I'm Jason. Hugh told me to come from the station. Are you Rosie?' He knew she was, from the photograph, and the same rank familiarity came over him at the sight of her.

'Yes.' She stood there on the doorstep looking hard at him, as if to identify for future reference all criminal traits visible to the naked eye. She was younger than she'd seemed in the photograph and her skin was dark. Not just from the sun. He thought of the bronze figure. 'Well come on in Jason, don't stand outside with the funeral of that old dear going past. I used to meet her buying salads down the road. Come in.'

She was wearing trousers, which she didn't really have quite the length of leg to carry off well. But she filled them, certainly. A feeling of despair took over, arriving from nowhere, just like that. It was the same as the rank familiarity, unexplained. 'I'd better ring Hugh and say I'm here,' he said, and she turned to look at him again. This time there was an ironical light in her eye.

'Let's have a drink first,' she said. 'Hugh won't be leaving the office for ages. Leave your bag there in the hall. I'll show you upstairs later.' Something had amused her, but what? Jason disliked being a source of secret amusement, also he thought her hard, harder than in the photograph. Her expression and the line of her mouth were hard. He hadn't liked her in the photograph, and he liked her even less in the flesh. And there was that feeling of despair she gave him, too. He wasn't sure just what he meant by hard, but the word stuck in his head. Perhaps because bronze is a hard material.

'You knew I was coming today?' he asked. Of course she knew. But apart from mentioning a drink, she hadn't been very welcoming. It made him think that all mightn't be right in her relationship with Hugh and therefore she didn't much want to make the acquaintance of his brother. The thought annoyed him further. Admittedly, Hugh used to have that timing snag, but surely two sensible people could sort it out between them? There were well-known techniques ... it depended on the woman's cooperation and grasp of reality. Still, Rosie looked pretty realistic to him.

'If I wasn't expecting you, I'd have been at the funeral with the neighbours,' Rosie said. 'Look, I found a bottle of rosé, Cassis rosé. To make you feel more at home.' She smiled at him. She stood in front of him, smiling fully at him, quite close. Her teeth were a good shape. They matched evenly and seemed aimed slightly inward, into the interior of her mouth, which was interesting. It probably had a character significance, like handwriting leaning backwards. The smile was like a gesture: it had some meaning too but he didn't know what it was. He only knew that this woman had taken the trouble to look for a bottle of Cassis rosé because she wanted him to see her as an ally. 'You've had a bad time,' she said.

'Hugh got me out,' he said, mentioning Hugh reluctantly now. You could love your brother but mention his name only reluctantly, in certain situations. What situations, for God's sake? Well, for example, when for some reason you were in no hurry for him to turn up. 'It's temporary.'

'Make the most of it,' Rosie said, and poured the wine. Jason wondered if she went out to work, normally. She didn't look like the sort of woman to sit around at home, waiting for the children to get conceived. Perhaps she wrote, or something like that. He rather hoped not, though it was nothing to do with him, obviously. He would rather she was more free. Of course she and Hugh hadn't been married long: maybe they were still in the planning stage. 'Cheers,' said Rosie, holding up her wine glass. 'Vote liberal. In every sense.'

They were standing just inside the gothic greenhouse, added to extend the sitting room. The late-afternoon sun was shining through the glass, and a shadow from one of the glazing bars fell vertically across Rosie's face and down her body to the floor. It was like seeing your own signature on a letter you'd forgotten. Now Jason knew why Rosie had seemed known to him like an invention. He'd dreamed her up in the cell of the Baumettes one night not long ago. The woman standing outside the bars, looking in. And with the electric agility you only have in a dream, they'd leaped the gap. In a cell you have to make out somehow. The rank sense of familiarity was accounted for.

'You're staring,' Rosie said. She passed her hand quickly over her face and moved away out of the sunlight.

'You just made me think—' Jason stopped short. He felt on close terms now, though not in a way you could explain to a woman ten minutes after first meeting. How had he thrown that dream together without ever seeing her? It was a time-warp phenomenon – if the same dream had occurred a couple of weeks later there would be no puzzle. So the unconscious had anticipated. 'I just felt we could have met before.'

Rosie laughed. 'You mean another life.'

'Yes, I suppose that's what I mean.'

They stood silently, neither looking at the other, the sun lighting up the pink wine in their glasses and the geraniums and begonias in the greenhouse in front of them. The silence felt peaceful to Jason at first; then it grew tense as if something was being stifled. Her presence just a few feet off weighed on him; he felt the weight in his back. How much time was passing, in this state of things?

He knew the telephone was ringing, had been ringing; but it

was a bell in the outside, real world, not in here. Then Rosie moved to answer it, turning back to hand him the wine bottle. 'Help yourself. I think you need it.' The telephone was at the far end of the room, by the window looking on to the street. Jason didn't listen to the conversation, the sounds reaching him indistinctly out in the conservatory, under the hot glass. He'd forgotten how hot London could be. But he heard Rosie's last words. 'No, not yet,' she said. Then, 'Yes, right, you do that. Bye.'

'Why did you say I needed it?' Jason asked.

'You looked thirsty. Actually you look knackered all of a sudden. Haven't you slept?'

'Only just woken up,' Jason said. 'Who was that who rang?' He asked this as if he was in his own house.

'Hugh.'

'Is he coming back now he knows I'm here?'

'Not straight away. He'll ring later.'

'He does know I'm here?'

'It's what he wanted to find out.'

Jason weighed this evasive answer, and decided to let it go. Did she mean by telling Hugh, not yet, that Jason hadn't turned up? He felt sure of it, but unsure of the implications. Like why he hadn't rung Hugh from Charing Cross to say he'd go directly to Fulham and not the office. But one thing was clear – they were each of them, Rosie and him, deceiving Hugh over a small detail. Trivial details setting up a complicity in deceit, that's what was going on here. Jason tried to recover his feeling of hostility but it was too late. It was up in smoke. Rosie had entered him. There she was, on the swinging sofa in the conservatory among the pots and trellises with her loose white shirt and long dark hair; spilling a bit of pink wine on to her trousers from time to time because she didn't care but kept her glass well filled up. 'Does Hugh drive to Southwark?'

'Yes. There's no tube here – or there, come to that.'

'How long does it take?'

'You mean, when's the earliest he'll be back?'

'I suppose so, yes.'

'Why else would you ask? What do you care how long it takes him unless you're wondering how soon he'll show up?' Now it sounded as if hostility had crossed over from him to her. She sounded angry. But with who?

'I wouldn't want to upset Hugh at all,' Jason said.

'Are you afraid of—?' Rosie asked. 'No. I don't think you are.' There was an aviary on one whole side of this glasshouse that Jason hadn't taken in before. Some pink doves were shuffling along a bar, cooing and gargling. Rosie nodded in their direction. 'They're Hugh's. On a Sunday he goes in there with them. I suppose they're not badly off. They've got a relative liberty. They don't have to shit on the same spot every day. They're so free if I let them go they wouldn't know where to do it. They'd be lost without him.'

Jason turned towards her. This was getting too much. The white shirt moved across margins of skin due to the seat swinging back and forth in the tropical temperature, while her feet performed their arc in the air three inches above the smart Spanish floor tiles.

'You know I have to go back and give myself up, don't you?'

'Yes, I know.'

'In a few weeks. Any time. When Hugh says. They can send me down for five or six years. They prefer foreigners who don't fool with the drug laws.' He'd stopped pushing against the floor with his feet to make the seat swing. Everything in the conservatory was still as nature.

Rosie turned to him. 'Weeks are miles and miles away. They can't put you down here and now.' Her hands, one of them holding up the glass, came forward together so the knuckles were within an inch of his shirt, open at the neck. 'It's a lifetime away.'

From somewhere behind them in the house came the sound of a door closing sharply. They were still sitting in the same position when Hugh came through and found them. 'So you made it on your own, Jason. I thought you would,' he said.

'You were going to ring again,' Rosie said. She sounded bright but breathless. 'How ever did you get here so quickly?'

'I was using my mobile in the car.'

Jason was on his feet, and he and Hugh embraced each other again. This time Jason felt a lack of authenticity in it. He kneaded Hugh's shoulder. 'Hi,' he said.

'When did you arrive?' Hugh asked.

'He turned up in a taxi five minutes ago. I'll get you a glass, you must be hot.'

'A whisky and lots of ice, my treasure,' Hugh said. His eye was on the empty bottle of Cassis rosé standing on the floor, with the newly opened one beside it. 'It's sure thirsty weather for London. Five minutes ago? Well I'm glad you didn't waste any time coming to the office. We've got a lot of things to work out together.' He put his arm through Jason's and led him back to the swinging seat where they sat down side by side. 'Welcome to Ricardo's Fulham folly. Didn't I tell you she was lovely?' With his fist still through Jason's arm he nudged him in the side. This time it was more a punch than a nudge. Jason didn't feel able to say anything about it.

Instead he waved a hand at the surroundings. 'Good to see everything looking right for you, Hugh. I mean the future, and that. Here's to it.' Hugh turned and stared at him. Jason stared back. What was that watchword? They raised their glasses, looking away.

'The rosy future,' Hugh said.

Chapter Four

'YOU MAY SPOT something vaguely familiar about Brian. Be polite. You could wake up one morning and find he's your step-father.' Rosie giggled and choked on her coffee. A flush appeared under the dark skin. Like him, coffee was all she'd had for breakfast while Hugh got on with bacon and eggs. 'He's a terrific admirer. Thinks the sun moon and stars shine out of your mother, I know.'

'How do you know it, love?' Hugh asked. He had hold of one of Rosie's hands and was playing, rather ostentatiously Jason thought, with the fingers and the diamond ring. But he sounded bored by the subject of Brian. Jason had thought Hugh only too interested in that side of their mother's life. Maybe just when it was Seker. Was Seker some sort of special red rag to Hugh as well as Alex? Jason was impatient to get a sight of him.

'I can see he's a lover who knows about taking his time.'

'Oh can you? Where d'you see that?'

'In his eyes.'

'When he looks into yours?'

'No. Into hers.'

There was silence for a bit. Hugh withdrew his hand. Jason

thought about the *Kendal*, to have something distant to think of. Rosie's last remark meant, to him, that Hugh's problem still gave trouble. For some men, the regular set-up of domestic love has a negative effect. They deflate. They depend on outside professionals as naturally as the professionals depend on them. They just need relief like the professionals need to live. No one feels anything except mutual recognition. Come to think of it, he wasn't so brilliant himself in the theatre of regular love. He separated the heart from the groin, in fact he knew next to nothing about the heart. It was an organ he'd neglected. He turned to look at Rosie again. She was sitting there at the table looking expectant in the sunlight already striking fiercely through the conservatory glass. A female agenda in waiting.

'Smartarse,' Hugh said. No one asked who he meant. His pleasure in bacon and eggs had been spoiled.

'What did Brian do for Charlie Seker, I mean when he was working for him?' Jason asked.

'He dogsbodied,' Hugh said. 'While Charlie and May were off busy together Brian answered the telephone. The door. The fax. Made himself necessary, against the day when he would dogsbody no more.'

Rosie was in her dressing gown and Jason waited for her to finish and go back upstairs. 'Did she give Charlie the sack or was it the other way round?'

'I think Brian fixed it. He was informed on plenty of things about Seker that Seker didn't want May to know. So naturally, he chose his time and passed them on.'

'How did you find that out?'

'Guesswork.'

'Brian was just on the make?'

'It's not what Rosie thinks but it's the obvious thing all the same. Rosie sees good motives everywhere. She loves the world, all of it. Love and beautiful motives are what she sees all around.'

Was there some sarcasm in this remark? If so, at whose expense? 'Lucky brother,' Jason said. 'You found a wife who'd never hurt a feeling till she had to. Not even then.'

'Yes,' Hugh said. He stood up and moved to the window. 'There's the car at the end of the street. Be careful. Brian may be useful but keep him in the dark till you're sure of him.'

'Sure of what about him?'

'When he sees it's worth it. Stops thinking we aim to ditch him as well as Charlie.'

'Do we? I didn't know.' So Hugh wanted to clean up May's private life as well as cutting the connection with the refugees. Perhaps he knew what was best. Hugh had become more decisive since he'd married Rosie and moved into this road of greenhouses and up-and-over garage doors. Round the corner from the street market. 'So that's Brian,' Jason said when the car drew up. 'Why didn't she come too? She hasn't seen me in five years. This is like a summons to the presence.'

'She doesn't come here.'

'Wrong postal district?'

'Wrong son,' Hugh said, sounding unmoved. True, May had once been out to stay aboard the *Kendal.* Jason remembered a long weekend of festivity. In the port, she'd made a sensation with her laughing freedom and the way she burst into song when her spirits went over the top. 'Are all your women like your *maman*?' he was asked. '*Ça ne fait pas très British*,' they complained.

Jason went out into the street and shook Brian's hand affably. 'Let's go,' he said, and climbed in. He felt he'd be at a disadvantage if the meeting was under Hugh's roof. He wanted his own first impression of this career boy who was making his mother so happy.

'Whatever you say, Jason,' Brian said. Jason studied him studying the traffic and the road as they started off. If you were used to a lot of Mediterranean faces at close quarters and you'd more or less forgotten your own, Brian's was very English. The skin was less hard than the structure under it. It was true there was something familiar. 'So how's May? Okay, is she?' Would there be some kind of smile? Pitying, or possessive?

'Your mother's on very good form. She's excited about seeing you after so long.' It was a conventional answer giving nothing away, and there'd been no smile at all. Brian was taking care to avoid anything too familiar. Obviously Hugh made him feel like a gigolo.

'I've only met Rosie for the first time,' Jason said.

'Rosie's good news. A real bloom like her name.' This time there was a smile – a brief one. Not a lover's, Jason was sure. That was something. He hadn't realised before how he'd been worrying at the back of his mind about it. And why should he? Because she'd gone on about Brian's qualities? And on whose behalf had he been worrying? His mother's? Hugh's? Or his own? He saw it could only be his own. Rosie's favourable report on Brian was so innocuous that only jealousy could account for being worried by it. He was jealous of Rosie's sympathies – not her preferences, just her simple, harmless, generous woman's sympathies. Hang about. Whoever heard of a woman's generous sympathies being harmless?

'Hugh says my mother doesn't go to them. Does Rosie go to hers? Is that where you've seen her?'

'They sometimes come over on a Sunday,' Brian said.

'For lunch? Things like that?'

'Yes, sometimes.'

'Who cooks it?'

Brian looked at him quickly, then back at the road. He probably thought he was being got at. 'I do that,' he said. There was something old-time about Brian in spite of being a domestic toyboy. He wore a grey flannel suit and even in this heat kept his jacket on. Was he some kind of closet case? Jason didn't think so, on the whole. He didn't want to think it, because of May. If there's anything worse, it seemed to him, than a middle-aged prima donna with a good-looking youth in her bed, it's one in bed with a youth who'd rather be in bed with a man. Too pathetic all round.

They were on the Embankment at Chelsea Reach now, tide up, gulls circling the bridges in the light hot morning breeze. He'd sailed a dinghy on this stretch; it was a scene from the past. The first girl here too, a summer night after they jumped in the river. It was on the next flight of steps – just here, the first after Albert Bridge. They'd made a pile of their wet clothes. Not that the flight mattered. He put a hand to his groin because there was unrest down there. It would hardly do to enter the presence with a hard-on. Still, this made him feel easier-going towards Brian, for a start. Age had so little to do with the thing. She was sixteen at the time, that girl, so she'd said. Give or take a year. Name of Daphne.

'You know what it is about London?' Jason said, as if he and Brian had sailed the estuaries together and known one another for ages. 'Why London's alive compared to Paris? It's the tide.'

Brian turned again, this time the eyes less hard. 'I worked in a bar in Paris for a few months once,' he said. 'London's much wilder. Far freer.'

'Right. It's the great equaliser.' After this, they continued the drive to St George's Square in peaceful silence.

May's flat, which she'd bought at the time of her marriage,

nsisted of a big studio for parties and a warren of little rooms, half a dozen of them, strung along the southern side of the building so their windows looked over the tops of trees with the Thames below, surging back and forth. A lift had been installed in the stairwell since he was last here, but Jason chose to go up on foot. He needed exercise for his legs. Brian followed him, two steps at a time, and by the fourth floor was less out of breath than Jason was. Well so he should be: May probably subscribed to an up-to-the-minute Pimlico fitness centre for him. Jason was out of condition and still wore a prison pallor.

Already at the second-floor landing the sound of the strong contralto floated down to them. The door of the flat must be open. May had a powerful, true voice and took lessons in Italy when she was a girl. You could never say she was off the note, or cocked up the phrasing, or went wrong on time. She didn't have a marked tremble and her voice wasn't harsh like some in the Marseille Opera House who scream curses at the audience. She claimed to have perfect pitch, whatever that was. So it was difficult to say just why the general effect was less pleasant than it should be, with all those qualifications. Jason knew she was singing to welcome and challenge him. She was signalling that he'd been away too long and she was uncertain about his motives in coming back. It was a Schubert song, that he did know for sure. Probably about an unstable wanderer fresh out of prison. She was at her piano, accompanying herself with less skill than in the singing but plenty of confidence and no pretensions, which made a rather touching effect. Maybe pretensions were all that was wrong with her singing anyway. Perhaps the damage was done by those lessons in Italy. She should have stuck to Manchester, the nearest big centre to Byland. There she was, at the piano under the sloping glass roof light, the sun barred by a Venetian blind. Jason hadn't been looking forward to this meeting, knowing he was here for the first time not in his own right but as Hugh's agent. Still, now that he stood actually on the doorstep he felt a familiar pleasure. He knew the place, every inch, and his mother's qualities, good and bad, which he recognised like his own.

Evidently she wasn't going to stop before she reached the end of the song, five years' absence notwithstanding. He walked across the wide planks of the floor to stand behind her at the piano, taking care not to make a noise with his shoes. She could be very confrontational about anyone doing that while she performed. When the last phrase of the accompaniment had faded from the sound-board, May looked up at Jason and laughed. He laughed with her, joining in though no joke was in the air. It was a laugh of pleasure, nothing to do with the words. May stood up and kissed Jason on both cheeks without holding him, then folded her music and shut the piano lid.

'Do you want something to drink?' Brian asked, in the background. There was a note of disapproval in his voice. Was that to discourage anyone from drinking so early in the day? Or a negative reaction on seeing mother and son together? Likely, if his own relationship with May was that way. But Jason wasn't at all sure it was so. His idea was that Brian was somehow much older than his years and so a natural partner for May who was much younger than hers. It looked as if Brian just liked control for control's sake – no approved drinking before he reckoned it was an acceptable hour. There was no reason to put up with that.

'Yes, I do,' Jason said. 'A glass of wine.'

'We'll have some champagne,' May said in her ringing voice. 'Brian won't mind us doing that, will you, Brian darling?' She wasn't exactly asking permission, but almost. If this hadn't annoyed Jason, it would have amused him, it was so unlike how she used to be. With older lovers, she ordered the drinks when she wanted them.

'Why should he?' he asked when Brian went off for the bottle.

'Brian says there's a lot of calories even in a glass of champagne.'

'He doesn't like you putting on weight?'

'He would never say something as crude as that, Jason. Brian has the lightest touch.'

'Good for him.'

'And me.' Side by side, May was nearly as tall as he was. There was a lot of her, too, always had been. She had a dense physical presence due to health and dynamism and the philosophy of freedom, the whole thing reinforced by a powerful, delicious scent. He'd smelt it from the stairs; you could practically smell it across the Square when she went out to the car or the taxi. Her scents were as challenging, as welcoming as the laughter and the singing.

'And it's good to see you,' he said.

'Tell me all about being in prison,' May said. 'It must have been exciting.' She admired extremes and those who underwent them. You'd think that, restricted by the condition of being a woman, she yearned for the rigours of male experience however unpleasant. When Jason was a boy she'd often enquired with interest into the hardships of life in his various schools, particularly the physical ones. 'But you look thin.' She touched his shoulder to feel the bones, then pulled her hand away. 'How stupid to get caught doing that,' she went on. 'But I dare say someone betrayed you. You've always been absurdly trusting. Not like Hugh.' Her voice went down as she mentioned the name. Poor Hugh. She was unjust because his existence reminded her of demands she couldn't meet, the obligation to keep liking your children just because you once had them, and then be milked all your life long.

'It was bad not seeing the sky,' Jason said.

'Yes, that would be terrible. Did you have a room to yourself?'

'They're called cells and I certainly didn't. There were three and sometimes four other men in there.'

'It must have smelt bad.'

'It stank. And it was hot, very hot. And there were fights.' He could remember saying that when he was at school.

'Did you get in them, Jason? Did you fight?'

Before he could answer, Brian came back with the champagne and the glasses. Two glasses. Evidently he was not running any calorie risk himself. While he opened the bottle, May watched him and Jason watched her. For the first time after a long absence he noticed changes. There was something reduced about her, but also something enhanced. It was easy to see how the relationship with Brian, younger than either of her sons, might reduce her because any woman in that situation would be worried, secretly or frankly, about her age and the passing years. What was enhanced was the impression she gave of appetite for pleasure and freedom while there was still time. Her colour was higher too, and it seemed to him that her eyes were more heated. The light they spread around looked likely to burn out. He wondered about her blood pressure. On reflection, Brian's strict views on alcohol were more understandable. Jason wondered if Brian was equally strict about other appetites. He didn't give much for his chances if he was.

May was already helping herself to a second glass. 'Here's to you coming home,' she said. The first had been emergency treatment; this was celebration.

'Here's to Ravenglass,' Jason said.

'But Hugh says it won't be for long. What about money? You know I haven't any to give you, Jason darling, don't you? Every penny goes in just keeping alive.' She looked over at Brian who was turning the financial pages of *The Times*.

'And on the refugees,' Jason said incautiously, and Brian lowered the paper.

'They're my refugees, no one else's. I was born lucky, my father gave me everything and left me everything. It's a debt,' May said. Her tone of voice had changed. She spoke more sharply as she always did in defence of her freedoms. 'I expect Hugh's been moaning to you about it. It's nothing to do with him. Not his business at all.'

Jason knew better than to argue, or even appear to notice. With her, distraction was the way round awkward moments. Bring her mind back from philanthropy to the good things of life. 'You're still in fine voice, you've been practising,' he said. 'Sing me something else. You don't hear that sort of music in prison.'

'Perhaps you do in Italian ones,' May said, and went back to the piano, taking her glass which she put carefully on the floor beside her.

'Seems you got in hot water in the wrong country,' Brian said, and his pinkish face had gone a shade deeper when Jason looked his way. Probably he was too careful to make jokes very often.

'I'll sing you Wolf's *Blumengrass*,' May said. 'All about the little flower and the bumble-bee, just made for one another.' This time the accompaniment, if not the song, was just about within reach. When she'd finished she sat still for a moment at the piano. 'The words always put me in mind of Hugh and Rosie and him pressing her to his heart hundreds of thousands of times. As in the lyric. Some story.' She laughed her joyous laugh, mouth open and head thrown back, like a last phrase written into the song. 'There. No more now.' She picked up her glass and emptied it, then held it out in the direction of the table where the bottle stood. 'So now tell me what you make of Rosie. I think she's far too good for him.'

'You shouldn't say that,' Jason said. He felt the level of provocation was rising. In a family it's like a flooding ditch. And they would be in it together, May and him. 'Maybe he's too good for her. You're unjust with him.'

Instead of fighting back, May looked at him with humour. His reaction suited her. 'Obviously she appeals to you, Jason. She's very attractive. So are you. You must be really starved; women who like it recognise that. And your brother lives for the office.'

'Ravenglass depends on him.'

'Ravenglass is mine, not Hugh's. My grandfather created it after the first war and it doesn't depend on any of us. It has a life of its own. Grandfather built the ships and sailed them and flew the Ravenglass flag all over the world. The flag will still be flying when we're all buried and gone.' This was an item of religious belief with her. Ravenglass wasn't a shipping line, it was an incarnation. Her grandad. She'd never run the business herself and, in her eyes, Hugh only went into the offices because he was a repressed person and someone had to pay the wages. And the insurance premiums. She probably didn't know the *Kendal* was one of the last Ravenglass ships still in the water. If she thought of the *Kendal* at all it would only be to remember the all-night party they'd had on board – a long time ago it seemed, now. And there was no point in trying to bring harsh realities to mind. Too much of that could tip her over like a boat with no keel. What she needed was stabilisers. And that meant looking into her relationships. Freedom is good, but no one can expect it to be perfect, particularly if they have children, and especially if they're a woman with sons. That stood to reason, Jason thought, and he turned his attention to Brian. Brian was one of the parameters here.

Brian must have decided the conversation was taking a more interesting turn because he now had a glass in his hand and was looking alert, *The Times* abandoned beside him. Jason considered that a man who didn't drink when others were drinking was suspect, so he approved of this development. Was it the mention of Rosie that woke Brian up? Or was it May's declarations about Ravenglass? Brian, it seemed, didn't any longer have a job: his work was May and her interests. Jason at first thought his mother's enhanced state was to do with liberated appetite; now he could see it was her equilibrium that was shakier than ever. And now Brian was gazing at her with admiration as though all the Ravenglass profits since 1920 were accumulated about her like leaf on the *Golden Hind*. Definitely, he should be made to be useful.

The dining room of the flat was next to the kitchen, both small, low-ceilinged rooms with a communicating hatch. May used to employ a woman who prepared meals which she left to be warmed up by whoever was going to eat them. Now, the dividing wall had been knocked down and the resulting space redecorated, with three windows looking over the river. The sun was streaming in and an air-conditioner was blowing cool into the summer light.

'Brian saw about all this,' May said. 'Isn't it lovely? It's his domain – one of his domains. I'm the other.' She laughed that open-mouthed laugh again, so infectious, with its touch of mania.

'And lovely too,' Jason said to show indulgence. And of course because a woman needs a compliment. And because he liked being with her, liked having her beside him with her scent.

'If I've matured well it's from being laid down,' May said. 'If your father hadn't run away I'd be vinegar by now. Someone should warn Rosie about that.'

'All right.' She seldom mentioned his father, and Jason didn't like it when she did. 'Rosie doesn't look to me to need warnings. She's like you.'

'What do you mean, Jason, she's like me? We're not alike at all.'

'She's real. Brian says she's sweet as a bloom.'

'Does he? And the thorns?' If it made trouble, so much the worse. Who knew where Ricardo senior was now? Probably, if not certainly, dead.

It was a light lunch, much lighter than May's lunches used to be and with no sign of butter or cream or sugar. Whenever she looked restless, Brian would quickly put a new featherweight titbit in front of her, a lot of taste packed in no bulk. To refuse her something was always a mistake, you must substitute a more harmless pleasure. Yet she could sacrifice her welfare and means to a cause; the cause of people she would never know, who would never acknowledge her. She liked to give, impersonally, like a spring. She gave the management of Ravenglass to Hugh just as she would give a cheque to a refugee, without expecting any closer relationship in return. The spring doesn't care about the drinker. Pouring is its function.

'I have to go up to Byland soon,' Jason said when the fromage blanc with coulis of unsweetened raspberries was swept away before anyone had a chance of a second go. There was a silence.

'What for?' May asked.

'To fetch something.'

'I never go there any more.' Her voice was full of sorrow. Jason looked at her and saw there were tears in eyes darkened by memories and regret. Byland had come to her from her mother and so, for reasons too deep for a son to penetrate, she loved it like the blood in her own veins and also, as she grew older, dreaded it like a grave.

'No reason why I shouldn't.' He would have to insist here, obviously. There were rights at stake. Jason didn't want Byland, he didn't covet the forest or hanker after raising sheep in the rain but he did have an urgent need of that bronze figure.

'What do you want to fetch? Everything there's mine. There's nothing there that isn't.' She sounded a good deal less tearful now. Anything to do with Byland had this double effect – refusal and repossession. 'Brian,' she called, 'I want some more cheese. Or chocolates, or something. Jason's upsetting me about Byland.'

'Here you are, my love,' Brian said, coming across from the clever zone of cooking with coffee cups and tiny black tablets of chocolate. 'Jason wouldn't upset you knowingly, I'm sure, would you, Jason? Remember what he's been through while we watch the tides sloshing in and out.' Leaning forward to put the coffee on the table, he gave his hips a twitch as if addressing a golf ball. You might think he was a doubtful case, by his way of moving and the hint of a lisp. Or an undecided mimic of a doubtful case. But Jason didn't believe any of that. It was only a manner and behind it was an ordinary bloke, unsure, in the long run, of how to make a living.

'It's a Ricardo thing,' Jason said.

'Well nothing stops you flying to Manchester. Or take the train to Blackburn unless you're terrified like me of the rotten old railways.' May drank down most of her small glass of Rivesaltes. She kept a drop in case Brian allowed her no more, as he certainly wouldn't. A lot of calories in vin doux. It seemed almost like masochism, to Jason. Indulgence had always been her standard. 'But you can't get in the house.'

'What d'you mean?'

'It's let, on a lease.'

'Furnished?'

'Of course furnished. Where would I store the junk of ages?'

'Who's it let to? A school or something?'

'No. To someone you've never met. A colleague in my refugee work. A friend.'

'Who?'

'He's called Seker. Charlie Seker. He's a star to the refugees: he works for them night and day. They think he's a great man.'

'Is that here in London, like you?'

'Yes.'

'He has an office, for helping refugees?'

'You're very interested all of a sudden. Of course I suppose Marseille must be full of them.'

'It is,' Jason said. What was new here was the letting to Charlie of Byland. Hugh hadn't mentioned that. Perhaps he didn't know. 'If his office is in London, what does he want with Byland? For banging at the woodcock?'

'I expect so,' May said vaguely. She didn't like the noise of guns: it hurt her musical ear, she said. 'Darling woodcock, they nearly always get away. In any case Charlie's got people there now.'

'What people?'

'It's a resettlement organisation. That's why they need room.'

'How do they resettle anyone up there in the middle of nowhere? Refugees who probably don't speak English?'

'There are jobs in our industrial towns. They learn enough for simple work. Charlie's helpers place them where they can earn a living and save up for lessons.' May said this confidently. She always spoke with confidence when she didn't really know, or want to know more. The details of resettlement were for someone else.

'I hope you're getting a proper rent,' Jason said.

'The organisation's in its infancy. They haven't the money for what you call a proper rent.' May emptied her glass of the last drop of Rivesaltes and stared into it with a dissatisfied air. Then she looked over at Brian and away again. Obviously she didn't dare ask for more. Jason reached for the bottle and filled her glass for her.

'So how's this infant organisation financed?' he asked. The result wasn't what he'd expected. He'd thought the top-up of Rivesaltes would cushion the impact of the question and oil the wheels of her reply. This didn't happen. Her hand tightened round the stem of her wine glass and the colour of her face rose higher. Jason recognised the advance signs of a storm. It was liberty – to do as she liked with what was left of her Ravenglass fortune – being questioned. And this by the son who set the same store as she did on deviating from the ways sanctioned by people like Hugh. Now she was much angrier with him than she would be with Hugh, for that reason. Jason raised his glass to her, with a smile. 'Only interest, that's all. *Santé*,' he said. But this wasn't a formula capable of checking the fury. Actually, he wasn't even sure he'd meant it to.

'What interest? You've got no right to any interest at all. In Byland or the refugees. Sometimes you're too like your father. Always trying to get on top of me – telling me what to do.' She drained her glass and put it down with a bang, breaking the stem. Then she looked at her hand: 'You've made me cut myself. Look. I'm bleeding.' She sounded absolutely trium-phant. This small accident got her out of answering questions about the financing of Seker's operations, and should even prevent Jason from asking more of them. To make sure, she raised both hands to her face. 'After six years away and months and months in prison when she was in agonies of worry about you,' she said between deep breaths, 'you come back and interrogate your mother like the Spanish Inquisition.'

Jason laughed, watching her. 'You thought I was having an interesting time,' he said. 'Seeing more of the world and getting in fights.' Unlike Hugh, he didn't really mind the scenes when at last they came. They should be played for what they were worth. Scenes were one weapon, laughter another. 'Perhaps this Mr Seker can give me an appointment soon, and I'll ask permission to fetch what belongs to me.'

'Exactly what is it, you say belongs to you?'

'A thing my father gave me before he went away.'

'He didn't have anything to give.'

'Just this one thing.'

'Where is it? I never saw it.'

'It's hidden. I wanted to be sure of finding it.'

May got up from the table. She looked quite calm now, holding a paper napkin in the hand she'd cut. If she mentioned his father, it was for good reasons of her own. If Jason did, that was different. The current went cold. 'You can't make an appointment with Charlie and he's ex-directory. Don't inter-fere. I never interfere with you. Own lives. You know we agreed that long long ago, when you were very young.' She leaned down and kissed the top of Jason's head, holding it for a second between her hands and leaving a bit of blood on his ear. 'Now I'd better go for my little rest. Come and see me again. Don't disappear for ages without seeing me, Jason darling, you know how I miss you.'

'And I miss you. Scenes and all,' Jason said, and May smiled.

'I'll go down with him and feed the meter,' Brian said, clearing the broken glass like a routine.

'Don't be too long,' May said, the usual energetic sparkle back in her eyes. Burning up the life force, but good for ages yet.

In the lift, Brian handed Jason a page torn from a notebook. 'This is where you're likely to find Charlie Seker,' he said. 'The Nauticlub. It isn't what it sounds. Not really a club, either. You can join at the door, as long as they think you're clean. It's a swimming pool. You'll be able to take a good look at Charlie before he knows who you are. He's the sort of man you need to suss out before you have dealings – if you know what you're doing and what's good for you. And good for your nearest and dearest. He's usually there about four in the afternoon. Every other day with one or two of his hangers-on. Best of luck to you.'

So Brian hadn't needed to be recruited. He'd joined up for his own reasons. Those would have to be explored later. There could be more to it than just watching jealously over May. Money, for example, one way or another. 'How will I know him?'

'Did I say hangers-on? More disciples.' They were out on the pavement, beside the Rover. May bought a new car every three or four years and always a Rover. Rovers were a four-wheeled expression of the Ravenglass spirit, to her, keeping afloat in hard times. 'They don't look the part but he does. When you see him, you'll see what I mean. *Ciao. A bientôt.*'

'Just one thing – what makes you think I've any more interest in Seker than getting into Byland?'

'Oh, come on, Jason. Shape up. You've been out of circulation in London town far too long. You're transparent. Your mother falls for any unlikely story but even she didn't go for the

60

one about you hiding a treasure up there.'

Evidently Brian didn't know her as well as he'd thought. In her private world, belief or disbelief weren't primary. What counted was dramatic value. 'Stick around,' Jason said, 'and you'll find out that doesn't matter as much as you seem to think.'

Chapter Five

CHANGE WAS IN the air. The London groin stirred and spread. Last time, five or six years ago, Jason had wondered how it was he'd missed this sad town so much, in absences on the sea and elsewhere. Now, the whole animal strained with vitality. And it was a different heat from Marseille – heavy, humid, the sky pressing on it. And the women everywhere, all ages and kinds, in full leaf.

He was going to need a dealer in bronze antiquities. Not necessarily honest, one who'd recognise the thing he saw for what it must be. Jason had faith in his father's gift. He'd said, 'For the day you really need it, son,' and he was a Mediterranean with antiquity in his heart hard as a bell. Well, the day was here. Jason came up from the tube at Green Park, gazed about Piccadilly and wandered along Bond Street. The dealers round here were the eunuchs of Aladdin's cave, they were into nothing but decorating and furnishing for the grossly rich. What he needed was a middleman at the centre of a spider's web for serious collectors, not a golden supermarket. What he needed was someone like . . . of course – what he needed was Alex, the heart of a hundred webs.

Give Alex a buzz, that's what he'd do, after he'd seen Charlie
Seker at the Nauticlub. Jason wanted his own opinion about
Seker now, having heard the others. Was it his mother's obvious
inclination that disposed him rather in favour than against?
Due to hoping she'd end in the arms and bed of a man with a
heart not as hard as bronze? But she wasn't in Charlie's bed any
more. She had Brian in hers, and surely he did there whatever
was wanted. Required. Odd that you could face your mother
having requirements and wish her the best of luck, yet be
unable to dwell on details. Anyway, sympathy for Seker
wouldn't protect May from exploitation. It would be simpler if
he proved to be the imperial shit Alex said he was. Jason waved
down a taxi lingering along Aladdin street like a predatory
widow, lit up within and for hire in black.

The Nauticlub was in a quiet square beyond Regent's Park.
There were pleasant girls at the reception desk who took in
Jason's Marseille clothing at a glance but accepted his entrance
fee all the same, being of blond, not swarthy colouring. He
hired a bathing towel and bought a pair of trunks from the stall
presenting necessities for the unready – goggles, caps, body
shampoo. The girl in exercise tights behind the stall didn't give
the impression of being unprepared – far from it, she looked
ready for anything.

'These are nice and snug and they've a handy little pocket,'
she said.

'They think of it all.'

'Would you care to take a swimming lesson?'

'I can swim already.' The girl turned her back on him.
'Maybe another time when I'm freer. And you are too,' Jason
said.

'Who knows?' Should he ask her if she knew Charlie? And

whether he was here now and if not, when he would be? Too late. The swimming lesson was an offer and he hadn't measured up. As a possible ally she was lost.

These premises were a conversion of the ground floor and basement of some Victorian parvenu mansion. Coal or beer or cotton. Even shipping. The swimming pool was across a sloping yard now paved and covered over, in a vaulted building like stables for the house facing on to the square. The whole thing, the rise and fall, had Ravenglass written all over it. Not Ricardo, though. Nor Byland. Between this sour earth and the leaf mould of the forest, spongy and fertile, was a world – like between the cell in the Baumettes and the sky over the sea. Jason changed into the snug swimming slip with the handy pocket and went to sit on the rim of the pool with his feet in the water.

It was a good-sized, L-shaped pool under a roof light like a glass pyramid, with a jet stream at the far end for fitness swimming and so on. Nothing Olympic about it – this was a fun-pool. There were about a dozen people, adults and children in and out of the water, in the jacuzzi, on loungers near the bar. The splashing and voices and rush of the jet stream made a confused, hollow sound echoing round the vault and off the tiled floor, so you couldn't make out anything said unless spoken close to the ear. That must be why the group of men near the bar had their heads together. One of them, the tallest, was leaning upright against the brass rail while the others inclined towards him, like cats at dinner time about to rub themselves up your leg. He was the focus of attention and he was speaking. This must be Seker. Jason put his goggles on, slid into the pool and swam along the side where the bar was, on his back. When he drew level he slowed down and floated, watching through the yellow lenses. He could see the Christ likeness.

Seker looked like Jesus after a trim and set. He had thin tragic features and eyes awash with a sense of self. As he spoke, his mouth moved elastically as if mobility was part of the message. It was a mouth to watch, and the disciples watched it, apparently fascinated. What could he be saying to them, here in the busy Nauticlub? What was his parable? Jason drifted nearer to the edge of the pool and lifted his ears clear of the water.

'—dawn flight on the Wash,' the voice was saying, intonation rising at the end of each phrase; '—pink-foot in thousands off the North Sea. I once killed more than seventy in a morning. Flighting geese in the dark over your head – nothing to touch it.' There was something exaggerated about the accent. Of course there was. Synthetic. Not native wildflower. Mainland bullshit.

'Only someone like you, Charlie, touching seventy of them,' a disciple said. Jason thought of prisoners in an exercise yard – the boasting, the brown-nosing of the one with the strongest will.

'Geese don't vary greatly in air-speed. You're catching them after a long flight as they drop to the water. If you can hit one, you can hit them all. Of course not everyone can hit even one. Not by any means.'

'Of course not,' said another disciple.

'Now partridge on the Hungarian Plain – there's something else,' Seker said.

'Over furlongs of stubble, I expect, Charlie.' The one who said this, who had his back to the pool, moved his hips from side to side as he spoke, like Brian serving the coffee in St George's Square. It must be a new signal of subordination. Not a gesture you'd see tried out in a ship.

'Over miles of steppe,' Seker corrected sternly. 'With the wind behind them – incredible curl – the real test of a gun.'

66

Jason wondered if any of the disciples would point out that partridges don't fly beyond their own nesting parish. No one said a word. By the look of them they wouldn't know one end of a partridge from the other until it shat on them. But he could be prejudiced because Seker was from the Hungarian Plain and these were English crawlers. One thing was for sure – they weren't making gestures of submission on account of Charlie's alleged prowess at murdering geese in the half light but because there was money in it, somewhere. This was a business gathering going on at the edge of the Nauticlub azure pool. Seker was here to give orders and the others to receive them. The geese flighting into refuge were allegorical. The real game was human. Jason swam further off so as not to seem to eavesdrop.

'—my place up in Lancashire . . . woodcock. Totally private . . . another century.' The voice came in waves, always with that rising intonation which left you wondering what was really being got at. 'If some of you've never tried woodcock, you can learn in your time off.' That bit of the message was perfectly clear and spoken more loudly, like across a classroom, and Jason knew he hadn't missed any of it. These hangers-on were being sent up to Byland with a project for their leisure hours. Probably the conference was at an end. Jason turned at the L and swam back underwater towards the bar. When he surfaced, he saw that Charlie was staring hard at him. He then pointed in Jason's direction and issued an order to one of the aides. This man, blond with a pony tail, stepped across to the side of the pool.

'You,' he said loudly to Jason. 'Mr Charles Seker wants a word with you. Over here.' He sounded a bit American. Was Seker a majority shareholder in the Nauticlub? Or did this aide think his personal law applied to everybody? Either way, Jason was here to meet Seker and now was as good a time as any.

'What's your first name?'

'Raoul.'

'Okay, Raoul, hop back and tell your governor I'll be with him in a minute.'

Jason fetched his towel and crossed to the bar. The towel wasn't exactly for protection but more than he'd have had in just the Lycra slip. 'Hi, Mr Seker,' he said, and held out his hand to Charlie who was now sitting in an armchair with long legs crossed under a kind of gown he wore, like a caftan. Charlie took the hand in his and let it go quickly, as if a longer hold could commit him to something he hadn't yet thought through.

'Your face looks familiar,' he said. 'We've met before?'

'I don't think so.'

'I seem to know you though.' Had Charlie seen a photograph of him? May didn't have photographs on view, she lived strictly in the present. But she might have one in a drawer in her bedroom. Was Seker the kind of man to rummage in a woman's furniture? There wasn't much doubt about the answer. He was. He would rummage for information. The narrow face and features were made for women's secrets.

'You're thinking of someone else. I haven't been around these last years.'

'I guess he puts you in mind of that little scumbag Brian,' Raoul said, then laughed. 'There's a likeness.' Jason looked over at him. This could be the start of unfriendly relations between him and Raoul. But more than that, the idea of a resemblance to Brian was new. He didn't like to think of the implications. Not on his own account, on May's.

'That may be it,' Charlie said. 'Fetch this gentleman something to sit on, one of you.' He smiled at Jason, a smile full of sweetness, like a woman's. 'No offence. Raoul's a simple boy, full of fun.' That wasn't Jason's assessment. To his mind, Raoul was a good example of someone whose strength had out-stripped his intelligence – not, in his case, an exploit. Still, he looked pretty strong and never stayed still, one muscle group or another kept in constant play.

'Is simple fun what you pay him for?' Jason asked, sitting upright, ready for take-off, in the chair pushed forward by Raoul with the back of his fist.

'Ha ha,' Charlie went, carefully. When the smile ceased, Jason noticed, Charlie's eyes lost sparkle as abruptly, com-pletely, as a soaked firework. What replaced it was the look of a prisoner deprived of humour, like food or air. 'No no. I give work to a number of young men who could otherwise find themselves at a loose end – missing out on the new opportun-ities of the day. Which must be caught like woodcock in flight. Might you be one of those, Mr—?' The smile returned. All that smiling could make you wonder a bit, but Jason believed it was nothing but routine Central European charm. Not that Alex often smiled, come to think of it. But his teeth weren't anything special. Charlie's were absolutely brilliant.

The moment of truth was here. To give a false identity would be no good, because if he planned to look into Seker's activities he'd be found out sooner or later, causing unnecessary difficul-ties. 'Ricardo,' he said. 'Jason Ricardo, seaman.'

'Yes. Quite.' Charlie showed no surprise. He must have known even when Jason was hiding behind the goggles. 'On leave?'

'Ashore.'

'Your brother Hugh is an acquaintance.'

To surprise him? Better show surprise anyway. 'What a coincidence. Extraordinary. You know Hugh who's mentioned a brother Jason. I'm staying at Hugh's place.'

'With his charming wife.'

'Like you say.'

'I think he mentioned too ... I believe he said you had trouble with some French administration. I know what that is. I've lived in France. Glad to see you let off the—' Charlie stopped for the right word and didn't come up with it. Hugh wouldn't have told him all that. Neither would May. She could keep very quiet when she wanted to, on things that were no kind of business of the people she spent her nights with. It was a good quality not expected by those who didn't know her well. They usually thought she was a woman to spill the works down to the last detail. So the only source must be Brian. More than ever he appeared in an uncertain light. A gambler on information.

'Off the hook for now,' Jason said. 'You know how their administration has a long arm.'

He'd slipped up. Now Seker knew something he wasn't likely to forget, that Jason's liberty was conditional, and you could see him register it. 'What will you drink, Jason?' he asked. 'Name it. Raoul, call that barman.' If you listened carefully there was a trace of American in his voice too. It was like a drop of Angostura to sharpen things up. And his tongue when he spoke was working near the front of his mouth, ladling out the *l* sounds. Charlie Seker was unencumbered with precise nationality, like Alex. It was another kind of freedom.

'I don't drink in the afternoon.'

'But at lunchtime.'

'Not usually.'

'Today was a special occasion?' May's champagne still on his breath must register even in the air of the Nauticlub.

'I'll have a lager,' Jason said. Seker was learning things about him, and not the other way around. He tried to take stock. On reflection, it wasn't quite so. He now knew that Seker was thinking of enrolling him. The quick way to find out what the disciples did was to join them. 'Cheers, Charlie,' he said when the lager was handed to him. 'So what about these opportunities of the day? What are they?'

'You're interested?'

'If I wasn't I wouldn't ask.'

'It could be a polite question.'

'I'm not so polite that I like hanging around doing nothing.'

'Good,' Charlie said. Raoul handed him a glass with a lot of ice and a colourless drink, possibly mineral water, possibly vodka. He drank some of it now, turning the liquid round his tongue as if weighing it before he swallowed. All his movements including speech were like that – deliberate, pondered. You could imagine him willing to wait for Alex's mailing list in the post. 'We could be helpful to each other.'

'Charlie—' Raoul interrupted.

Charlie pivoted on his chair like a fisherman off the Florida coast. 'Raoul. Go jump in the water and come up when I tell you,' he said with his smile. 'Mr Ricardo and I have connections to explore.' Obedience counted for a lot in the Seker outfit. Raoul dived into the pool and disappeared round the bend of the L, flailing the water. This would be marked up on the tally of his relations with Jason, to be settled some time when Charlie wasn't around. Raoul didn't look like a patient man but one who could wait, if he had to, for the right moment to get even. Charlie watched him go and then turned back. 'He's a hasty boy,' he said. 'You and I are old enough to be his father and we know the trouble too much hurry can get us into. I think it's a mistake you wouldn't make.' Jason nodded his head and said nothing. He was probably about twelve years older than Raoul. 'Not even when your days outside are numbered.'

71

What was Charlie really saying here? Was it a warning? An invitation? To do with May, of course. The bankroll. Have the errant prodigal tied up as soon as he surfaces. Keep him for Raoul. Jason wondered if Raoul carried a weapon. It seemed likely. 'I must be a bit younger than you, Charlie,' he said. 'I'd put you nearer my mother's age. She had me when she was sixteen.'

'So the regretted Ricardo took her before the age of consent.'

'As far as I know, he's still alive. And he wouldn't be the only one into minors.'

'It'll be found to be universal, when the hypocrites come out of the woodwork,' Charlie said. The smile was so frank, you had to believe in it. 'Are you a hypocrite about that?'

'No,' Jason said. 'If you've worked the North African ports you're used to anything.'

'And tried it all?'

'Mostly,' Jason said. Admit anything to learn something.

'Polymorph?'

'Could be.'

'Welcome to the club,' Charlie said.

Okay. Some people lean on it. Most pass on. 'I don't bother about other people's tendencies.'

Charlie laughed. His laugh was very different from his smile, it was corrosive. 'So what would yours be, Jason? Twelve to thirteen? Or midshipmen? Commodities can be supplied if you have the right friends in this town. Ask Raoul.'

A classic. Charlie really wanted him in. And there could even be a bit of fellow feeling. They were both mercenaries on the outside. The gang, by contrast, was orthodox. Charlie must feel lonely with people like that even if they did exactly what he told them. 'I'll think about it when I have more time. Right now I'm looking for liquid assets to tide me over.'

'On dry land?'

'That's it.'

Charlie reached into his gown and produced a card from a little silver case, convex to sit comfortably against the ribs. 'Call me some time, Jason,' he said. 'But don't leave it long. I might forget you.'

'Thanks for the drink.' Jason took the card and stood up.

'Cheers, Jason,' Charlie said. It sounded like a foreign idiom in his mouth.

'Cheers Charlie.' Jason was glad of the towel as he walked away. Raoul, not a good swimmer, was watching him from the shallow end.

In this weather London seemed even more a hotbed than Marseille. Each street a strip scene. Jason felt his clothing tight for the conditions. Relief would be a fine thing but for some reason he recoiled from the quick way out. That selection of cards in the nearest telephone box. When he entered one it was for a different reason.

'*Oui, j'écoute. Ascolto.* I'm hearing.' Alex's number had rung for a long time before he answered. Probably he had to connect a recorder, just in case.

'It's me, Jason.'

'Yes?'

'I'm in London.' Alex offered no comment on this. True, he hadn't asked. 'I've met Charlie Seker.'

A click at the other end suggested that the recorder was now turned on. 'How did you find him?' Alex asked.

'My mother's young friend pointed me in the right direction.'

'No I'm not enquiring your logistics, Jason. I'm interested in your impressions.'

'I liked him. He was friendly.'

73

'And charming?'

'That all right.'

'So what was your real impression?'

'He's certainly got something going, but no idea what. He's surrounded by educated rough trade.'

Alex gave his high-pitched laugh. 'Educated ignorant.'

'I mean guys whose fathers paid so they'd turn out like they are.'

'That's what my own father did,' Alex said. 'He sent me to the Benedictines.' He sounded sad, regretting advantages fouled up. He could have gone straight to the Quai D'Orsay and by now be well up the ladder to ambassador. An Excellence, think of it – instead of videos. 'And you?'

'I was not educated,' Jason said. 'It somehow got blanked out of the CV.'

'Well. Not as much as you think. What else was there?'

'I want advice about selling something, Alex.'

'Why would I advise you?'

'Because you owe me money, morally.'

'Moral money? Never heard of it.'

Jason laughed. He'd known all along there would be no easy way. 'It's an antiquity. I mean a real one. Not just a couple of hundred years old.'

'That has to be proved.' Alex's voice had changed. He sounded careful.

'I thought of showing it to Christie's first of all.' In the pause following this remark Jason could hear breath drawn in. That was a good sign. Alex, like a whale, only seemed to breathe occasionally. Getting interested usually set it off.

'I wouldn't do that in too much of a hurry,' he said. 'There are people with few scruples. If it's any good you want to keep quiet and get a private opinion.'

74

'Like from one of your expert friends.'

'You haven't told me what it is.'

'It's a bronze figure. Some kind of Venus, I think. About twenty-five centimetres high.'

'Did you borrow it from your mother?'

'My father gave it to me. He said it came out of the sea near Marseille. Marseille was founded by the Greeks, you know.'

'I see,' Alex said. Now he was really interested. His voice on the line was all the more cautious. 'You've got this piece with you?'

'It's up north. I'll have to fetch it. Or I dare say Christie's have a representative there. He could pick it up and save me a journey.'

'Be reasonable, Jason. You didn't ring me to say you'd make this thing over unseen to Christie's man in the savage north of your country. Be fair. We're old friends and you rang for help. I'll scratch you if you scratch me.'

'So you'd like to see it?'

'I would. And before anyone else. Meanwhile I'll look up my contacts in the right world.'

'What world would that be?'

'Collectors for collectors. The provenance of your figure if it came from your father must be dubious. It could have been stolen. But if we play it carefully we may find the right exit. Planning, Jason. Authentification on engraved paper from the address of one of the known authorities in the field – a signature – you see, the sort of thing that can't be hurried. Carbon dating, too, that needs time.'

'Are these collectors for collectors so hard? I mean when they see the beauty—?'

'They're agents. They have to satisfy the principals. And we know where those come from, most of them.'

'I can guess.'

'What colour's your bronze, by the way?'

'Greenish. It's in a damp place and I haven't seen it for years.'

'Look, Jason. As your friend, I'd like to help. But if you haven't seen the item for years you could be all wrong about it. I think you must get it in your hands and then we'll talk again. You could send a photograph. No, don't do that if it fell off the back of a Greek boat. Find it wherever it is and bring it over.'

As Jason hung up he heard a cry of pain from the other end. Alex suffered from lots of minor complaints – belly-aches, headaches, piles. He took no exercise and lived on chocolates as he listened to the *putes* and their clients tramping up and down the stairs. He was a champion of unfitness. He must have had a worse twinge than usual. On the other hand, he might have been assaulted by someone. If so something should be done, and at once. Jason rang again.

'Are you okay there, Alex?'

'Thank God you called back. I've no number for you. Forget everything I said about bringing that piece to Paris. The metal detectors would pick it up. Then you'd have problems. They all link instantaneously.'

'Who?'

'Where can I reach you?'

'I'm at my brother Hugh's.' Jason gave the number. 'I don't know for how long.'

'He may throw you out?'

'I don't think his brand new wife likes me around.'

'Keep me *au courant*.'

'*Ciao* Alex. Don't leave any messages.'

There was a grunt from the other end. 'Why not?'

Chapter Six

TOMORROW WAS THEIR wedding anniversary. The first. Subject of so many down-market jokes. But Hugh hadn't forgotten, in fact he'd been thinking about it for days. He'd take her to Cristabel's again. His feet itched and twitched at the thought like a signal. Moving to music, his body could say so much that didn't come out in words. Or in bed. Those techniques – squeezing the gland just in time, so it was claimed – didn't seem to work too well. He couldn't help it, it was maddening, he ejaculated however hard she squeezed, and on to the squeezing hand. Rosie didn't say anything but it must be a disappointment not to have cured him yet. She must feel it – that she hadn't succeeded. But love would solve all, he felt sure, given time. By the next anniversary. And for now, there was Cristabel's. And the floor. And the newest thing from Brazil, he was already into that.

He wanted a word with Deakin & Deakin. He wondered where they used to meet, him and May. An image formed up in his head, involuntarily, of May and the legal adviser hard at it. The striped legal trousers down, *habeas corpus*, *mens rea*, and no *ejaculatio praecox*. Hugh rang the chambers in Lincoln's Inn and asked for an appointment.

★ ★ ★

Jason crossed Regent's Park among the sunbathers and those others who like in the Brassens song prefer their loving on public benches. He ought to go back to Fulham, though he wasn't sure why. Hugh probably came home from work between five and six, boss's hours. It was four now. He skirted the lake, crossed the footbridge, and came out at the top of Baker Street. There was no hurry to go down into the dark stink of the underground. He kept walking. He was at Marble Arch before he realised how fast he was going. He slowed down and found his way through the underpass into the dark. Might as well walk on. Fulham wasn't going to run away. It drew him and he resisted. But he was soon walking again with a long stride; he was aware of crossing the ground among trees like a roe. When he reached the Serpentine he slowed down again. He hung over the balustrade of the bridge. He watched the swans. He observed the bathers in the black-green water. More love-makers in rowing boats hove to under the willows. This was one of the many hearts of the town that could never die. It was good here but it wasn't where he needed to be. Needed? He didn't need to be anywhere, actually. No lading, no embarkation depended on his presence. He was free and unneeded.

Of course he didn't believe that. The roe doesn't bound for nothing. He strode on past the museums without seeing them. When he hit the Fulham Road and read the name on the street sign it was like the end of a remission. He waved down a taxi and gave Hugh's address.

He had enough in his pocket, with not much over. A few hundred francs he could change tomorrow but that would clean him out. He must have a talk with Hugh and he didn't relish it. For this evening, he hadn't even enough left to buy himself a dinner. He was a dependent guest. That was one of the reasons for cold feet about this return to Fulham, while he was speeding over the grass and down Exhibition Road, almost at a run through the South Kensington squares and gardens. What other reason was there, could there be? None. There was no sign of Hugh's car. Jason let himself into the house, hoping to find it empty, and closed the door quietly behind him. He might look out those francs straight away, now, and then see if any banks round here stayed open late. His foot was already on the first step of the stairs when he felt watched. Or perhaps there was a sound – tension confused the senses. He turned back.

There she was. The stairs in this house were new, rising out of the centre, all aluminium and underwater-green glass planks with furniture to match. Including the huge sofa taking up one angle of the room. That's where Rosie was, hidden in the corner with a book in her lap and her legs folded beside her on the green leather. It was a fat, important book with a photograph of a great spreading tree on the cover. Jason liked great trees but he thought that if you found one you should keep your mouth shut. Putting them into a coffee-table book was as bad as signposting them from the road.

'Have a drink,' Rosie said from the far end of the sofa. She didn't say it in a hospitable way and she wasn't smiling. On the contrary, she looked unhappy, angry, like any woman dealt a bad hand by nature. Her evident feelings about the situation reflected Jason's own. He didn't want to be her guest and she didn't wish him to be. Anyway, nature had been generous to her, she couldn't be angry about that. They stared at each other in reciprocal, trapped resentment. She had good ears, they made you want—

'Thanks, I'll wait for Hugh.'

'Up to you.' Rosie had no drink herself, as far as he could see; she wasn't smoking, she wasn't reading, she wasn't noting down thoughts for later use. Now she seemed to retreat further into the angle of the sofa like a child about to hide behind the cushions. Her hand moved towards the tree book, then she drew it back. Without thinking what he was doing, Jason came a few steps closer so he was staring down at her from a couple of yards. She looked up at him, and away again. Eyes shifting like that tell you all you need to know, they can tell you something you don't want to know about yourself by what they've recognised.

'If there's some of that wine—'

'There's a whole bloody case.'

'Minus two.'

'Minus two or three.'

'Do you want a glass?' Rosie didn't answer. Whether either of them really wanted it or not, they were going to drink a bottle again because a bottle of wine defers commitment. 'I'll get them.' Jason went into the kitchen where he'd seen the case earlier on. He found two glasses and a corkscrew and returned to the living room. Rosie wasn't there any more. The tree book was planted in the hollow where she'd been curled up and the scent led towards the conservatory. Jason followed it, expecting to find her on the swinging seat. She wasn't there either. He walked out into the narrow garden, planted with sub-tropical evergreens including a couple of palms. There was an oleander growing in a pot and a smell of lavender in flower. Rosie was standing with her back to the wall in the far corner under the spreading palm fans. When she saw Jason she drew nearer the trunk as if she'd been driven into the garden to escape an intruder. But the truculence in her voice when she spoke made a quite different impression.

'It's Hugh who looks after this garden,' she said, as if he'd asked about it.

'Good.'

'What d'you mean, "good"? You mean it gives him something to do with his spare time?'

'No, I didn't mean that. I didn't mean anything.'

'He likes exotic plants. He's gifted.'

'I can see. Why don't you come away from them? I've brought the wine.'

'It's me lives here, not you,' Rosie said, her voice unsteady.

'I know. With Hugh.'

'He could be back any time now.' She wrapped her arms round herself as if she was wrapping Hugh to her breast.

'Come and sit on the swing. Shall I open the bottle?'

'For God's sake,' Rosie said, and came across the garden to the conservatory. When she reached Jason on the step, she stopped and turned. 'Hugh can be a bit two-faced but he has good qualities. He's tender. He's a marvellous dancer. Acrobatic. People stop to watch him. It's what I fell in love with. Silly, I know. He admires you.'

'I can't dance. We've never fallen out in our lives.'

'Poor Hugh.'

'We're like that.' He crossed the index and middle finger of his right hand and laid them like a penknife on his left forearm, below the rolled-up sleeve. 'It can't change. It kept me going when I was banged up.'

Rosie laughed, a dry laugh. 'I suppose most of the others felt separated from women, not brothers,' she said.

'You don't know about the Mediterranean,' Jason said. 'Down there, even the women recognise it.' From inside came the sound of the telephone. Rosie walked past him and then he could hear her speaking at the other end of the living room.

'All right. Later then.' And after a pause, 'No. No sign of him.' She came back into the conservatory and sat on the swing.

She looked tired. She closed her eyes as the seat took up her weight and began to move under it.

'Hugh's held up. He won't be back for dinner,' she said. 'And I didn't mean you were up each other.' Jason thought she piled it on like that because she was near the end of her tether. He drew the cork. The new wine let go a momentary pink sparkle into the sunlight of the conservatory and a flavour of fruit. Peaches, perhaps.

'Cheers.'

'Oh yes, cheers indeed,' Rosie answered. Sitting next to her, Jason heard his heart going. The system wasn't waiting for the okay from the will. He looked at Rosie and smelt hostility coming off her like an animal. But there was the other odour spread about too, the fatality. Her eyebrows were raised and eyes wide as if taken by surprise. 'Too hard on Hugh, being delayed like that,' she said, and leaned towards him. It looked like an involuntary movement to do with balance, the wine glass, and the swinging seat.

'Hard all round,' Jason said, and turned so they came together almost at once, their glasses clashing in mid-air, wine spilt, the seat rocking like a dinghy. After a bit, Rosie sat up straight.

'Not here,' she said. 'Upstairs.'

'Right,' Jason said. He drew a breath. 'Fine.'

When she was near the top of the green glass planks she turned her head. 'Are you coming Ricardo, or what?'

'I'm here.' As he climbed he repeated to himself over and over, 'Criminal intent—' The words took him towards the half-open door and Rosie waiting in the middle of the room. She was laughing now, strain broken at last.

'We did all we could,' she said.

When Hugh got home at ten Jason was in the shower and

heard the front door bang shut. He didn't go down. The order of life had changed, whatever that meant. Not the same as evolution. More like turning a coat.

Alex was coming by Eurostar, and bringing cash. Jason waited for him near the money-changers' desk at the exit from Customs. It was an emergency and Alex had responded to it, not just from kindness of heart. He must believe in the potential of the bronze figure, and could have another motive besides. Alex had had time to think and maybe he'd like to see something more of Charlie, in different circumstances. With the advantage of preparation. Probably Alex needed an ally as much as Jason, each supplying what the other lacked. Cash back-up, to begin with.

Because he'd left Hugh's house first thing in the morning, without breakfast and without saying goodbye to anyone. Inside him he carried a cargo not lashed down. Remorse. The only thing to do with it was take it away. He hadn't thought yet how to explain his sudden departure to Hugh. Probably tell him he'd found a woman, that's what Hugh would expect anyway. Jason's thought veered off from Rosie and her image. In a day or two he would think less about her, that was how to see it. And once he thought less about her, he'd find a way back. He hoped. Everything else – May's affairs, Byland, the examining judge in Marseille – seemed less important. They'd shifted into the distance.

He could hear Alex's voice calling him. His attention had been off wandering like a child. Alex was standing just six feet away, staring at him; an obese mass of pornography-peddling, sweating flesh. He wore a raincoat and carried a bag in each hand. 'Wake up, Jason,' he wheezed. 'Am I to carry my own luggage half across London in this temperature?' His English sounded more foreign here. There was a slight lisp, plus a touch of guttural. The effect was much more endearing than in Paris. He sounded like a central European tourist who'd made money out of the end of the Cold War. He didn't look like one, though. He was unshaven and his clothes were dirty. You couldn't call them ill-fitting – no clothes could fit him, his physique wasn't made for clothes. But they were a sorry sight. Under the raincoat was a grubby white shirt and crumpled trousers of synthetic fibre. God only knew about his under-clothes.

'Glad to see you, Alex. Sorry, I was on the moon.'

'Where are the taxis?'

'The queue's down there.'

'My God. Half a kilometre in the distance . . . miles away.'

'Nothing like. It looks a long way because it's a brand new building. Here, I'll take your bags. We won't hurry.'

'Oh yes we will,' Alex said. 'I can't bear being about in public places. Among all these—' He didn't finish the phrase but rolled along down the slope at an alarming rate considering his bulk. If he fell, life would get very difficult.

In the taxi, Alex fished a bundle of notes from his pocket. 'This is an advance,' he said, spacing out the words. Jason counted the notes. There were ten fifties. A minimum to get on with. He could go as far as Byland with that, easy. 'You said you were in trouble.'

'A family problem.'

'Have you got Charlie Seker's card on you?'

'Here it is.'

Alex took the card and wrote the details in a notebook. 'That's very useful. He isn't in any directories and his videos go to a post-box number in somewhere called Putney. Is this address in Putney too?'

'I shouldn't think this is his address,' Jason said. 'I suspect it's some sort of run-down office and if you went there it would be Raoul or one of the lads who opened the door to you.'

'Raoul?'

'Charlie's number one assistant arsehole.'

'Who does anything he's told?'

'I'd think almost anything.'

'How lucky I have you with me,' Alex said. 'Where are you staying?'

'The same hotel as you, for tonight.'

'I thought you were going to your brother's?'

'It didn't work out.'

'That wasn't long, but say no more,' Alex said, his voice livelier from the curiosity that can bide its time. Jason was tempted to confide. Alex was about the last person likely to pass hard judgement. He owed no obedience anywhere. But on reflection, no. The confidence wasn't his to give. It was in a way – the only way that mattered – Hugh's confidence.

'Thanks for the cash,' Jason said instead.

'I look forward to seeing the bronze. I trust it'll be as good as you say. The advance is returnable if it isn't.'

'D'you mean it wasn't your money?'

'I have been in touch with a possible client, yes.'

'There's a complication. I'll tell you about it in the hotel.'

'You didn't say anything about any complications,' Alex said, and his eyes turned hard.

'It's not a fatal one. It just needs working out, that's all.'

'I hope so.'

In the hotel bedroom Alex at once produced a bottle of Pernod from his bag. 'This is to sterilise the water,' he said. 'God, the heat here, the humidity.' Once he had a glass in his hand he crossed to the window and looked out. 'Where are we?'

'Near Paddington.'

'What is Paddington, please?'

'A railway station. You go to Oxford from it.'

'I don't wish to go to Oxford. The Sorbonne was too much for me. After Charlie took the girl . . . why did you choose this district? It's depressing I find. It's bourgeois but down-market. Bourgeois in Paris always means going up.'

'Because there's a lot of cheap hotels here. And restaurants, near the station.'

Alex sat on the bed with his drink already half finished. 'I never eat in restaurants. You must fetch me something prepared from outside and I'll eat it here. I've brought my chocolates.' He took a box of them from one of his bags. 'Tomorrow we must look for a room with a little kitchen. I need to be absolutely private.'

What was he afraid of? Perhaps it was just the anonymity a wise pornographer needs. Not that Alex – as far as Jason knew – wrote or filmed any works of pornography himself. He was a merchant, a distributor, a turner-around of wealth, not a primary producer. But it was a trade where you could attract enemies, and probably blackmail. 'You might have to take it by the week. A non-returnable advance.'

'I expect to be here at least a week.'

'What about business?'

Alex went into the shower cubicle to add a dash of water to his second drink. 'The beauty of my business is, all traffic reaches it from other sites. It's like the spiritual plane – no exact locality.' He was sounding much more affable now, even jocular.

'So whereabouts count for nothing.'

'The whereabouts that count,' Alex said, coming down to earth; 'is your bronze figure. What are these complications? Have a little Pernod, by the way . . . ring for another glass. Is

86

there a bell? Will anyone answer it? Accept my apology. I was thirsty. I didn't think of you. An oversight.' It was a French exercise in politeness – strictly gratuitous, too late, and not from the heart. Better than nothing, all the same. Anyway, Jason needed and even liked Alex enough to put up with it.

'There's a glass here.'

'I'm waiting,' Alex said.

'Years ago I put the figure in a safe place. I hid it. In my mother's house up the other side of Manchester. In the middle of a kind of forest.'

'Manchester? Can you get there from Paddington too?'

'No. But you can fly there.'

'First you tell me on the telephone there's no hurry and you'll think about it. Now you bring me from Paris by train and you talk of flying to Manchester. Obviously there's a hurry after all. I suppose it's to do with the family matter. So what are you waiting for?'

'My mother's let the house and everything else to Charlie Seker. It's closed up. His gang go there to learn to shoot woodcock. It's a difficult thing to do,' Jason explained.

'Can't they be caught with snares?'

'Not in England.'

'Never mind all that,' Alex said, waving it away with the back of his hand. 'If Charlie is the tenant of your mother's house in the country, and he keeps it closed, he won't only be using it for sports . . . hunting . . . I think.'

'Just what I think too.'

'How big is the house?'

'Not big. It was built for shelter, to stay a few nights. It's hardly a real house. More what they call a folly.'

Alex looked as if this didn't surprise him, over here. 'And the forest? Is it a state forest? Who owns it?'

87

'It's just a big old wood, really. Not cultivated. It goes with the house.'

'It too belongs to your mother?'

'Belongs? I suppose so.'

'And all this property, you say it's not exploited commercially?'

'Perhaps Charlie's exploiting it.'

'Yes. Commerce abhors a vacuum. That's how it's always worked; that's how to work it,' Alex said, and poured himself another Pernod. 'I'm feeling much more cheerful.'

'I'd noticed that.'

'The situation is interesting. We have Charlie Seker in our sights. Your mother must tell him, as his landlord, that you need to go to this folly in the forest and find something of yours.'

'She won't do that.'

'Why not?'

'Because it's more amusing to watch me get myself in and out of trouble. It's hard to explain. She's adventurous by nature, but hung-up on just being a woman.'

'I understand. Vicarious fantasies – the male in jeopardy. Rewards and punishments. Quite common.'

'If you like,' Jason said. He felt he'd given too much away. His mother's mysteries should remain private.

'You see, it wasn't so hard to explain after all,' Alex said. 'In business, you learn a lot about women. More than most of the people who have carnal relations with them.'

'Don't you ever . . . haven't you—?'

'I told you. Charlie robbed me.'

'There's still time.'

'Look at me,' Alex said, simply. He didn't really seem to mind. If he was a eunuch because alcohol and chocolates and imaginary longing had shrivelled up his tackle, what had he lost? Something he had no more use for. 'All the better. Approach Charlie directly. Go to this address where the arse-hole Raoul opens the door. Demand to penetrate the unex-ploited forest. I'll wait here but before you go you'd better bring me something to eat.' A worrying thought seemed to occur to Alex. His hand shook and he spilled some of his drink on to his trousers. He made no move to rinse it off. 'Don't be gone too long,' he said. 'Don't go to Manchester or anywhere else without first coming back to see what I need. You know I haven't been away from my room in Montmartre for years. Don't let me down. Don't abandon me, Jason.'

It was a small, blind-looking house in a back street between the Regent's Canal and City Road. Not yet smartened up and sold on. There was no name on the bell which rang – if it did ring – silently somewhere behind shuttered windows. Jason checked the card. He pressed the bell again. He could wait if whoever was inside had to put his trousers on to come to the door. Usual cause of delay at an address like this. While he waited, he examined the fabric of the building. Potentially, it was attrac-tive. The brick was a blackened yellow like teeth once gleam-ing, laughing; and if you looked closely enough, with flecks of violet in the mixture. London Stock. His Ravenglass grand-father, second or third generation of merchant adventurers, had put money into a brickworks, somewhere down in Kent. Jason remembered being brought there as a boy, shown round, urged to see how bricks were made. To encourage him to grow up as a merchant. It hadn't taken. He was only an adventurer. Anyway, the brick business had collapsed soon after, his mother said, as if his visit had convinced the spirit of the place that there was no future for it. Suicide of a brickworks. But London Stock was still a historic material, the brick of a great town.

'Yes? Oh, it's you.'

'Is Charlie here? He told me to look him up.'

'Listen, cuntface,' Raoul said without preamble. 'We know about you, and we don't want you around. You could have caught something nasty in prison. We don't want to sit in any chairs where your ass has been. Be advised. Fuck off and stay fucked off.' He stood four square in the doorway, blocking it completely. Jason inspected him. Raoul now wore a grey flannel suit with a wide chalk stripe in it, broad in the shoulder, waspish in the waist. Jason didn't know much about clothes but this suit rang a bell. He'd seen suits like it in Valetta, or Cairo – suits impossible to wear in good faith, anywhere. They told a studied lie about the man inside. He wasn't a respecter of dress or other civilised convention. He was a hun in loungewear. No prisoners taken.

'Here's his card your boss gave me.' Jason held it towards Raoul, while keeping out of reach. 'And here's what he wrote on the back – "admit without fail" – pretty clear, I think.'

'Let's have a look at that.'

'Oh no you don't,' Jason said, returning the card to his pocket. 'If he's here, go and tell him I'm on the doorstep. If not, I have other ways of finding him, and I'll mention what's happened.'

'You'd better come in.'

'Thanks, I'd rather not.'

'Here's hoping you drop dead of Aids while you wait then.' Raoul slammed the door behind him and the first few of his footsteps were audible from beyond it. Then silence.

Jason believed Charlie was somewhere about. Otherwise the interview with Raoul would have turned out rougher. He could have called one or two of his mates from inside to lend a hand.

They were an exclusive group and wanted no intruders. They were up to no good, yet on to some good thing here. Jason waited patiently in the street. After a couple of minutes a shutter opened in a second-floor window.

'Ricardo,' Charlie called, leaning out, showing his smile. 'Just a minute and we'll go for a coffee.' The head disappeared and the shutter closed. In no time at all he was on the doorstep, spreading harmlessness all about him. 'Good to . . . we'll have a talk in private. There's a café round the corner.' He led the way. It was a small, newish café with coffee-coloured furniture and lighting and personnel. The coffee smelled good, too. 'So you want to work,' Charlie said when he'd stirred his cup. 'I thought you would. I'm not surprised to see you. We must think what we can do for you – or you for us. Friend Raoul, between these four walls, is wood from the collar up. Useful for apish tricks. I need a man with a bit of something grey between the ears. You're a Ricardo, you might do.'

'Hugh's the intelligent one.'

Charlie looked at him. 'You don't really think that. It's to compensate. Abel and Cain. Perhaps there's even more to it. You can confide in me. Myths are my—'

Jason noticed how Charlie spoke in short sharp sentences, like a Frenchman used to long ones and fighting for a stranglehold on English grammar. 'There's nothing to tell.' Charlie looked unconvinced. The moment had come to bring May into the conversation. 'I didn't find you to ask for work, anyway not today. My mother says she's let you Byland on a lease. There's something I left there years ago, just a bit of my belongings. A piece of identity, in a way. She says I have to ask you.'

'I see. Did you know about that when we met at the Nauticlub?'

'No idea at all. Pure chance. You can imagine my surprise when she told me.'

'Yes, I can,' Charlie said. Whether he believed it or not, he looked more wary than before. 'The whole place is closed till I go next month. You wouldn't be able to get in. There's no one there.'

'May said so and I've thought about that,' Jason said, 'and I've got an idea.'

'We'll hear your idea.'

'Brian Foley. It seems you know him; she knows him too—' Jason paused. He hadn't meant a joke and he wanted to seem neutral regarding May's lovers, past and present, talking to Charlie who'd filled the post for quite a time. He *was* neutral about them. At least he thought so. 'Brian could come up with me as your agent. Give him the instructions and the keys, I'll pick up my stuff, the lease will be respected. And you won't have your shooting disturbed.'

'It's not as simple as that,' Charlie said. 'It's a lease with an option to purchase. I plan to exercise the option while the lease runs. There are affairs of mine . . . which are—'

'The sort of thing it's Raoul's job to see to? Monkey business?'

'Private. Read the Landlord and Tenant Act. I have exclusive enjoyment.'

'It's why I'm asking permission. Otherwise I'd just go. I know my way in, believe me.' Jason regretted saying this. Never give gratuitous information. He could see Charlie take it on board.

'I don't advise that,' Charlie said. 'Come next month when I'm there. Meanwhile we'll write you into the payroll.'

To draw a wage out of funds originating from May, that's what. If she'd offered a provisional subsidy to tide him over Jason would have taken it. But she hadn't, and he didn't mean to get one through Charlie Seker. 'If you're converting your lease to a purchase, the sooner I get my property away from the place the better. I could talk to Foley tonight and fix it.'

'Next month.'

'Then I'll have to take it up with May.' He would rather not have fallen back on this threat. It could imply suspicion. He wanted to seem neutral and ignorant. But he had no choice. He'd made it impossible to accept even temporary financial help from Hugh. He was a bastard, but he'd fix it to be an independent one.

'Send Foley to me. He knows where to find me. I'll give him his instructions. In, and out. Fetch your belonging whatever it is and leave.' Charlie was showing how a good leader does a volte-face without wasting time. 'I'll expect to see you when you get back to London. What is this famous belonging, by the way? I ask in case it's part of the contents covered by the option.'

'You've got an option on the contents too?'

'Yes. Your mother's tired of Byland.'

'It's only a memento from my father.'

'He left none in her mind.' Now Charlie had said something too much, too familiar. That's the trouble with feelings – they turn to quicksand when you're not thinking.

'I didn't know you knew her so well,' Jason said, and stood up.

'Oh, I think you did. You and I, we're people who know so much more than we . . . even realise,' Charlie Seker said. Jason decided this didn't mean anything exact enough to worry about. It was too fluid. It was a piece of piss, really. Charlie was basically that, nothing for anyone to be afraid of. All wind-up.

Chapter Seven

IT WAS BUCKETING down. Well it would, up here, while London sweated in the heat wave. Brian was from this neck of the woods and he knew what to expect. From Bingley, to be exact. July fog on moors. Drenching mists in towns and villages. Swollen watercourses everywhere. Perfect weather for the mill. So he wasn't surprised. All the same it was depresso. He'd come because May told him. 'It'll only be a day or two out of our season of love,' she'd said, histrionically as always. He loved her histrionics; they didn't embarrass him at all. He saw her as Latin, essentially, though she came from north of Manchester, and he often told her so. In return, she took his advice about other things. Practical matters. She was a great lady. If only she hadn't sent him with backward old Jason, up here where they all originated one way or another. Specially another in Brian's case. The best of it, the consolation was that once Jason was finished with bloody Byland and the forest, she could be finished with it too. Liberated. She could flog the sodding, sodden forest and the hunting lodge folly. That was well understood between him and Charlie, with a bit of a backhander. Not enough to be ashamed of. Pricewise, well north of nominal, in a good cause, and she'd escape the upkeep and all the crap that went with it – dry rot, taxes, worries, sons, God knows what else. Of course – Charlie Seker too. Because once the deal was through, it shouldn't be difficult to sink Charlie. Rub in, retrospectively, the prices of comparable properties on the open market. And with Charlie well and truly sunk, then May would save a lot of money that would otherwise go down the pan in subsidy and she could buy something in Ischia, mythical isle of girls, and boys. They could both be perfectly happy there, either way. On permanent working holiday in facing-both-ways island. Good causes never far from mind. With e-mail, you could almost still be in Pimlico—

'You drive,' Jason said. He'd had some drinks on the train, had Jason, as if there was something he needed to forget. Like a cat to drown.

'Okay.'

'You know the way?'

'It's up behind Blackburn, isn't it?'

'A long way up behind Blackburn.' It would be. Imagine the Ischian sea, from there. 'Haven't you been to Byland before?'

'Only ever heard tell.'

'May was very fond of it. It was where she could always be happy. Summer or winter.'

'I don't think it is any more.'

'She thinks it isn't,' Jason said.

Brian didn't like the sound of that. It sounded like filial pressure to come. It looked like leaning. However, without being unkind, it was a relief that Jason would soon be back in prison in Marseille from where leaning would be a difficult exercise. He wished Jason well, up to a point, but he wanted the benefit of his wish to be enjoyed a long way off. It was bad enough Hugh being around. But May didn't love Hugh and Hugh didn't love her, that was the big difference. There was no oedipussying about in their hostilities. In Jason's case, Brian knew there was. He could hear it in her voice when she spoke to Jason. It rang from the heart, similar to when she spoke to him, Brian. In bed. And there was another strong reason to believe it. Something that had only occurred to him very recently. In fact, Charlie pointed it out, as Charlie would.

'There's a generic facial resemblance between you and Jason,' Charlie said. 'You don't know what generic is? It means you're of the same kind. Quite a compliment to you.' That's how Charlie was – always finding a word to make you feel less than yourself. Since then he'd examined himself in the mirror, and inspected Jason with a more critical eye. Charlie was right, in his snakelike way. There was a resemblance, and the more he looked, the more he saw it. It made him feel like a substitute. Once she was rid of Byland at last and they were in Ischia the illusion would fade. Between now and then, play it very cool with Jason. With May also. No one must be able to even suspect he had anything in mind.

They drove a long time in silence. 'After Clitheroe we turn off and begin the climb,' Jason said. 'It's a narrow road. Anything coming down has priority. If it's a truck, you want to look out.' As they rose, the sky, surprisingly, seemed to lift off, cloud thinning out nearer the sun. Mist moved in waves up from valleys and across the bare slope of hills, sucked like steam into the heat above. Round a bend, a huge view opened out over the plain to the west, and the distant sea. All the horror of the industrial towns between here and Manchester was gone, as if it had never crawled into being. And Bingley along with it. 'Not so bad, is it?' Jason said, his voice full of the nostalgia that comes to out-of-date people after a few drinks.

'Very good,' Brian said, though actually he loathed anything and everything north of a line from Bristol to Southend. He'd seen too much of it. His people were out of those industrial streets, they'd bred and knuckled under and died in them. 'Why does May have this wood up here with a ruin of a house in the middle of it? Where did it come from?'

'She's never told you?'

'She shoves it away. The only time I asked, she just sang one of her love songs.'

'This is where she's from. She had it from her mother. She was an only child.'

'The family's out of this street? Exactly here, up this hill?'

'Yes. They were sheep farmers before,' Jason said, still with that sound in his voice. Funny what different feelings two northern exiles could have. Bingley wasn't that far off as the sooty crow flies. Of course Jason's was the sentimentality of a son of folk who reared children in clean air well above the chimneys. It wasn't an honest feeling, in his case. His honest feelings were for overseas. And probably some woman there. He was out of place in Britain. If he had to choose his prison, Brian was sure it would be the one in Marseille.

'Before what?'

'They put their savings in a mill. It did well.'

'So they gave up the sheep and built a folly instead? Gentrification?'

'That's about the size of it,' Jason admitted.

'Stopped growing wool and took up fleecing the workers.'

Jason turned his head to look at him. 'Yes,' he said. He sounded less dispossessed already. Brian believed he'd done them both a favour. He, personally, didn't give a toss for the workers; he'd got away, he was May's lover, and he had plans. But the less Jason entertained archaic feelings about Byland and the hill, the better. And the sooner he'd buzz off to his natural habitat.

The road ran into a village of a few houses built on either side of a gully with a stream in the middle. In angry brown flood, naturally. The grass on the common ground flanking the gully was tall and there was no sign of people. 'Doesn't anyone live here?' Brian asked.

Jason didn't answer. How would he know, come to think of it? He'd hardly been here since he was a boy, he'd said so. 'Keep going,' was all he said. Beyond the village, the moor began. Walled fields gave place to open grassland with a lot of unfriendly looking vegetation signifying to Brian the eternally soaked, spongy bog underfoot. Then, on the brow of this slope, with the summit of the hill beyond and above, a wood. A big wood, spread darkly across all the view in front of them like a pubic bush, though that wouldn't normally be green, granted. The road ran round it to one side and could then be seen wandering off up the higher ground, a long way on. Closer to, the wood was surrounded by a high wall, and beside the road was the gully, still deep. If the house had drains, this was where the raw effluent would run, bang through the middle of the village. Unless by some freak they'd built a giant septic tank to receive the nightsoil of the new gentry. The height of the wall gave the measure of the trees inside – stunted by wind and cold and soil – trees hanging as close and dense to the ground as sheep would, up here. Enough to shudder, and this was July. To make the point, the sun suddenly came out and the whole hillside, the tops of trees, bracken and reeds, heather far off, the sky itself, broke out in colour. You saw what was hidden in grey before – the beauty to take your breath away and bring tears to your northern eye; untouched beauty almost, of this country way above chimneys. Untouched it might be, but it didn't damp down Brian's longing for the crowded coastlines of Ischia. The *spiaggia degli Inglesi* where the pair of English lovers like patron saints had lived on *frittura mista* in a cave above the sand. How good it would be to camp in a beach cave with May, a familiar deity rising when he called her. That would make him a bit of a deity himself, which was what she was for, after all. To raise him up. The sun went behind a cloud again and as they reached a pair of iron gates in the wall, the rain started. The gates were chained together. 'Is this where we go in?'

'Stop and we'll have a look,' Jason said. He got out of the car and went to piss against the wall. Those gins. Then he walked up to the gates and inspected the chain and lock. 'They're new. It looks like we're meant to arrive and leave on foot.'

'Why?' Brian asked from the car window.

'A way to keep visitors under control.' Jason pushed at a narrow door in the wall. It swung half open. From the distance, somewhere inside the wood, came a sound of barking, a single, repeated deep bark like a signal. 'With dogs, for example.'

'Why would anyone want to do that?' Jason didn't answer the question. He was inside the door, examining the gate. 'Is there another way? How far is it to the house anyway?'

'By a cart track, round the top of the wood. You have to cross a ford.'

'This is a Citroën. They go up and down – they're made for fords and that.' Brian thought Jason looked at him with a certain respect on hearing this. This was because Jason might know about seafaring but probably not much of anything about cars. He was a simple soul, in many ways. And a bit paranoid with it, so it would seem. A closed gate was just a closed gate, that was all. Of course prison gates were always closed. And there would be dogs behind them too, and guards and guns. Just for starters. No wonder, then.

100

'The track goes in at the top where the wall swings left and the road right. You follow the wall round as far as the stream – you'll see. I'll go from here. I'm going in through the wood.' The gins were making him repeat himself.

'I'm supposed to stick with you, Charlie said so.'

'Screw Charlie. When you get to the house, wait. No, take your time. Make a row. You've got the keys, go in the front door. I'll be inside.'

'How are you going to get in?'

'No problem,' Jason said, and slipped with surprising speed into the wood. Looking down the drive, if that was what it was – just a track between trees and bushes – there was no sign of him at all in the dead silence. You could tell Jason had been around, and in some out of the way places, like a rat. In London, he resembled a resting actor who looks to any dodge going. And beginning to find the dodges fewer and farther between. Here, on the contrary, he was more like a commando or enquiry agent. And that was the odd part. What could there be to enquire about?

This time it was at the Wig and Gown in Chancery Lane. Deakin explained on the phone that May's affairs were regarded as strictly off-the-record. A personal interest. Even a lawyer has those.

'What'll you drink?' Hugh asked.

'Campari and soda. And not a lot of soda,' said Deakin, probably not long home from holiday in Portofino or some-where. His mouth when he approached it to the glass opened itself outwards – eager, fleshy and red like a creature from behind an underwater rock. When he'd got half the mixture inside him he looked a good deal more laid back. It made it easier to imagine him out of the striped trousers. 'How's the prodigal getting on?'

'It's why I wanted to see you. He's disappeared.'

'Gone prodigal with his seed I expect. I'll have another.'

Fair enough. There was no fee for this consultation. When Hugh got back with the glass of pink mind-bender he tried again. 'I don't know how much use Jason's going to be. I'm worried.'

'It was your idea,' said Deakin. Hugh didn't argue. He knew that professionals don't care to be wrong.

'If Seker and his lawyer get caught in a refugee fiddle, what's the likely penalty?'

'A massive fine. More profitable. It costs money to keep people in prison.'

'And anyone involved would catch the same?'

'Who do you mean?'

'The sole owner of the Ravenglass company. Where there's no thin red line.'

'I see,' said the legal adviser. He pushed his Campari away unfinished. 'If you think that, you should get her out of harm's way while there's still time.'

'I think you must do it,' Hugh said. 'Ring her. As an old friend. She'll listen to you. And the sooner the better.'

'She'll dig her heels in,' Deakin & Deakin said.

'Lean on her with the full weight of the law,' Hugh said.

When he reached the ford, Brian got out. The stream was an angry brown torrent off the hill and you couldn't see how deep. He was wearing suede shoes and he had no raincoat or parka. Two minutes out of the car and he was already wet more or less through. He wondered if he should give up and go back to the gates with the heater on. Jason would turn up in his own time, he only had to fetch some item or other and if he could get in without keys, he could get out again. But Brian's curiosity was itching him. He wanted to see this folly that he must wean May of for ever. Also he wanted to know what Jason was up to, what exactly was the itch in *his* mind. He raised the Citroën and eased forward into the waters, keeping the engine racing and the other foot on the clutch. That should be audible enough a long way off.

He was through and out the other side. There was water on the car floor and he'd hit a rock or two, but the engine was still running and the brakes worked. The track continued up the slope to where the wall and the wood turned away downhill. Beyond was just grass, rising to the crest not far below cloud level. Rooks circled, disturbed by the noise of the engine – or were they disturbed by something inside the wood? Like a man with a dog? There was an opening in the wall, barred only with a couple of big branches. This wasn't like the new lock and chain on the main gate. Brian didn't believe in Jason's theory. There was no one here taking precautions about visitors with cars, and his opinion was confirmed when he looked back up the hill. He saw an encampment of caravans among a clump of trees, in the middle of nowhere, in the grass and sedge. Travelling folk – the chain and lock were for them. Keep travelling, that was the message. Beat it. And the dog earlier on, he was probably in charge of this way into the wood. He hadn't barked again so he must be muzzled. Hang about. That implied a guard. Jason's theory, though cracked, might still have some-thing in it. But guarding what, and why? A wood with a ruin? Brian sounded the horn and entered the wood, the car still on its high suspension like a heron crossing a ditch.

It was a good wood; even he, a town boy from Bingley could see that. It was primeval, if that was the word – nothing in it had ever been cut or thinned or made to toe a line. It was strictly uncommercial, and full of birds. There was a jungle of trees of no importance, all over the place, wrapped in ivy, and among them the oaks of England. Nelson, and all that. Not high, but broad and spreading. Something inside Brian's usually tight chest swelled up at the thought. This was a piece left over from where it all began, where his distant forefathers and those of the Ravenglass family were together lighting fires and sharpening flints. A classless society, among these trees. A long time ago. Now the trees were May's, the folly was hers, the land under his tyres was hers. He was a dependant – he was hers. He dispersed the idea like a dog shaking off water – things were going to change. In Ischia, it would be different. Brian smiled – in Ischia he would be living where gigolo was a profession with standing. The track widened out so branches no longer knocked on the side of the car as it crept along. The surface improved, not much but enough to know the house wasn't far off. He blew the horn again, like whoever it was to the dark tower came. GCSEs were some time ago now. The whole place was deserted. Apparently deserted, that is. In the teeming life of this wood was a dog and a guard keeping out of sight, and God knew what else: ghosts perhaps, travelling men with knives, carnivores never seen on pavements.

Through the trees ahead, a building. A break in the clouds at the same moment, and light on pale grey stone. Almost silvery in the sun. He was approaching from the back – outhouses, kennels, a stable, then a wide yard. The back yard where kitchen refuse would be thrown out for dogs and chickens. People, even. Barred windows, smashed tiles littering the ground. Tall weeds in every crack, some in flower. The Raven-glasses had come up from muck, and to muck they would return. Brian left the car and walked on round the side of the building to find the entrance. He had keys, he was licensed to enter by the front door. And here it was. He looked up at the façade. This was a folly all right. It was crazy. It was like a bit of abbey thrust out of the undergrowth. But it had a roof: he could see a corner of it. Three stories of pointed windows, buttresses, pinnacles, gargoyles. Or a wing of the Houses of Parliament, ivy-grown and stuck here, rooted and rotting in this Lancashire wood. There was no denying it, the Ravenglass sheep farmers had style. Dubious maybe, but style. This whole opera set a monument to social climbing. It was beautiful, in a way. But it scared the shit out of you like any spooky lunatic.

Three steps rose to the entrance, an arch in an arch, drawing you in. Brian tried the keys one by one. There was a mortice and two newer locks, installed without respect for the oak carving of the door. A pity. Still, May would soon be rid of all this. Fiddling with keys made him feel jumpy, like learning to blow a safe. The last lock gave, the high door swung and he was through. Inside, dim bars of blue and red and green fell across the floor from stained glass in two pointed windows. There were a few pieces of dark furniture and a piano in this hall; a lantern up there, deer's antlers, a pike and swords hung in a wheel pattern on one wall. What pretension. A crook and sheep shears would be more like it. It was gloomy, damp and ante-diluvian. Still, he rather liked it all, in a way. Here was May's secret origin and here was he in sole possession. Now there was nothing to her he didn't know. It made them equal, like those forebears rubbing sticks and chipping away at flints. The door was open behind him and now the sun came out again and he stood in a rectangle of light on the stone floor. Nothing to hide, nothing to fear, in the sunshine of the open door. From somewhere beyond the hall there was a sound of steps in the silence. A cawing of rooks some way off, that was all. Then Jason appeared, carrying something wrapped in a sack. He looked at home here, at ease, less fouled up. They met in the middle of the hall under the wheel of swords.

'That's it,' Jason said. 'I've looked round and there's no one here and I've got what I came for. We can bugger off again.'

Brian wasn't ready to go, not yet. He wanted to look around too. 'I had enough trouble with those locks. How did you get in?' he asked for the second time.

'There's an ice-house here – you wouldn't think it was wanted, but there it is.'

'To chill the champagne,' Brian suggested.

'That could be. It's at the back.'

Brian was glad to know about this ice-house. It was an intimate detail. 'What about it?'

Jason looked round. 'There's a passage. So the ice wouldn't melt in the blazing heat before they got it in.'

'Underground?'

'It's part of the wall. You'd never notice it unless you knew it was there. That's the way out, if you don't want to be seen.'

This really was crazier and crazier. These children of privilege had not only a front door and a back door but their gentrifying forefather, like a rabbit fearing a stoat, had tunnelled a hidden exit. 'And a way in,' Brian pointed out.

'And in.' Jason laughed for no reason like someone a bit off their head but in a good phase. 'For girls.' So there was a reason after all. Old Jason was peculiar, because he was born to a peculiar world, but he wasn't that out of touch. May was the same, perhaps more so. 'Let's get going,' Jason said, and moved towards the door.

'Did you and Hugh bring girls in by the ice-house?'

'I did, once or twice.'

'Schoolgirls?' Jason didn't answer. He was already outside on the steps. If he'd heard, he didn't like the question, you could tell by the way he turned his back on it. They probably weren't schoolgirls anyway: Clitheroe would be the nearest school and it was too far off. They would be girls off farms, or out of an orphanage somewhere grim in the hills around. Easy prey. 'What does Charlie want with renting this place?' Brian called out, following.

'For banging away at the wildlife, that's all. Come on,' Jason shouted, now out on the mucky drive. At the same moment Brian heard a noise inside the house. A door upstairs, it sounded like, knocking against a wall. It could be a draught. Jason could have left it open. All the same, it was creepy. Intriguing too. Brian went out on to the steps.

'I think there's someone in here,' he said.

'Yes?' In a few strides Jason was back under the arches. He was heavy, Jason, but quick. A lot of force there, you felt. When he moved like that his feet hardly seemed to touch the ground. 'You saw something?'

'I heard something.'

'Keep quiet.' They stood in the hall, listening.

'A voice?'

'Only a door. Upstairs.'

'I didn't go upstairs.' With that same walk Jason was at the back of the hall. 'Over here.'

Trying to be as quiet, Brian followed. His leather soles made a sound like light, patting, public caresses on the stone floor. They were wet, too. Perhaps he'd imagined that knocking. At the far end of the hall was a staircase with an iron rail and one window, high up. Brian had time to notice several portraits of past Ravenglasses, a rough bunch by the looks. Jumped up from the market place in Clitheroe or Blackburn. Thank God, Brian thought just before he heard the scream from up above, cut off at once, thank God I'm free of it all.

A scream like snapping cat gut – pain or anger? A rational

person tries to analyse a shock like that straight off. Was it the scream of a girl attacked? Or only disciplined? Now there was that door banging again, against its own frame this time. A sharply closed door. The one who had screamed was shut back in: that was what the sounds suggested to him. And he decided it was more anger than pain.

Jason was already running up the stairs. Brian followed. 'It was at the top,' he said.

From the first floor, the way upward was by a spiral staircase of stone. On the landing above were four doors. 'Those are bedrooms,' Jason said, and opened them in turn. The rooms beyond were empty. 'Nothing, a ghost.'

'You believe in that?'

'Ships get ghosts,' Jason said.

Brian knew that seamen were superstitious but he could be right about the ghost, this was a place for one of those. Still, there had been a scream and they'd both heard it. 'Hadn't we better make a search?' Brian said.

'No, it was nothing. This is a peculiar house. Come on,' Jason said again, impatiently, 'I want to be in London by the first train.'

'To cash in whatever it is you have in your sack?' Only a guess.

Jason looked down at the sack, then at his other hand holding a crumpled envelope which he put in his trouser pocket. All he said was, 'I've some other reasons.' This didn't take Brian in. Jason had been fired up all day, from first thing in the morning at King's Cross. Now he looked on the run. Brian tried to read it. Not running from here, from something in himself. Another guess – *towards* himself, the part that made him want what he had to want. Therefore there was a woman behind this, some-where. Stood to reason. And not just any woman. A woman you fought a losing battle against wanting. That was it. May often praised Brian for his intuitions about the love life of others. It was the feminine part in him and he enjoyed setting it loose. Jason was being driven mad by wanting some woman he shouldn't want, that was what intuition came up with.

But back in the car Brian began to worry. Jason mustn't burn up in the atmosphere while there was use for him. As they laboured through the ford with the engine roaring, he thought of something. Out on the other side, he said, 'I wonder if Charlie pays any rent. Your mother has a great heart. All ready for breaking. You know she backs this refugee game of his. I mean—' he lifted his left hand off the wheel and rubbed the thumb and index together in a gesture he'd seen in a French film, '—liquidity.'

'So Hugh says.'

'Charlie's belief is there's no bottom to it. Whatever her great heart tells her, Ravenglass forks out the necessary to the end of time. But my idea is there isn't all that much liquidity left for Charlie to suck in.' That should be enough to get Jason on side in the cause of May's freedom. And Charlie and Jason might, with luck, cancel each other out. May would be liberated from both of them. The great heart brought to earth in keeping with her years.

'Thanks for the company Brian,' Jason said as they parted at King's Cross. 'When you give Charlie the keys, forget all about the ghost. It's fatal luck. The first to tell is always the first to go.' Was Jason being ironical at his expense? Brian didn't think so. Jason was too hard a case to bother much with irony. He was straight, and heading for the exit. After that the wheels should be off him in no time at all. Leaving him flat on the skids.

Chapter Eight

HE'D THOUGHT AFTER that first time it was finished. A one-off. Bad enough already to make him sling his hook. Now he knew it wasn't finished, and he'd always known. Thinking is one thing, knowing another. He'd lost his precious freedom, maybe for good. He lifted the telephone.

'I must see you,' he said. The message sounded flat, not urgent.

'Where?' she said.

'I've taken a room.' He gave the address and phone number.

'Whereabouts is that?'

'Off the Edgware Road, east side. It's comfortable, there's a good bathroom.' That was important.

'I don't know what side's east of the Edgware Road.'

'Take a taxi.'

'When?'

'Now,' he said. He'd meant to say, when you like, but the now came out on its own, urgent enough for anyone.

'All right,' Rosie said, not wrapping it up. He thought he could hear the note of hostility like he felt himself. He'd seen cats on docks mating in mutual hostility like that. 'In half an hour.'

Alex was back in Paris with the bronze, leaving him with a further advance. 'I'm just doing it as a good friend,' he'd said. 'This may be some kind of copy. Only an expert could tell. I'll ring you at this hotel.'

'No don't, I'll be moving on. I'll call you in Paris when I know where I am. I'll leave a message.'

'So Charlie hasn't burned your mother's house down? Did you see his friends? Was there shooting in the forest?' Alex was seething with curiosity. He'd scented something.

'There's another thing. Can you tell me what these words mean?' Jason handed over an envelope.

Alex took a quick look and gave it back. 'It's Romanian,' he said. 'Where did you find it?'

'What does it say?'

'It says, "help women very bad". Just that. No punctuation and not addressed to anyone.'

'Message in a bottle, then.'

'I thought Byland-in-the-Forest was a long way inland?'

'I never said that's where I got it.'

'And you haven't said it wasn't.' When Alex was on the trail of something he was like a greedy dog. But he was far too necessary to give him the elbow. Jason knew no one else who spoke Romanian, for a start.

'Okay, this envelope was on the stairs at Byland. But it could have lain there blowing about for years.'

'Oh yes, of course,' Alex said. 'Ever since the last Romanian guest came for the woodcock.'

'That's right,' Jason said. The whole thing needed cool thought, and he wasn't in a condition to give it. All he could think of was finding a quiet room with the cash Alex had brought and then making that phone call. As near to now as . . . 'We'll get you a cab to Waterloo. I'll ring you tomorrow. I must think about it, but afterwards. Later. About my mother too, where it leaves her.'

Alex laughed at him. 'That's the catch for *mamans*. At first they come first. Later, only after.' Jason hadn't thought of it like that. It sounded like a hang-up.

Now Alex was gone and Jason stood at the window of the room he'd taken, watching for Rosie in her taxi. His heart led and he followed, seeing nothing but the patch of road in front of the house, feeling only the pulse. A thought of Hugh flashed across his mind and out the other side, leaving a dark smear of guilt. Now a taxi was coming along the street, going slow. It drew up two doors off, then started away again. Had she changed her mind? He felt sick, he had a pain.

There was another taxi. The pain cleared and the sky was bright. Of course she would come: he understood one thing about this woman he hardly knew – she was driven the same as him. There – she was out of the taxi and looking up at the windows. Jason raised a hand. From above, there was more red in her hair than he remembered from three days ago against the bedclothes. Effect of light. Or she'd used a henna shampoo. It caught the sun, while she paid off the driver. She looked up again, and this time too there was the sketch of a smile. Nothing committed, just reflex. Jason ran down.

'Here you are,' he said stupidly.

She leaned against him for a second, in the doorway. It made him feel needed, which was new. She looked as if she was delivering herself like a patient in an ambulance. 'It's hot. Let's get off the street,' she said.

Upstairs, between the locked door and the comfortable bathroom, the knots and tethers undid almost of their own accord. If he'd run from this it would have lasted the rest of his life. As it was – 'Is it all right?' he said.

'All right now.' She smiled, widening her mouth unexpectedly as if most of the time she kept it narrow to hide the happiness it could show. Some people fear happiness till it's forced on them. 'It's good here,' she said, and he noted she wasn't a woman to waste words. So each one she gave you was worth its weight. If she said it was good she meant it was going well, something you're always glad to know. And later, when she came the first time, it was messenger and message in one, you couldn't have any doubts.

'How long have you taken this place for?' she asked, as they lay separated because of the heavy heat. Distant thunder sounded, somewhere up the Thames valley.

'A couple of weeks.'

'Not so long.' He knew what was on the way, because it had to be. 'Hugh's worrying about where you got to.'

'I expect so.'

'He doesn't understand.'

'Let's hope.'

'He thinks you've run away again.'

'He's kind of right.'

'You're not helping me,' Rosie said, and withdrew the hand she'd kept on his arm. Without it, Jason's arm felt like an empty sleeve.

The trouble was they were wounding the same person from opposite sides. And you couldn't expect the wife to give priority to the brother's problem. 'Sorry,' Jason said, 'I was still out there.'

'It was as good as that?'

Jason didn't reply in so many words. 'You know the rocking horse?' he said after a bit. 'This way—'

There was a pub down the road with a garden, and when the sun was lower they walked there and sat under a plane tree. 'We shouldn't be here,' Rosie said. She sounded relaxed enough not to worry for a long time. About a year, say.

'This is no one's stamping ground.'

'In London you never know.' She drank half her glass of Alsatian in one go. 'I should get back by seven.'

Thunder was still rolling in the west and the heat was stifling. There was a small fountain in this garden, in the middle of an overflowing pool with empty cigarette boxes and crisp packets floating about; the spray, when Jason put his hand in, was as warm as water out of a tap. He was spilling over too, with an unfamiliar feeling. He recognised it from hearsay as happiness. Mixed in with that despair he'd got to know by now. But you can't fight the tide. 'To cook his supper?' he said.

'He always rings.'

Yes. Hugh would think he did that from consideration, but really it was so as not to surprise an unwelcoming face if he wasn't expected back so soon. It was part of his low self-esteem – the condition that made him assertive – to look ahead to a reluctant welcome in his own house. Hugh was someone who deserved backing, not getting cock-blocked . . . this way. Or any way.

'What are we going to do?' Rosie said. Jason had no answer. It was too soon. The situation hadn't set. There were still so many things they could do but wouldn't. Swear never to meet again. One of them chuck the other for good. Run away, separately or together.

'Will he guess?' Jason asked. The cop-out question. Whatever the answer, Hugh's unconscious must know already. Their
unconscious was twinned like a communicating vase. If one
filled up the other did too.

'I think so. He'll notice.'

What did she mean? In bed? About the house? In that wide
smile Hugh hadn't seen before? Like anyone, Jason wondered
about a woman's experience – with husband, lover, casual from
the café. This was different. He still wondered but he couldn't
decently ask. There was nothing decent he could do except
disappear. And he knew he wasn't doing that.

'There's something you should know about Hugh,' Rosie
said.

'I expect I do.'

She looked at him and then back at her glass. 'It's not that.
That improved.'

'I'm glad.'

'A bit.'

'Good.'

'Not much.'

'Sorry.'

So where did that leave them? Here they were, half an hour
out of bed, admitting to Hugh's unsolved ejaculation problem.
'What is it I should know?'

'You and him . . . it isn't just how it may still seem to you.'
She said this like someone who doesn't really want to make
things any clearer. And there was the problem of her being so
sparing with words. 'I'd like another, please,' she said, holding
out her glass, and Jason went back into the bar to get a bottle
this time. When he came out again she was sitting on the stone
rim of the pool watching the overflow and with her back to
him.

116

'Hugh and me, you know we've never fought,' he said.

'You already told me that. You were sorry for him.'

How was she so sure? Anyway it wasn't true. It sounded too patronising for anything he'd ever felt, and too incomplete. 'Here you are.' He filled her glass and handed it so she'd have to face him. 'Not sorry for him. He's four years younger. I looked after him a bit when our father lit out.'

'And he admired you.'

'I dare say – in those days—'

'Well, I can tell you it's turned into something else. Or the same thing but another side. You know what I mean? I think he was . . . angry inside because he wasn't sorted out. Like we hoped. Like I promised him he would be. The admiration turned to envy.'

'You knew before?'

'He told me.'

'That was fair.'

'It was insurance. The worst thing for him is when it happens with a woman who hasn't been warned. Seeing the bad surprise. Women have to make an effort, you know. The let down, that's the worst.'

The sun still beat down on the pool and through the spray, light shifting in shadow of leaves. She hadn't been so sparing there. And she was drinking at a fair rate. Jason didn't quite believe in all this. Okay – problem, even bad problem, competition, hard for her, yes. But she only said it because of what they'd done to Hugh in their heads. As long as he knew nothing, they'd done nothing to him in his. No. That wasn't right. You aren't much more than the idea other people have of you. They'd injured Hugh more in their heads than between the sheets. They'd cut him to nothing. But Hugh eaten by some envy, no. 'What made you do it?' he asked.

117

She looked straight at him as if the answer was to be sought at the back of his eyes. After a bit she said, 'A sort of power, I suppose.' She must trust him, to be so honest with herself.

'But not enough.'

'Not enough.'

'How did you guess, about the envy?'

'I watched it happening. All he ever said is that for your mother, the eye of heaven shines straight out of your arse. And he'd had to live with it.'

'Strong talk,' Jason said, and looked round him.

Rosie laughed. 'Actually, I could think it too, but I wouldn't say. I'm rather afraid of Hugh now. Didn't the Ricardos come from Spain, or somewhere? It's that in him – so bloody absolute, that's what I'm afraid of.' She emptied her glass and held it away in front of her, expecting more. There wasn't much left and Jason shared it out. It was after six and the garden was beginning to fill up, while from the direction of the bar the voices were getting louder. He felt they were being watched, perhaps overheard. They'd been drinking wine for forty minutes and the others out here had hardly started. Sitting on the edge of the pool with an empty bottle and talking about the eye of heaven, one could attract attention.

'When do I see you again?' he asked.

Rosie took his hand. 'I'll ring in the morning when he's gone.' It sounded bad, put like that. The earlier feeling of happiness had crossed the line. A telephone buzzed angrily like a trapped hornet. He didn't know till now that she carried a mobile. Probably it was totally archaic not to, like him. 'Yes?' She listened with a look of practised patience. 'No. I've really no idea . . . he just went. No, he hasn't . . . probably a skirt, it wouldn't surprise me, or you, I should think . . . of course I will, if he does but he won't . . . yes. Goodbye. Yes . . . oh yes.'

118

'Not Hugh.'

'Your mother wants to see you.'

'Tomorrow. After I hear from you. I'll see her then.'

'And Hugh.'

'And Hugh.' Who must be – what? To start with, faced. Jason remembered something he ought to ask Rosie. 'Do you know Charlie Seker?'

'I saw him around a bit with May.' She sounded guarded. She didn't want to talk about Charlie.

'And what do you think?'

'Don't arrange to meet him on a dark night,' she said. 'Take it from me.'

They were definitely listening, those silent drinkers on the far side of the pool. Rosie stood up. For a moment her eyes were like someone signalling for help in the water. Then they righted themselves. 'You'll remember?' he said.

'What d'you mean?'

'Tomorrow. After . . . he leaves.'

'What d'you think? Remember? Honestly.'

Had he ever asked a woman before if she would remember? She walked out through the garden door into the street without looking back.

He hadn't been near the Ravenglass offices for years. He was no longer on the strength. When he sailed the *Kendal* it was at his own responsibility, profit, or loss. But he often came when he was a boy. Their grandfather ruled and in his day May had a room here where she was supposed to master the business. She never did. She ran rings round him. To her, Ravenglass was a means, and she despised means. Ends were her thing. Means were good enough for people like Hugh, unfree people. So now she was under the eye of her bank and

119

lawyer as well. Liberty circumscribed. And the ends, how about them? Did they include whatever was going on under cover at Byland? The women very bad, scribbling words on a brown envelope?

There were several big newish trucks in the yard here, Ricardo on them in large letters, Ravenglass in small ones. The bottom had dropped out of grandfather's tramp steamers. And a couple of drivers loafing about smoking against the wall. They watched him cross to the main doors. A notice board – something else to read, a bit more time gained – he read about sailings of the Dover–Zeebrugge crossing; holiday rosters; an announcement on the pension scheme; profit-sharing – not a thing his grandfather would have gone in for, that. One of the drivers came over.

'Looking for someone?'

'Yes. Hugh Ricardo.'

'Upstairs. Got an appointment?'

'He'll see me.'

'Will he? He's a busy man. Who are you?'

'I'm Jason.' The name rang no bells. Just as well.

'You can always try your luck,' the driver said and returned to his mate. Jason heard a laugh. He went on reading the notice board – he was well into fire regulations and procedure in the event of an emergency in the Channel tunnel when he heard the voice behind him, the other side of the yard.

'Hasten, Jason,' it called.

They were right. What was holding him up? He was hanging about. Why didn't he hasten? Because he wasn't ready, that's why. If Hugh knew how he'd been shafted it would be almost better. There'd be less fraud in the deal. And less shame. Face value and market value would match. Entering the offices, Jason tried to prepare himself. The secretary who showed him in was attractive in a numbed kind of way. Or maybe it was he who was numbed, for once.

'So where did you speed to, departing guest?' Hugh said from behind his desk. Hearing the tone Jason was relieved.

'I met a girl,' he said carelessly. 'Went to Byland, too.'

Hugh got up and closed the door into the secretary's room. 'Well?'

'I picked up what I went there for.'

'Which was?'

'A thing to sell.'

'You're sure it's yours?'

'And I've sold it, more or less.'

Hugh didn't look so pleased. 'So you're not here for cash,' he said.

Jason counted up to ten. Would Hugh say that if he didn't know that morally Jason was at his mercy while they stood face to face? Wouldn't Jason rise at once otherwise to the affront? 'No. Something more important.'

'To do with what I fetched you out for?'

'If you want to put it like that.'

'I do. I'm a businessman. But we'd better not talk here.' Hugh lifted the phone. 'I'll be out for half an hour,' he said. No first name, no endearment. For Hugh, the secretary was a mechanism, not a woman. 'We'll walk down to the river.'

'What's wrong with here? It's business. You're a businessman. You're the boss.'

'Exactly. Drivers all over the place with their ears open. And Charlie Seker uses drivers.'

After the power station like a giant evolving caterpillar, St Paul's filled the air and sky ahead; then you saw the unfinished footbridge, the khaki Thames. Always the same pull, as if every tributary gathered here to go out and rule the waves. They leaned against the wall and watched the low water in silence. As when they were boys and still believed their mother was a power for good who could be trusted to look after herself.

There was a flight of steps down to a patch of oily shingle, parody of a Thameside beach. 'Remember Daphne, by any chance?' Jason asked.

'Remember her? Daphne Velveeta? Spread like butter?' They both laughed though it wasn't funny now. A joke from the time when it came naturally to laugh together at nothing. At the big win.

'That's the one.'

'Your first.'

'Awake.'

'But not hers.' That was like Hugh. Jason had forgotten and he stopped laughing. 'A pity, in a way, we had to switch over to road haulage,' Hugh went on after a bit. 'But it's where the money is, not all this.'

'And it's coming in?'

'What's coming in?'

'Money from road haulage. Not the tide.'

'Well,' Hugh said cautiously, 'restructuring by definition takes time.'

'I find that too.'

'What have you got to restructure? Oh, you mean your life.' Hugh didn't sound much interested in that. Not business. He looked at his watch. 'Sorry, brother, I haven't all afternoon,' he said. 'What did you want to tell me?'

'Charlie Seker – I thought he wasn't someone you'd hang out with for long but nothing to get worried about. Now I don't know so much.'

'What do you know then?'

'At Byland I heard someone. A woman. I'd say she was there against her will.'

'What did you hear?'

'A door banging, and a scream.'

'If it's on a lease to Seker he could leave a caretaker. A caretaker can have a family row.'

'You knew about the lease?'

'I told you.'

It was a relief to hear a lie, even if it was only a straw off your back. 'We were told the place was empty.'

'Who by?'

'Charlie, when he handed over the keys.'

'Who was we?'

'Brian Foley. He was Charlie's idea, to keep an eye out. Charlie wasn't keen. He quoted the Landlord and Tenant Act at me.'

'Brian?' Hugh sounded suspicious. 'He was at Byland with Seker's approval?'

'That's what I said.'

'And did Brian hear this yell too?'

'Yes.'

'What did he make of it?'

'I didn't ask him what he made of it, Hugh. At the time, I didn't give a toss what he thought. Now I can see how it might matter.'

'Yes, it could,' Hugh said.

'If May knows anything about what's going on.' Jason looked at Hugh, still watching the water. There was something about the way he did this that raised a doubt. He was too intent on watching; it didn't convince. Hugh had information he wasn't sharing round. It was no real surprise. Hugh's agenda could hardly coincide with his own as it seemed to do twenty years ago. And his own agenda – what about that? It included Rosie; it included their meetings. She was one of the few things his agenda and Hugh's still had in common. Shouldn't in any circumstances have in common, but did. Things? Rewards. 'We must think how to protect her from herself,' he said.

'You mean May?'

'Who else?'

'I think she just knows about subsidising refugees. Byland's let. She can't have any idea what's happening there, if anything is.' Hugh sounded as if he'd worked it out carefully while he watched the river. 'But you could have made sure of that by chatting to Brian on the way back in the train.'

'Maybe, but I didn't. I must go and see her.'

'Rather you than me.'

'Obviously.' Jason felt there was haze in the atmosphere between them, it was like watching a dubbed film of himself and Hugh. He'd started off this meeting unhappy with himself and now he felt there was some kind of bullshit on both sides, though he didn't see just where. Something nagged at the back of his mind. 'She'd be an accessory after the fact, and if it's a crime—'

'You'd better find out and prevent it,' Hugh said, watching him too. 'Keep me informed. Where are you staying? Rosie wondered what on earth happened to you. She took a lot of trouble, getting the right wine, and all. I think it was a bit rough, Jason, you disappearing like that. Of course you're not used to women like Rosie and their ways. You chose the free life.'

'Apologise for me. You know how it is. I ran into this girl and we both realised—' what could they have both realised that would neutralise this situation? '—that we're lonely people just now.'

'That's the price you pay for turning your back.'

'You don't turn your back on anything till they shut the lid down,' Jason said.

'You can leave things too late. Like finding a proper wife. I did it in time. You may find the sort of woman you fancy doesn't want you any more, not on a permanent basis. I know what you'll say – you can buy it. But there's nothing like having a home to go to and a girl like Rosie waiting for you in the evening. And nothing to pay.' Hugh laughed, a different laugh from the shared one about spreading Daphne. 'Well, back to the office. Give me a number to reach you. Here, write it on this.'

While he scribbled the number, Jason pictured Rosie in bed with Hugh after his hard day. It was unbearable now in a new way. What would Rosie do on future evenings when Hugh said he felt like it, and insisted? Trying to hold back . . . contracting the pelvic floor . . . cursing the thing that wouldn't wait – not another second – 'There you are. There's an answering machine. Anyway I'll call you when I've—'

'Ring me at home, not the office. You never know. And if you speak to Rosie, don't tell her anything. We'll keep her right out of this. Women and their mothers-in-law—'

Jason watched Hugh wave down a taxi coming from the Globe Theatre, then he turned back and walked westward along the river. The sky was hard and hot and bare as if no depression had ever hit these islands, but the irritation at the back of his head cleared up as soon as Hugh's taxi turned the corner out of sight. How did Hugh know that he and Brian returned to London by train? They might have flown from Manchester. They could have hired a car down here and driven back. That was where his sense of bullshit going both ways came from, Hugh's inside information. He tried to remember

125

what indiscretions he'd let slip in Brian's company. He didn't think he'd been careless but he wasn't sure. With luck he was protected by knowing that AC/DCs such as he supposed Brian to be, and of which every ship's crew includes at least one, are good at locating the shadowy sectors in other people's lives, pinpointing the hiding places, storing guesses like information. He wouldn't have been too incautious with Brian, he thought.

Through the arches of Blackfriars Bridge appeared the *Wellington* and the *President* moored against the opposite bank: idle, landlocked, dressed in bunting. Sham seafarers, massaged annually for rust; better off at the bottom. Jason marched on beside the river towards Westminster, his coat slung over his shoulder, shirt open, back to the tides like the stern of those superannuated ships on the far side; headed upstream against the flow of fresh water into the last sun.

Chapter Nine

IN THIS PART of town, history and pageant could crush you like a beetle but they let you go. The buildings are too accidental to get the upper hand. And there's the seven-metre London tidal drop that scours the leavings twice a day. Jason went into a pub called the Samuel Pepys in a small street behind Westminster Abbey, just to try it out, and because he'd walked a long way in the heat. He recalled that Pepys pissed himself from sheer excitement in a ship's bunk off the Dutch coast, fetching the King from exile. All mopped up with the next tide.

The only other customer was a woman, sitting up at the bar. The inside of the pub was decorated with frescoes showing the Great Fire on one side, the burning of Parliament on the other. The woman wore trousers and a striped shirt and had blonde hair plaited in a short pigtail ending below her shoulders. The effect was uncontemporary, like passing herself off for a cabin boy. Jason wondered what to drink. It was too hot for pub wine and he wasn't keen on beer. What was she having? Something fizzy with a slice of orange and a bit of mint. Probably sweet. He ordered a glass of wine after all, and drank it at the bar while he stared at the mural of the Fire of London, his mind a blank.

'It cleared a space for St Paul's, the old fire,' the woman said. He turned to look at her. She had a rather square face and small blue eyes with a hard expression, but she was smiling as if someone had made a good joke. A woman older from the front than the back. Was she trying to pick him up? Interested, or just friendly? It surprised him to find he didn't know, and when he'd thought about it, he still didn't know. He made the effort to smile back.

'People scrambled into boats. Hundreds drowned. They'd have done better staying ashore like Pepys,' he said.

'Good old Sam,' she said vaguely. Pepys wasn't what interested her. She finished her drink and held on to the glass in the air in front of her. At least Jason knew what that meant.

'Let me get you one. What's it to be?'

'Cheers. Make it a brandy and ginger,' she said.

Ordering it, Jason decided the choice of drink meant this woman was game and on the lookout. It wasn't what she was drinking when he came in. Over another glass of wine he took stock. Here could be the chance to escape before he burned any more boats of his own. Nothing could be less of a commitment than a walk-out with this lady for the time he had to remain in the homeland. She would like it, and he would like it, probably. She looked a good sort. In Marseille, a woman like this in a bar would pretend to be sizzling with passion, which he was sure this one wouldn't; moreover, the woman in Marseille – Greek, Armenian, North African – wouldn't have the humour in that square face and the wary eyes. He looked at her again and she looked back, steadily. 'Is this your local?' he asked. Not exactly lively, as a gambit.

'No,' she said.

'Not your part of town?' She didn't bother to answer this. She was beginning to appear a bit disillusioned, he thought.

What a good sort expects is stimulus, and Jason felt leaden. Try again. 'Very nautical, your pigtail,' he said. 'I should know. I'm a ship's master.' That was stretching the truth, but in a good cause. Even if nothing comes of it, women appreciate your attention all the more if they think it's built up over long nights on the water.

She raised her glass to him. 'I'm Sandy, who are you?' she said.

'Jason. Glad to know you, Sandy.' He meant it. She might save him.

'So where's your boat, Jason? I thought these days there were only oil tankers. Is it one of those? I'd better warn you, I'm a Greenpeace supporter.'

'Don't worry. She's only an old tramp I left behind in Marseille.'

'Sounds more like a wife,' Sandy said fatalistically. Then she cheered up again. 'So, on the loose are you?'

Things seemed to be going faster than he'd bargained for. He wasn't yet sure he really wanted to get into this. But if he did, it would be for others as much as himself. Hugh and Rosie were all right before he turned up; he hadn't any reason to believe otherwise. Their commitment to each other was recent; it should be given the best chance possible. 'You know how it is,' he said.

'Do I, Jason? How is it? You tell me.' He didn't know how it had come about, who had moved, but they were now much closer to each other than at the outset. Almost touching.

'Like another?'

'It's my turn,' Sandy said.

'No no. It's me on leave.' He wondered if Sandy had anything to be on leave from and if so what. Then he ordered the new drinks, wishing the wine was less acid and at the same time less sweet. That was the genius of pub wine, uniting opposite vices. God knew where it came from or how long ago it was opened. Even brandy and ginger would have been a better choice. Too late now. 'Cheers again Sandy.'

She put an arm through his. 'You're a decent bloke, I can see that Jason,' she said. She sounded very slightly pissed. 'I knew you were, as soon as you came in. You don't suppose, I hope, that I'm in the habit of getting into conversation and taking drinks from just anyone. Do you?' Her manner of speaking was variable as if she came from no particular background but had passed through several, stopping long enough in each to pick up some of the voice. Taken with the clothes and pigtail and face, the effect was rather sad. If she'd been better looking, by now she'd be solidly set up by someone, somewhere, and in no need of brandy and ginger with strangers in the Samuel Pepys at five o'clock in the afternoon. On the other hand it might well be that she was an independent woman with a business and timetable of her own, answerable to none and free to pick up whom she chose, where she fancied.

'Where are you from?' he asked.

'I was born in Portsmouth,' Sandy said. Jason decided she wasn't an independent businesswoman. She was some kind of life refugee. She didn't ask where he was from. Displaced people don't do that; for them it's not origin, or accent, or memory that count, it's keeping going. For a few minutes they remained silent, her hand still in the crook of his drinking arm, their glasses neglected on the bar in front of them. The outcome of this meeting must be in her mind as in his. 'Drink up,' Sandy said.

'We're going somewhere?'

'Why not?'

She was right. Why not? Well, one reason was absence of

ready desire. Still, there were solutions for that and Sandy, by the look and feel of her, knew all about them. 'Not too far off?'

'Too far off for what? Are you in a hurry, Jason? You have an appointment? I wouldn't want to keep you from it. I was actually quite happy here before you turned up.'

Jason drank about half the undrinkable white wine and pushed the glass away. He'd offended her. 'Well I'm glad you were, otherwise you wouldn't have been still here for me when I arrived. My good luck,' he said, and she looked mollified, except for her eyes which stayed hard as ever. He decided that hardness in the eyes was a defence. Sandy was touchy and expected to be badly treated, that was it. 'You lead and I'll follow. And we'll find a taxi.'

'A taxi? I'm round the corner.' Sandy took him down Marsham Street and, to his surprise, into a block of flats where the hall had a lot of polished brass and a porter in uniform. Most of the tenants here would probably be MPs. Sandy occupied a flat on the top floor consisting, apparently, of two small rooms. Even so, unless you'd had it for years it would cost a pile in this part of the world. The decoration was faded and the furniture nothing much, yet there was an atmosphere suggesting former opulence as if there'd once been items of value, disposed of one by one to keep afloat. It might be the chandelier, a French-looking thing with fat crystal drops, that did it. She was standing under it as if it was mistletoe, watching him expectantly.

'Nice gaff,' he said. Then he approached and put his arms round her. He felt at once that he was holding a woman older than she appeared. There was a lack of resiliency betraying it straight away, and a faint odour like upholstery kept clean but in use a long time. Also there was his own lack of desire: that was enough to make you judge the situation as not all it might be in the best of worlds. He kissed her under the mistletoe/ chandelier and felt her response but not his own. She turned and went into the other room.

'Give me a couple of minutes, Jason,' she said, and soon afterwards he heard flushing sounds from the bathroom beyond. It looked as if effort was going to have to be injected into the enterprise. He waited to be called.

This was a new experience, a thing like falling ill with something deadly, which sometimes happens to others. Cajoling and goodwill on Sandy's part, various familiar and even unfamiliar passes on his, had failed to do the trick. Nothing meshed. Lying back with his hands linked under his head, Jason considered the position. He was, of course, sorry about it for Sandy's sake. She'd taken to him at first sight and he'd let her down. She'd murmured enthusiams a good deal warmer than he'd expected. She'd brought him to this hideout which represented for her, he was sure of it now, her days of success when someone, probably an MP, had told her she was everything a woman wanted to hear. And he'd given her a demonstration of the contrary. Then, he was sorry on his own account. It was humiliating of course, but that wasn't important. It had been humiliating to be in a cell with three others and a bucket but he'd survived. No, the serious thing was what this proved. He'd lost this freedom too. Even the thought of Rosie took his mind away from Sandy and the current delicate situation as completely as if they'd happened to someone else. Not his responsibility.

'Well,' Sandy said. 'Not exactly far-out.' Her voice was very different from the murmurings of fifteen minutes ago. Jason returned to earth.

132

'I'm really sorry. All my fault, of course. Not yours at all, that goes without saying,' he said.

'Yes, it could have.'

'Thank you for—'

'You'd better get dressed,' Sandy said. The hard look no longer seemed defensive. She was throwing him out. Well, she had every right to; he shouldn't still be hanging around in her bed as if he'd earned a place there. 'Thinking hard about someone else didn't seem to help much, either,' she added, and Jason had enough sense not to answer this.

When he had his clothes on he turned back. He ought to find words to say goodbye and express some sort of appreciation, even if low-key. The idea was to get himself back in the street with the least possible added embarrassment. Sandy was sitting up in bed wearing her striped shirt and with the sheet pulled up above her waist. 'I'm glad we met and I wish it had turned—'

Sandy interrupted him. 'On your way out,' she said in a voice of fury, 'you can leave the sixty quid on the table in the hall.'

In St George's Square, the shade of the great plane trees reaching their branches as far as the highest windows was some kind of consolation. London heat was cruel. It made you understand that lightning was in reserve if the Turkish bath treatment didn't break your resistance. It was lucky he'd had sixty quid on him. As he walked, he'd worked it out. It was revenge, not a tariff, she'd sounded too angry for that. She'd just named the figure that came into her head. He was relieved about this because it meant he wasn't so far gone he'd misread the motives of a woman picked up in a pub. Sandy was on the level: she'd been insulted due to accident outside anyone's control, and now the best thing she could do was go out and stand herself a good dinner on the proceeds. He rang his mother's doorbell and waited on the step, watching the mast of a pleasure boat drift by above the parapet of the Thames.

There was no music echoing down the stairwell this time, and the door of the flat wasn't open when he reached the top landing. He knocked. It was May in person, not Brian, who opened up. Showily turned out as always, in a silk dress with a pattern of fierce-looking birds, all beak and claw. And she wore a necklace of presumably false, dark pearls the size of small eggs. She looked older to Jason than last time.

'You took your time coming to see your mother again. She expected you as soon as you got back from Manchester. But you were in no hurry,' she said, and he recognised her temper by the old trick of referring to herself in the third person. It's what she always did when he or Hugh annoyed her. 'And now you're here you can give me the address where you've moved to. And the telephone number.'

Jason gave her a kiss which she received coldly. That would usually have disturbed him, recalling the coldnesses of childhood which at once set you to work finding a way back into favour; but now his reaction was only an echo. Something had changed in him; there'd been a shift such as can happen on the sea bed. 'Where's Brian?' he asked.

'Gone away for a few days.'

'Where to?'

'He's got friends in Italy. Brian speaks Italian. Near Naples. He's gone to see them.'

'Good. I need to talk to you on your own.'

'I hate being talked to.'

'We must,' Jason said firmly, and walked ahead into the big room with the studio window through which you saw the leaves of the planes motionless against a sky so pale with heat it was almost white. 'Why haven't you drawn the blinds? It would make it cooler.'

'I haven't been in here.' Curt sentences denying everything were another of her signs of anger.

'Well I'll do it now.'

'I like the light. I don't like sitting in the dark with a man I hardly know just out of prison.'

Jason laughed. 'Some of the men in prisons are a lot more harmless than some people outside claiming to do good works.'

'Jason, I don't think you know anything much about good works. I think you should keep your mouth shut about what you don't know.' Decidedly, tension was on the rise. Knowing her, it would end in an explosion sooner or later, like the weather outside. Better bring it on than waste time while it rumbled round.

'Sit down now and listen to what I've got to say. You've lived too long without anyone to answer to. You're a spoiled woman, mother.'

'You used to call me Mum. Mum's more affectionate.'

'We've both grown out of it.'

May smiled. This remark didn't seem to put her out at all. She was in an upright chair by the piano, upright herself, a statuesque figure in high colour. Her smile was one of full satisfaction. 'I'm not spoiled, I'm an independent woman. I don't have to listen to any man and least of all my own no good sons. But now you just be a darling and go into the kitchen and fetch me a glass of wine out of the fridge. You can have one too. Off you go, Jason, I'm thirsty. And bring the bottle.'

When he got back, Jason decided to come straight to the point. Otherwise she would go on running rings round him with various forms of emotional infighting and evasion. 'How much do you know about what's going on at Byland?' he said.

'What is going on there, according to you?'

'Charlie Seker said the house was empty. It isn't.'

'I don't think that's any of my business.' She held up her wine glass to the shaft of light passing between the slats of the Venetian blind, inspected the contents, then emptied it. 'Top me up,' she said.

'It could get to be your business if the law's broken. You're the owner. Besides, you're a patron of charities. I think something very uncharitable may be happening at Byland.'

'Brian told me he heard a noise. That's all he knows and it's all you know.'

'But you – is it all you know? Give me a straight answer. I never lied to you. We don't lie.'

'Oh, men and their honour.' Her voice was rough again. 'Ricardos and the Mediterranean code and all that *machismo*. Don't you know yet how women despise it and laugh about it and have a code of their own they keep quiet about?'

'You haven't answered.'

'Well you tell *me* something. Why did you run away from Hugh's house so suddenly, without saying where you were going? Well? If your honour never lets you lie?'

Jason rose and approached the upright Victorian chair so he was standing over her. Neither of them feared the other, but there was what you might call moral leaning, if necessary, even on your own mother. 'Come on now,' he said, 'you've got to say.'

She looked up at him as if he was a long way off, assessing the threat like a dark cloud on the horizon. Tears came into her eyes. Now he was sure she was going to lie. 'Since Charlie had it I don't know anything at all,' she said.

'Is there a formal lease?'

'It's an agreement between friends.'

That much was true, anyway. 'Nothing written down, then?'

'Charlie and I understand one another.'

'I think there's a woman there, probably locked up. A foreign woman, maybe several of them. Did you know that?'

'If they don't like it they can always go down to the village and ask for help.'

'They? So you know there's more than one?'

'I thought you said so.'

'I said maybe.'

'Well, I'm saying maybe too. That's all I'm saying.' She seemed to draw herself deeper into the chair.

'The whole point is, if these women are shut up they can't run down to the village. The gates are locked and chained. There are dogs, big ones. Anyone shut in the middle of that wood might as well be in Ravensbrück. And I think you know something about it. If you didn't, I'd get on to the Lancashire police. But I can't do that, if you're—'

May interrupted him by standing up in a sudden rush of movement. 'I'm not. I'm not involved in anything,' she said so loudly it was as if she'd hit him. 'You've just come back to torment me. Why did you go away? Now you can go away again, I know you will anyway.' She advanced to the table where the bottle stood, three quarters empty, and poured the remains into her glass. 'You're only ever done what you wanted and nothing else. You're very like your father. You're as bad as him.' That was always the last insult, signalling anger which could take a long time to be forgotten. Jason's tactics hadn't worked. She'd admitted nothing and now would certainly admit nothing more and part with no information. 'Anyway,' she said, 'I help Charlie help refugees from his country of birth and other places. They have to be housed and some of them need protection when we get them over. That's why I let him have

Byland, if you insist on knowing. And if some of these poor people come into the country in . . . unusual ways, they need even more help than the others. I'm proud to be able to give the help I do. Now go away, Jason, like I said, but first fetch another bottle of wine for me and open it. And this time, you can't have any.'

On this errand, Jason remembered that whenever May was really angry it was because she was alarmed by something and afraid of the consequences. Locking people up against their will was false imprisonment and that took you to the Crown Court. But it was no good telling her so. She must be protected in spite of herself.

'Write your address and number on this,' May said, giving him an envelope and a pencil as soon as he got back. 'I didn't mean you were to go away without telling your mother where you are. You know she always wants to know that.'

She took the opened bottle out of his hand, and then a sly half-smile crossed her face. 'If a woman's voice answers when I ring, it wouldn't surprise me at all if I recognised it.' When he looked quickly at her, the smile had vanished. 'Go out and grab it,' she said, but whatever she meant by that she'd forgotten all about it a moment later, and on his way downstairs he could hear her strong, clear voice singing in German, and the sound of the piano. Brahms, he thought it was. A rhapsody. And he'd noticed a couple of suitcases in the hall, not put away.

Jason felt in need of an ally. Hugh was the obvious one, but he'd made Hugh into part of the problem. Rosie would be at home now, waiting for him, organising his supper or swinging back and forth in that seat among the plants, feet clear of the ground. He saw a telephone box on the Embankment and crossed over. It was Hugh who answered and Jason hung up.

Doing that always makes you feel futile and deviant as a heavy breather. He tried Alex's number in Paris but not even the answering machine came on. He was on his own. He rang the number Charlie Seker had given him.

'I'm listening,' Charlie's voice said.

'Jason Ricardo.'

'Ah, Jason.'

'I'd like to see you.'

'Your mission to Byland was satisfactory?'

'I expect Brian told you it was when he returned the keys.'

'We had a talk.' There was a pause. What else had Brian told him? Jason suddenly saw a possible connection between the talk and Brian's discovery of friends he must visit in Italy. 'Come to the Nauticlub. I'm on my way there now. We can converse in the bar.'

'I'd rather see you without your friends. Raoul, for example,' Jason said.

'I'm going alone this evening. You'll find me in the sauna.'

'I think I'll wait for you in the bar. That's a good place to converse,' Jason said.

'Sauna is very purifying – eliminates poisons from the pancreas, and elsewhere.'

'Then by the time I see you, they should be clear of your system.' Charlie laughed loudly, as at an unfunny joke with no harm to it at all.

At the Nauticlub, the same girl as before was on duty. 'You again. The club closes at nine, where will you go then?' she said. He had a quick swim and then sat in the bar, wrapped in his hired towel. It was after eight and the place was almost empty, a couple of elderly ladies going slowly up and down the pool by sidestroke like wounded moorhens. At eight fifteen he ordered a glass of wine which turned out to be a very drinkable dry Australian. At eight thirty there was still no sign of Charlie. Was he playing games? The appointment at the Nauticlub, if Charlie wasn't here, would be a way of making sure of where Jason would be at the hour when the club was known to close. Raoul and co. could be waiting for him outside in the fading light. Jason got up with the glass of Australian and went into the hallway where he'd seen an arrow indicating the sauna, down at the end of a passage. On the door there was a notice to warn members that it was a mixed sauna and the decencies must be respected. Thank God for that. If Charlie was inside he would be wearing something.

Charlie was there, apparently asleep on the upper bench. There was no one else. 'Hi, Charlie,' Jason said in a loud voice. Charlie stirred, opened his eyes, and slowly sat up. All his movements were slow-motion, deliberate, like raising yourself from the dead. His hair was held in a kind of net. He was sweating heavily and Jason had the impression of his long, thin, wiry body covered in some precious fluid. Prepared for resurrection.

'Close the door,' he said. Jason sat on the lower level as far away as possible from the stove. When he took a mouthful of wine it already tasted warm. 'Alcohol's banned in the sauna but between us—'

'You want one yourself?'

'No. I live by the rules. I'm not native and I take care. It's different for you.' Charlie removed the net and shook out his hair so that it hung over his ears and each side of his face like a hood. 'Tell me, Jason, wouldn't it be wiser for you, with your Maltese passport, to get away somewhere – South Africa, for example – beyond the long arm of the French law? Here in London you'd be picked up in hours.'

'How do you know about the passport?'

'Naturally, from Hugh. He thought it very clever. And doesn't it all depend on him? Your remission I mean? If anything ever got to him – something he didn't like – that he'd rather not hear, perhaps?'

What was Charlie suggesting he knew? Nothing, he could know nothing. It was a ploy. 'I'm not jumping bail. When I'm called I'll turn up.'

Charlie ignored this. 'A flight to Cape Town could be funded. With contacts, good ones,' he said. 'There are always pickings in disturbed regions of the world. And where there are pickings, there are businessmen. Lonely businessmen, pockets full of money. Have you any money, Jason?'

'Me, no, but my mother has. And that's why I'm here. To have a look at how sensible she's being with it.'

'It was a rhetorical question. So you haven't any money, and you need some. And soon. You're not getting any younger. Who is? As for your mother, she's a very strong-minded woman,' Charlie said. He thought for a moment. 'She's a woman prepared to pay for what she wants. And who she wants.'

'I know that.'

'In her wisdom, she expects to pay.'

'And I don't suppose the expectation is often disappointed,' Jason said. He was usually more direct, leaving irony for people with time to spare. 'Byland's what I wanted to see you about,' he added.

'You recovered the belonging you went for, I think. But it won't take you far. Not far enough.'

'It's nothing to do with that. That's my business.'

'Only up to a point. The day your business crosses mine is the day I get interested in it.'

'And the refugees my mother helps you help, are they a

philanthropic interest, or a business one?'

Charlie stood up and moved to the door. 'You're overheating, Jason,' he said. 'Was there anyone in the bar?'

'No one.'

'I'll offer you one for the road. Or the street. Shut the door behind you.'

In a recess of the bar half screened by a bamboo partition were a couple of comfortable chairs. Charlie installed himself and called out for two large glasses of Australian white. When they came he turned to Jason. 'You remind me more than you know of your mother. That must be why I like you. Because let's face it you haven't done much to help me there. But seeing I like you, Jason, and feel a bit sorry for you as a loser, because of that, I'll give you a polite warning instead of a rough one. Keep out of my affairs and don't ask questions I won't answer. Better for you, better for me, better for Raoul not to get his hands dirty.'

'I don't think I'll worry about Raoul.'

Charlie laughed. 'No, I seldom worry about him either. I mentioned him as a sign of what could be.'

'I get the message,' Jason said. 'So you wouldn't like to save us all trouble and just tell me what's going on at Byland? Who the people there are, what they're doing? I hoped you'd say my mother has nothing to worry about.'

Charlie finished his wine and stood up. 'But of course she hasn't, dear May. Now I'm going back to relax in the sauna. I don't think it suits you. You're too hot-blooded. Don't wait. Take care going home, wherever that is. I don't want anyone hurt. *Not anyone.*' When he reached the doorway he turned back. 'Your mother and I hide nothing from each other. We never have. Think about that.'

Jason overtook him in the corridor. 'By the way, Charlie.

Does the name Alex Békassy mean something to you?'

Charlie looked at him without blinking and shook his head slowly. 'Never heard it before. Some misapprehension.' Every so often, Charlie's *r* sound came from somewhere at the back of his throat. Probably it had to be surprised out of him. He disappeared into the sauna, bowing his head as he went in because of his height, and closed the door behind him. His skin was dark and so was his long hair, and from the back he looked like a sepulchre attendant, in his towel like a loincloth.

It was the same car parked two days running on the other side of the street, by the corner. But a different man in it. The similarity, of course, which Jason didn't register until the second afternoon when it was too late, was that both men stayed in the car all day. He'd first noticed it from the window and took it for someone waiting to pick up a woman. Or meet one who shouldn't be having rendezvous in cars. But when Rosie was leaving at about four thirty he put two and two together. 'Someone's watching the house,' he said on the doorstep.

'I don't care. Let them watch.' She took his hand, turned it over and held the palm against her face. 'Your hand's nice and cool. It's too late in the day to hide anything,' she said. Once she'd caught a taxi and driven off, the car pulled away in the other direction. Mission completed.

Who knew this address? Not Hugh: he only had the telephone number. And May wouldn't have passed him the address: she never gave Hugh anything, especially not information. It wasn't just protecting herself from curiosity; she took pleasure in withholding it. Therefore the conclusion was an unpleasant one. She must have given it to Charlie, for the same reason that she'd been angry the other day. She was frightened. Jason picked up the telephone. 'Is Brian still away?' he asked as soon as she answered.

'Yes.'

'Are you all right?'

'Of course I'm all right,' she said. 'Why shouldn't I be all right?'

To Jason, she sounded nervous. He was used to her never telling more than relative truth, at best, but now he had the impression she'd dropped even that. 'Why did you give Charlie my address, where I'm staying?'

'I haven't seen Charlie for months.'

'You rang him then, or more likely he rang you.'

'No. I haven't spoken to him for months either.'

'You're lying to me, May.' She rang off. Jason called Hugh at the office.

'Mr Ricardo is out,' the secretary said.

'Out where?'

'He's busy.'

'Tell him it's his brother. It's urgent.'

'I'll tell him, if he comes back.'

Everyone was lying to him. This girl was, he could tell. He enjoyed that more than his mother lying. 'If I had you on my ship, I'd soon get you telling the truth,' he said.

'Ooh,' said the secretary.

'Be good and fetch Hugh for me now.'

'Hang about, sailor,' she said, and a minute or so later Hugh came on.

'I gather it's urgent,' he said.

'Yes. I have to see you.'

'Do you? Why not come to dinner tonight at home? Or tomorrow? Rosie'd be pleased. She thinks you disappeared because she didn't make you welcome enough. She thinks you

144

don't like her. I want to see you two together again.'

'Thanks, Hugh. I'll call when . . . For now, I have to tell you Seker wants me out of the way. Offered a passage to South Africa and lucrative contacts. Pimping.'

'That's not what it's called on the international business circuit. Hosting's the word.'

'He'll try leaning on you somehow. I don't know how. He'll find a way.'

'I don't think so,' Hugh said. He laughed. 'Blameless life. Blameless wife.'

'Yes.' Jason wanted to put the phone down but what good would that do? To the brother network? Strong, elastic, and adhesive like a cobweb. 'On May then.'

'Too late.'

'What d'you mean?'

There was a hesitation. 'Oh I only meant Charlie's lost his purchase there,' Hugh said.

'Someone like Charlie never lets go. Not if they've once had the woman. And it must have been a lot more often than once.'

Silence. Part of Hugh's problem, Jason thought, was that he couldn't accept their mother's right to a chosen sex life. Couldn't be light about it, as about anyone else's. It made him feel protective of Hugh, it was so unreal. But protectiveness can be just as unreal. You go on feeling it long after it isn't needed or wanted, and even after you've turned into the predator yourself.

Part Two

Chapter One

THEY WERE WOKEN at four forty-five sharp each morning by the racket of iron-bound casks hurled on to the quayside. It was the water ship from Pozzuoli without which the island would dry up and the hotels drain of clients. Soon after, Brian wandered along to buy the bread and yesterday's *Times* fresh off the first ferry from Naples. When he got back, May would be sweeping and swabbing the tiled floor like a fisherman's wife. She seemed happy here, as he knew she would be. She drank less and fooled about in the sea like a big schoolgirl. In the water she looked unsinkable and, beside the dour Latins, still more exotic, to his eye. The locals watched her, men and women, with wonder. Another English lady with temperament, like the one who'd lived in a cave on that beach. And like a Roman woman, she'd taken a young lover for the holidays.

On his return today she was sitting on the washed terrace with the coffee ready. The empty casks were being loaded on board and there was a tender, warm breeze off the gulf. He handed her *The Times*, folded back. 'Have a look at this,' he said, pointing to the column. She read it quickly and pushed the paper back at him across the table, then turned away to stare at the sea, dead calm near the island and with a ripple farther out in the Procida channel where the air came from.

'No one knows where we are, thank God,' she said.

'No.'

'You were right to tell me to take out plenty of cash. No card withdrawals.'

'Yes.'

'How much have we got left?'

'Plenty for a quiet life.'

'I don't know how long I can manage a quiet life,' May said. 'I mean it's lovely now, but suppose in a month or so—'

'You can write to the bank in confidence.'

'I told you, the lawyer watches my account like a buzzard whatever I say to the bank. I had to agree to that. And now when I want to buy a villa on Ischia I can't do it without everyone knowing. This flat's too small. I need my own bath-room.'

He must get her off the tragedy of her situation or the next thing would be a glass of wine at eight in the morning, chased by another. He looked again at the brief item in *The Times*.

The Fraud Squad is to investigate a London law firm suspected of running a bogus asylum scheme ... last September, the firm in question was awarded immigration legal aid franchise worth up to £1m ... suspicion of legal aid irregularities and misconduct ... the firm has been shut down by the Law Society.

'No names,' he said, and then remembered the rest of the phrase his father used to repeat. 'No pack drill.' Who would have thought he'd ever scan memory for a phrase of his father's? Youth must be coming to an end. 'Nothing to do with Charlie, I hope.'

'I shouldn't think so. But once they start—'

'One law firm leads to another. Still, if they get as far as him I expect he doesn't keep records.'

'He's got a photographic memory.'

'But he'd keep his mouth shut.'

'As long as it suits him to,' May said, 'like any man. I rather think Charlie may turn out one of my mistakes. Brian darling, be good to your May and bring her a big glass of Ischian wine.'

Now they'd got away, Brian didn't want to know too much about her dealings with Charlie. That option to purchase Byland was for the back burner. He was sure of one thing – with Jason around there was going to be trouble. For the time being here they were, living their idyll. May had faith in the union of beings. She felt free for the first time in her life, and he thought she meant sexually. It wasn't always easy to know what she did mean, and in this case he didn't ask. It wasn't something she was likely to tell you the truth about, he thought, even if she knew it herself. In sexual matters truth is too compromising, as he knew well. So he was content with the implied flattery, and in exchange she'd taught him a lot. For one thing, he'd learned to hear her kind of music which before he'd always considered irrelevant to modern life. A far cry from Pink Floyd and they were said to be pretty well over the hill nowadays. Also, what he felt when he thought of her, and when they lay on the bed on this terrace, must be love. It wasn't what he'd ever had before. But as for union, he knew that each one is alone and communication chancy, and that's how it would always be. May believed the idyll would last for ever. Not the best thing to say, really, not if there was a financial cloud on the horizon. The idyll wasn't likely to outlast the money. And when you're young, there's a lot of lasting in front of you.

No reason to stop looking at the market in villas, though. There was one round the other side of the island at Forio they could visit today, with a garden above the sea, and a private quay. With a fast boat you could be in Naples in half an hour. You wouldn't be cut off, not seriously, from the real world. He took May's glass into the kitchen and rinsed it, and when he came back he spoke to her about the Forio villa.

'Let's go and see it at once,' she said. 'And get away for the day from all those American queers in the town.'

'You shouldn't say queers.'

'I know. It reminds you how much older I am than you.'

On the winding coast road, he sometimes had the impression that, instead of watching the scenery, May was watching him. He turned to look. He was right. And he knew what she was thinking. In spite of the perfect union of beings, how long could she hold him? Would he be carried off, in this paradise of beautiful people, by a younger woman? Or some American? But what she now said was far removed from all that.

'I wonder if Jason will have seen that article.' She hadn't mentioned Jason since they'd been here. It was an unwelcome subject. Brian would rather she kept her mind on him. Bringing her to Ischia was meant, among other things, to help her forget all about Jason.

'I doubt it. He's busy with his love life.'

'Love life? Jason has affairs, not love. He walks in, and he walks out.'

'It may be different now.'

'I hope not. I wouldn't like to think of him . . . herded into a corner.'

Brian understood quite well what that meant. Not being

cornered kept Jason much closer to her than he would be if he was. But there could be a way out of this, now. 'From something he said, I think he's got serious; he's caught it badly.'

'What was it he said?'

'I just forget the words. It's your family not mine. I don't stick my nose in. He doesn't want to hurt Hugh, that's really what he was saying.'

'I thought so.' When Brian looked at her next he saw an expression of quiet satisfaction, and this time he made no attempt to understand. All too deep for him and no one can really know about mothers anyway. All you do know is that every one of them's different.

'There's the sea again, look,' he said. 'That's the view we'll have from the villa.'

'Until when, I wonder.'

'You said for ever.'

'No one lives so long,' May said, and not for the first time he had the feeling that she was host to some secret sickness without knowing it. Maybe only in the emotions, but that can be mortal too.

Jason had read the same item in a different newspaper. Unwillingly, he rang Hugh.

'I've seen it,' Hugh said.

'Does your paper name the law firm?'

'No. But it says their bank accounts have been frozen. Whoever they are, they'll need money from somewhere.'

'There's no one at St George's Square. No answer. I came round. No sign of life. I'm in the Square now.' Hugh said nothing. Talking to him, Jason felt something like a burned skin wrapping him round. 'Did you hear me?'

'Have you asked on any of the other floors?' Hugh said.

'Not discreet.'

'You're so into discretion, these days?'

The remark was probably quite innocent. Jason laughed. 'Does she usually go away without telling anyone?' he asked.

'How would anyone know?'

'That doesn't answer the question.'

'I'll get on to Deakin & Deakin – he can check out cash movements with the bank.'

'Let me know what he says.'

'Oh, I'll let you know all right,' Hugh said.

You could tell nothing from his voice. It was neutral, there was no warmth in it either of affection or hostility. 'I told you Seker warned me off. It was a bit more – like he was expecting something,' Jason said.

'Keep away, then. The idea was he wouldn't know. How do you make out for money? Do you pay a rent where you are, with the old girlfriend you ran into?'

'It's too late to keep away. If May went before this story broke, maybe she knew something. She may have been told. Seker, in other words.'

'So what d'you think of doing?'

'I'll go round to his office and ask him.'

'He'll know all right then. Take care,' Hugh said before he rang off. Jason wondered which way he meant it.

He approached the building warily, until he could see it seemed deserted. The shutters were up and there was no name on the doorbell. He couldn't remember if there'd been one before, but now, with circulars scattered on the steps and no dustbin it looked like an empty house. The street was quiet and when he tried the bell and knocked, the sounds came back at him like a dead letter. He thought of the café nearby. Charlie was a regular client, he remembered the girl at the checkout saying, 'Hi, Mr Seker, how's it going?' It humanised Charlie to know he was on easy terms with the girl in the café. Jason walked round there.

'Mr Seker? Charlie? We haven't seen him for a few days.'

'Nor his friends? I mean the ones who work for him?'

'Don't know any of his friends,' the girl said.

'Raoul, a big guy who sometimes puts on an American accent and throws his weight about?'

'Don't know him.' She was sounding cautious. Jason asked for a coffee and sat down.

The coffee was brought by a thin, small, dark girl with a scarf tied round her head. When he thanked her, she didn't answer. Soon afterwards he heard voices from another room, speaking low in a language he didn't recognise. On his way out he saw two other girls in the kitchen with similar scarves, and several small children playing on the floor. Seeing him, one of the girls quickly shut the door, without looking up. He went to the checkout to pay.

'Sorry to miss Charlie,' he said. 'My mum helps out with the agency. She had to go away and his number doesn't answer so I brought the message.'

'Oh I see, that's all right then. I'll tell him if you like, next time.'

'Thanks, he'll know who it is.' Jason took his change. 'I suppose he finds you the kitchen staff, does he?'

'I only work here, I'm not the manager or anything,' the girl said. 'This bar's part of a big chain. A lot of girls work for it. I think quite a few come from Mr Seker.'

'Yes, I expect they do. I hope they get properly paid.'

She hesitated. 'More than they'd get in Albania, which was nothing,' she said. 'They owe everything to Mr Seker. They treat him like a father. I mean like one gets treated in their country. Plenty of respect.'

And a cut on the wages. 'I expect he appreciates that,' Jason said. He turned back at the door. 'Does he often go away? The house looks shut up.'

'Mr Seker's probably got somewhere in the country,' she answered.

'I bet he was too.'

The car wasn't there any more, at the corner of the street, when Rosie came that afternoon. She held on when he let her in at the door, and afterwards he felt her fingers digging into his back. When he straightened his arms she still held on.

'Hugh's being odd,' she said.

'How?'

'I think he knows.'

'You mean he guesses.'

'No, I don't mean that. I mean knows. When someone knows something they're more definite. Specially a man. You have this thing about *knowing*.'

'How's he odd?'

'I'll think and then I'll tell you.' Jason didn't stir. 'You won't get it.'

'Give it a try.'

'Well, men have a sort of film going on in their heads all the time. Quick sequences.'

'All the time?'

'I said you wouldn't get it. I mean with a woman. And the woman sees it from the other side of the screen. So, Hugh's changed his film.'

Jason didn't want to know how. So near home. Terrible that anything feeling as right as this – this simple – could feel so wrong too. But there was something he'd wondered about all the same, relatively painless, fairly safe. 'How did you and Hugh first meet?'

Rosie laughed. She stopped short, then laughed again. 'He was a client.'

A bit vague, that. 'Yes?'

'I did massage.' Jason said nothing. He was more surprised than he would have thought. Rosie laughed again, without embarrassment. 'I'm qualified.'

'Hugh had a problem with his back? His knee?'

'I worked in a clinic. Tense people came regularly. Hugh was a new client. It's not what you think. He was so – dark and neat. He told me the problem. I liked having him under my hand. Power of a sort, like I told you.'

This was film all right, Jason thought. One he wouldn't buy a ticket for. So the problem had introduced them and brought them together. As if every woman was a nurse. Some on both sides of the fence love that. He looked down at Rosie, the hair all spread about like a peacock's tail. Power, that's why a woman with hair as beautiful as that let it grow so long.

Later he rang Hugh. 'No sign of Seker,' he said. 'The house is closed up.'

'Deakin says there's been a transfer of ten thousand to another bank. Cash withdrawals every day. She's well past her credit zone. Ravenglass has to plug the gap.'

'From whereabouts are the cash withdrawals?'

'Manchester, then Blackburn.' It was true there was something odd in Hugh's voice. A familiar note. He was lying, but about what?

'Blackburn?'

'Yes.' He didn't think that was the lie. Hugh sounded definite. However, your own lie can convince you, that's true, and then, in a sense, it stops being a lie.

'What date is it, Hugh?'

'Why? September two.'

'Opening of the woodcock season,' Jason said. 'Byland. That's where Charlie is.'

'Of course, you're right,' Hugh said. He sounded relieved. Some difficulty was resolved for him. 'They must both be there.'

'With Brian? And Charlie's chums? I don't think so. You know how she hates shooting and she's let it. She'd never go there under a tenant.'

'What about the withdrawals? Where else can she be?'

There was no answer to that. 'The woodcock may not be the only reason,' Jason said.

'You mean the thing in the papers.'

'Yes.'

'If that's so, then she knows,' Hugh said. 'Always supposing she went of her own accord.'

'What're you getting at?'

'You said she wouldn't go there as a guest. I agree.'

'I'll try ringing and let you know what I find,' Jason said.

It didn't take long. The number at Byland was changed and the new number ex-directory. When he reported this to Hugh, there was a silent pause.

'What do you plan to do?' Hugh asked in the end.

'Go there.'

'It's the only thing,' Hugh said, and Jason felt nudged in the right direction. More than nudged. Push was turning to shove. 'When will you start?'

Jason looked at Rosie. 'Tomorrow morning, first train I can catch,' he said.

'You've got yourself a mobile?'

'Mobile what?'

'Telephone of course, a telephone.'

'No.'

'Well, ring Rosie now and ask her to lend you hers. She only just got it. She can manage without one or two little amenities while you're away. Call round and collect it this evening, she'll be happy to see you. The mobile's a great invention. Then we can all reach you anywhere, any time.'

'You mean you can.' Whatever Hugh said seemed to Jason to carry a sting; hard to identify, concealed, sharp. Unless it was his own conscience. The only way to be was cool, as cool as possible with Rosie's hand on his forearm. 'Okay, I'll do that.'

'Keep me posted. I wouldn't like to buzz you at a bad moment,' Hugh said. 'By the way, what will you do if you're not welcome?'

'I can always get into Byland,' Jason said. When he'd hung up, he turned to Rosie. 'Hugh says to lend me your mobile phone.'

'Does he? Well he paid for it.' She put her shirt on and got off the bed. 'Well? Go on. Here it is. Brand new. Spare batteries still in original wrapping.'

Jason looked suspiciously at the instrument, neat as a watch. 'I'll have all your friends ringing me,' he said.

'No you won't. I haven't given the number to anyone yet. Only Hugh.'

'And my mother.'

'You said she's away. And if she reaches a telephone and rings you can find out where she is.'

'Right. I'm supposed to call round for it this evening.'

'What a brilliant idea,' Rosie said. 'Then we can be watched together instead of separately.'

'If I take it now, how will you explain?'

'I won't. If a gypsy told me this a year ago when I married Hugh . . . it's too late now for explaining,' she said. 'Even to ourselves.'

'Why did you do it?' She didn't answer this time.

Chapter Two

AT THE START of September the anticyclone moved north. When he left London it was raining and windy, but at Manchester airport the sun blazed in a clear sky nearly as blue and still as at Marseille. Alex was due on an Air Buzz flight from Paris. So cheap even he didn't complain.

'I have news for you,' he'd said on the telephone.

'Well?'

'That figure – it's Hellenised Roman. Probably third century and not a museum piece but good for a collector of curiosities.'

'Does that mean you've found one and there's some cash?'

'Don't you think it rather vulgar, Jason, to be in such a hurry over something as unimportant as money? We're talking here about an artefact made seventeen hundred years ago.'

'I never expected to hear you say money wasn't important.'

'I mean there are times when one should pretend it isn't.'

'It's too urgent to pretend anything. Can you fetch it over?'

'I think it's for you to come here,' Alex said. Jason knew what that meant.

'Add the expense to your commission.' He'd once met Alex's grandmother who'd brought him up, a fierce little Viennese with the beak of an owl. You wouldn't think of trying to do her, or any of her descendants, out of expenses.

'I've just been to Great Britain,' Alex said. 'It was hard. I'd need a better reason to come again so soon.'

'Well Alex, old mate, there is a better reason. Hear this item from *The Times*.'

When he'd heard it Alex said, 'Remember I'm from a refugee family. If this law firm helps refugees and breaks the regulations, I'm on their side. Like your mother, bless her.'

'Yes maybe, but today there's more. They say villains charge a couple of grand per head to import people in lorries, then half of them disappear. Particularly women. Some of the women get jobs in sweatshops and restaurants and others just vanish. Like girls in the forest of Fontainebleau.' It was necessary.

'Where are you? Are you still in London?' Alex asked.

'I'm off to Manchester in the morning. I think Charlie's in my mother's house at Byland where the guard dogs are. She may be there too. She disappeared without a word.'

'You're going to march in?'

'I'm going to look around a bit.'

'That's better,' Alex said. 'Manchester? It has an airport?'

'Quite a big one.'

'I'll inform myself. How do I find you?'

'I've got a mobile now, just like everyone else,' Jason said.

So there he was in the heat of the Lancashire afternoon, meeting the Air Buzz connection from Roissy where torrential rain and high wind had delayed take-off. He hadn't wasted time since he got here this morning. He'd found and put a deposit on a Volkswagen van with two bunks and a cooker. The nearest pub to Byland, with rooms, was fifteen miles away and independence would be better. Like the travelling people he'd noticed last time, encamped in the clump of trees up the hill.

Quite likely Alex had some words of Roma. A few phrases would do.

A crowd was coming out of the baggage reclaim area and being waved through customs. All except one whose case was open. The crowd thinned out, then dried up. Alex was standing there, shifting his bulk from foot to foot and looking exactly like the man you'd stop at a customs barrier – displaced, implausible. In fact, a pusher of paedophile videos. Probably that was what the customs men were on the lookout for. No, they were all laughing now; the lid of Alex's case was shut; he was on his way out. 'What was the joke?' he asked, taking Alex's stuff so he could waddle along unimpeded.

'Always keep in with customs men. You never know. Where are we going?'

'To pick up our van. How much cash did you bring?'

'Twenty thousand francs for you,' Alex said.

It seemed not much for his Venus but there were more urgent things on Jason's mind.

'It'll cover the van and a few weeks' keep. After that I'll think again.'

'What is this van, please?' Alex asked. Jason described it briefly. 'We're going to sleep and cook in that? You're mad. I am a Parisian. Have I the build for a mobile home?'

'It's as comfortable as your room in Paris and about the same size,' Jason said. 'We'll take a taxi from here.'

When Alex saw the van he made a pretence of not believing his eyes. 'But it's not even a mobile home,' he said. 'It's a *bidonville* on wheels. What are you paying for this wreck?'

'Fourteen hundred pounds.'

'You're not a practical man, Jason. No wonder you never have a sou. Leave this to me. You wait outside.' When he reappeared his expression was the same. 'That's settled,' he said.

'A thousand. We must find a bank and change the francs.'

While they crossed the sunlit moors, Alex asked about methods used for catching grouse. Jason explained that it was an overpriced sport for the privileged few, the very few. Alex seemed to approve of that. 'In France, it's mostly communists do the hunting,' he said. 'This is more like Hungary in the old time.'

'Have you ever been to Hungary, Alex?'

'Haven't you heard of folk memory?' Alex said. Later, when he caught sight of Burnley from above, with Blackburn in the distance and the long trail of industrial housing along the valley bottom, grimmer than ever in bright sunshine, he was silent as someone in the presence of hopeless grief.

'It's better over the next hill,' Jason said as if Alex was his guest in this awesome landscape. The van was a slow mover on hills, the engine was too small or it had been badly treated. But at last they were on the top with Clitheroe below them and the hills rising after, purple with heather. 'You see that spread-out patch of wood right over there? The last one on the hill in the distance? That's Byland.'

'Extraordinary,' Alex said. 'You're telling me that Charlie Seker, the rat of Pigalle, has his headquarters at this end of the earth?'

'Don't forget there's a massive population in an hour's drive from here. Less. Paris and London aren't the only places with people waiting to have their money bled off them.'

As they ground uphill with screaming machinery northwards beyond Clitheroe, Alex turned in his seat. The window on his side was completely blocked out by his bulk. 'Now, Jason, what are we doing here?'

'We're hoping the caravan camp in the trees hasn't moved on.'

'We're joining them?'

'If they'll have us. How's your Roma?'

'Won't they speak English?'

'Of course. But to get them on side—'

'I'll think some up,' Alex settled back like a neutered cat watching a hole. 'There's just one thing. If you think your mother may be there, what stops you going to the door and asking?'

'I thought you understood. If she's there, it can't be willingly. See what I mean? She'd never go as a guest in her own house. So asking for her won't help. And it won't help the woman who left the message in Romanian.'

'Balkan women. Very ferocious. Cross to the other side of the road,' Alex said. 'How long before you have to tell the London police your mother's missing?'

'It's her right to go missing. We've got as long as we need.'

The camp was still there, now down to one motorised caravan and a car. Washing on branches, a couple of dogs. Jason approached slowly and stopped the van a hundred yards from the clump of trees. They'd seen no one. The gates were chained as before and everything locked in the siesta of the hot afternoon now ending. The sun was already down but the air was warm and larks rose out of the grass as the two men walked uphill. Alex had the stained raincoat he always wore whatever the weather, and he was sweating. Jason thought he'd leave the van to Alex tonight so he'd feel at home, and sleep in the open air. The dogs barked as soon as the engine was turned off and now were running down to inspect them.

'They'll bite me,' Alex said. 'Not you, me. They go where the protein is.'

'Those dogs are just camping here. This isn't a territory.' He was right. The dogs circled them like sheep. 'They want to play.'

'I don't play with dogs,' Alex said, waving his fat hands at them. 'Go away. *Filez*. Shoo! Isn't that the English word?' It wasn't one the dogs knew. They grew more excited, concentrating their games around him.

Just then a man appeared from behind the mobile home and shouted some order; the dogs changed immediately into an escort trotting along beside Jason as if they'd invented him. The man was long and dark and thin, with narrow sloping shoulders and a presence in some way formidable. He looked as if he knew what he wanted, and got it. Or it might be the forearms that made the impression. They were far more powerful than the rest of him, and he held a hammer in one fist. More a mallet. The hair on his arms and chest was powdered with a honey-coloured stone dust. 'You can't turn us off,' he shouted.

Alex came puffing up behind Jason and approached the man, speaking some words of Roma as planned.

'What?'

Alex repeated his phrase patiently.

'Don't neither of you speak English?'

'Yes we do,' Jason said.

'This is common land, here,' the man said, 'and like I said you can't turn us off.'

Jason held out a hand. 'We were going to ask you if you mind us joining you with our van under these trees for a bit,' he said.

'I'm Nick. My girl's called Beral and she's breastfeeding the baby. B-e-r-a-l. How long's a bit?'

'A couple of days, probably,' Jason said. Nick, who sounded as if he came from London and took it for granted that everyone was up to as little good as he was, looked suspicious.

'And what do you and your friend want to be doing here, for a couple of days?' he asked.

'Surveying about,' Jason said, and this appeared to be just what Nick expected.

'Not a lot to survey.'

'You never know,' Jason said, and he could see Nick already trying to work out how to move in on whatever game it was he and Alex were playing.

'Looking for something in particular? Dolmens? Hill forts? Roman roads? Coins?'

'There aren't any round here. I know it all pretty well already.'

'I bet,' Nick said. 'What are you going to do about food in that van?' He stared hard at it, down the track. 'Those things don't exactly come with a two star restaurant. We've got a barbecue. You can join us, if you like. Beral won't mind.'

Jason thought Beral probably did pretty much whatever she was told. Nick didn't seem to him a man to put up with a lot of capricious behaviour, and if willpower wasn't enough, the forearms . . . 'Thanks a lot,' he said. 'We've got some steaks and plenty of wine.'

'Steaks'll be something else, on the barbecue,' Nick said, and went up the steps into the mobile home.

Alex had been studying him during this exchange. 'I'll tell you what I think,' he said. 'This man carves in stone. I recognise an artist. I think he makes abstract stone sculptures in this wilderness – this abstract landscape. Nowhere could be better. And at night he kills sheep and grouse to feed his starving family.'

'I doubt it about the grouse. Sheep, maybe. I was thinking he could be useful somehow.'

'Penniless artists are free of moral problems. He'll do any-thing you want if it's worth it.'

'I think so too,' Jason said as Nick reappeared, closely

followed by a very young, nervous-looking girl carrying a baby on one arm. Nick had hold of her by the other.

'This is Beral,' Nick said. You can usually tell when a poor girl's been knocked around a bit, and Beral looked as if that was the case with her. She looked both defiant and cowed. Usually, if the man's still there, the girl tries to take it out on someone else. Jason decided to be vigilant and friendly but not too friendly.

'Hallo, Beral,' he said, smiling. 'That's a good-looking baby there. Alex—' he indicated him, 'and me, we're hoping you won't mind us.'

'Nick says you've got some booze, so if you have that's all right with me,' she said. She smiled back at him, a smile full of charm despite a couple of missing teeth – charming because life's grudges hadn't got the better of it yet.

'Light the barbecue then,' Nick said.

'I've got the baby.'

'Well put it down, stupid.' Nick turned to Jason. 'It takes a good hour to get it going right. We could be having ourselves a drink. Your van'll fit okay the other side of that tree, the ground's hard enough. And when you want a shit you can go round that pile of stones. We've got a chemical in the mobile but I don't recommend it. Not with the baby.'

'Artists are always practical people,' Alex said, and Nick smiled for the first time.

Jason left them together and went down for the van. When he got back he found them beyond the mobile home inspecting a block of stone. Beral was busy with the barbecue and the baby lay on its back, studying its legs and arms waving about in the air as if learning to count to four. The stone block already had projections and hollows worked on it and smooth ground surfaces here and there, and at its top end the

168

chisel had cut out of the mass a domed shape like a skull coming into the world. Jason stood silently looking at it, beside the other two. He didn't read much there, yet it made him feel good. The work already done seemed to answer something in his own head he hadn't known was there, a question he hadn't put. That must be part of the trick. He looked with new interest at Nick, so concentrated, standing there with the stone below him, passive, marked with his mark. Like mother and father in one.

'What d'you think?' Nick said. Who was he asking? No one in particular. The world in general. His attention was turned inward. Jason found nothing to say.

'You've got it under control,' Alex said. Did he mean something intelligible by that? Naturally the stone was under Nick's control. No one else would touch it.

'You think?' Nick said. He squatted down with his chisel and gripped the stone between his knees, then struck it a few times, accurate blows making a new relation that looked immediately right and destined to be.

'That's what I meant,' Alex said. 'Control. Kinaesthetic empathy.'

'I've got a couple of bottles here, but no corkscrew,' Jason said.

'It's for sale when it's finished,' Nick said, standing up. 'Corkscrew? I keep one of those in my pocket.'

By the time the barbecue was ready it was getting dark and the second bottle of wine was about empty. Jason opened another. Nick looked after the steaks while Beral drank and puffed intermittently at her joint, relighting it each time a bit less deftly. She was on the ground with her legs curled under her and swaying so that every now and then she bumped gently into

Alex, to whom she seemed to have taken a fancy. If he noticed it, he showed no sign. The steaks were excellent, the air still warm with a light inland breeze from the hill behind. Jason saw that, across the glow from the barbecue, Nick was watching him.

'I think it's that wood you go for,' Nick said. 'If you know the surroundings that well then you know there's nothing else here. Just the wood.'

'Have you seen anyone there?' Jason asked.

'Oh we've seen them all right. Came up here with their fucking rottweilers and tried to get rid of us.'

'But you didn't leave.'

'Like I said, this is common land. And I told them if they gave me grief I'd be dropping off by the police station in Clitheroe.'

'You told them that?'

'I certainly did.'

'And they believed it.'

'Because it's right. But they said they'd be back. At first, that's what I thought you came for. I reckoned you could be some kind of . . . what's it . . . bailiff.'

A new experience that. 'Anything to do with the law's the last thing the people in that wood hope to see, if you want to know,' Jason said.

'More into rottweilers. And razor wire.'

'Where's the razor wire?'

'All round the wall on the inside.'

'Since when?'

'The last few days,' Nick said. 'Stepping up the security. Perhaps they knew you was coming.' He laughed, and Jason joined in.

'You can cut razor wire,' said Beral, surfacing unexpectedly.

170

'I was with some boys who done it, once.'

'But not if you're inside and there's no way of getting out and you haven't got cutters,' Jason said.

'So that's it,' Nick said. 'But if anyone's in there wanting out and can't that's a police job.'

'We've got a reason for not wanting the Lancs Constabulary, same as them. Different reasons, same result.'

'Yeah, I get you,' Nick said. Jason had the impression that what Nick got, well on the way into a third bottle, was that there had to be promising opportunities in this situation. 'There's a tosser in there I wouldn't mind having the balls off.'

'Raoul? Talks with a bit of American accent when he remembers?'

'Right.'

'Tell us what you've seen coming out and going in.'

Nick turned to Beral. 'You say,' he told her. Then he turned back to Jason and said in confidence, 'Not as thick as she looks. Sharp enough when she wants. Go on, girl, speak up.'

Beral stopped rocking and concentrated. 'It's furniture vans,' she said. 'I walk up the hill with the baby. You can see the road from there. Not the gates but the road.'

'That's right,' Jason said.

'I thought, they're bringing in a lot of furniture for just a house in a wood, and then one time a van breaks down, out there. After a bit they open up the back and some people get out. Three or four and a couple of kids. You could tell they didn't know where they were.'

'And then?'

'There's all this shouting and then the driver and his mate, they wave their arms and make them go on to the gates. Didn't see them no more after that, did we darling?' she said as if to the baby, then noticed she didn't have it with her at the moment. 'But when the van's fixed, they hump a couple of girls up in it and away quick.'

'Hump 'em and dump 'em,' Nick said.

'That's what you would think, you,' Beral said, and lit up again. She didn't sound much concerned. It was a rough world, she was under the heap and the weed was her exit, good for an hour or so. Or till the baby woke up.

'Does that tell you anything?' Nick asked.

'It fits the idea in my head,' Jason said.

'You're on the trail of missing persons?'

'We're looking for the owner of the wood.'

'That owns the house in it too?'

'Right.'

'And you don't go in because you don't reckon he's there, and you don't know where he's got to, is this it?'

Without the wine, Nick would probably be more round-about. But Jason saw the advantage. It saved time. 'The owner's a woman,' he said.

Just then the dogs, asleep since the offcuts of steak, rose up to bark. There was no apparent reason but dogs don't need that. Their noise was immediately echoed from the heart of the wood by more serious volleys. 'D'you know if they're loose?' Jason asked.

'You thinking of going in?'

'I might have to.'

'Well they are,' Nick said. 'If you went down and made a racket at that wall, in a minute you'd have them roaring away at you the other side.'

'Then you'd be on your own as far as I'm concerned,' Alex said. 'Unless we poison them first.'

'I don't poison dogs,' Nick said.

172

'We can do a lot better than that,' said Jason, 'we can use them.'

The first segment of a copper moon began to rise over the crown of the wood. Tomorrow it would be full. The dogs had their premonition. Soon the sky would be light with it and shadows of big trees would fall across tracks and clearings. All you needed now was the call of an owl; and soon enough there it was, repeated, floating across the hillside. 'That moon's going to be a help,' Jason said.

'I don't know. Beral goes funny when the moon's full,' Nick said. She seemed to be asleep now, propped against Alex's bulk, head hanging and hands folded in her lap. She looked at peace. 'Her rhythms go all to cock. You don't know what she's going to do.'

'We'll look out for it,' Jason said. In a minute the moon would clear the trees and up here the temperature begin to drop. For a northern hillside in September it was still hot; not a Mediterranean night but softened by the sound of the stream and the scent of mould and moss. He could never remember another like it here before. The moon itself seemed a source of heat, a night sun. In spite of the razor-wire and the rottweilers, it felt as if reality was left behind in London.

The mobile telephone rang, inside the van.

'Jesus,' Nick said. 'I didn't expect nothing like that.'

Jason took the mobile round the other side and walked over towards the pile of stones with his back turned. 'Yes?'

'It's Rosie.'

Something must be wrong. She was hoarse or breathless as if she'd been running. 'What's happened?' he said.

'Aren't you glad to hear me?'

'Of course I am.' He meant it. He'd almost forgotten how

her voice sounded, it had become the intimate voice you know in sleep without hearing it.

'Why?'

'Because I think about you.'

'Are you sure?'

'All the time.'

'Well here I am.'

'The mobile was a good idea.'

'One of Hugh's.'

'Yes.'

'He's had some others since then. It's why I've rung.'

Like the dogs and the moon, Jason had a premonition. 'What are they?' he asked.

'He definitely knows.'

'You're sure?'

'Quite sure.'

No point in asking how she knew, obviously something had happened between them. It would be unlike Hugh to come into the open. When he was a boy his rages were always aimed off the target. His attacks were underhand because he lacked self-esteem. But a woman, especially a wife, could be more at risk. 'I think you should get out of the way.'

'I have. I'm at Euston. There's a train in fifteen minutes. I must talk to you. Tell you something. If you'll have me, that is.'

'I'll come to Manchester and meet you.'

'No, better not. I'll find a hotel first and call again. In the morning.'

'Be careful.'

'You mean take care.'

'No, I don't,' Jason said. 'I mean be very careful.'

'Because you need me?'

'You know that.'

★ ★ ★

At first, Alex said he wanted to come too. Then he looked at the sky, at Beral under the trees and Nick beyond them chipping at his stone, and said he'd changed his mind. Obviously he felt safe with them. 'It's years since I spent a day in the country and I can see this is an emergency of a private nature you have,' he said. 'I prefer not to intrude.' His eyes were alive with speculation. 'You're a walking emergency, Jason. That's how in a few weeks of getting to London after five years—'

Jason laughed. 'It could happen to anyone,' he said.

Alex peered at him, took his glasses off and rubbed them, then peered again. 'Oh no. What's happening to you couldn't happen to anyone. It's out of the ordinary. It's Greek drama, I can tell. The gods are after you.' Jason thought of Alex's grandmother, never out of touch with the beyond. 'I don't want to know any details.'

'You're right. They're basic,' Jason said. 'I'll be back this afternoon. So what will you do?'

'Watch progress on the sculpture . . . bathe in all this uninhibited nature. It may never happen again.'

'Mind out. You're a conspicuous object.'

'Thank you. But no one pays attention to people who look like me. They think we're lost and frightened and that's good enough for them. Nick will keep an eye on me.'

The hotel was a modern one and the room a carpeted cube like a padded cell. It was hot and they lay under a sheet. Anxiety made Rosie seem desperate, as if this chance might be the last and she must burn up her reserves. For the first time with her he'd felt out of reach. But it would come back, the merging, they'd have that again. Or was it an illusion, something like being in the right place for an eclipse once in a lifetime?

175

'What happened with Hugh?' Jason asked. Whatever it was would divide him in two, he knew that. He wasn't sitting on any fence, he was impaled on it.

'When he went off yesterday I was in the street, he drove at me.'

'Are you sure?'

'What d'you mean, am I sure? I was there. I jumped aside. He didn't stop.'

'Had he said anything?'

'Nothing. He was on the phone, then he came out of the door white in the face, and there I was.'

So here was another consequence. 'Don't go back,' Jason said.

'I won't.'

'Where does Hugh think you are?'

'I left a message I'd gone to my sister.'

He'd never thought about her family, as if she'd come into existence just for Hugh to have and him to steal. He could imagine what May would say about that. You've never had a relationship before, that's the trouble with you, is what she'd say. 'He'll check up on it,' he said.

'My sister knows.'

'Whatever happens I won't let you go.'

'Won't you?' She looked happier again, at least he thought it was happiness. He wasn't sure yet of her every expression.

She said she wanted to come to Byland with him. She hated the hotel and didn't want to stay in Manchester alone. No one would know who she was, at Byland. She'd like to meet Nick and Beral, they sounded her sort of people – easy people. She would keep a low profile, out of the way. Share his beach mattress from the van, under the stars. They would make love in the eye of the full moon. That was a guarantee of constancy, where she came from.

Jason didn't know where she came from. 'Where's that?' he asked.

'Cornwall.'

'So you're a Celt.'

'Yes.'

If she'd said Scotland or Wales he wouldn't have credited the legend about constancy. But in Cornwall he could believe in love-making in the eye of the moon. All the same, it was impossible to take her to Byland. It would be like camping out with her in St George's Square. She seemed to have forgotten what quicksands they were on. That was the Celtic way with reality. He checked himself. He was beginning to think like Hugh. 'It wouldn't be safe,' he said.

'Who for?'

'Anyone. The fewer the better.'

'You're exaggerating,' Rosie said. 'This is Olde England. You're not going to bump into a gang of hoodlums in the middle of a country wood.'

'Lancashire isn't Cornwall. It's a huge industrial sprawl and a subculture. It wouldn't be safe,' he repeated.

The mobile sounded on the bedside table and Rosie picked it up. It was hers after all. Jason took it out of her hand while it was still ringing. 'Yes?'

'Jason.' Hugh's voice came through at its most relaxed, almost warm.

'Yes, Hugh.'

'Where are you?'

'Not far from Byland.'

'I mean where are you staying?'

'Out in the open. Why?'

'I might join you. I'd find a pub. I've got some news.'

Jason knew by a change in his tone that Hugh didn't mean it

about joining him. 'What's this news?'

'I've been asking round St George's Square. The old bat on the ground floor spends her time at the window. She saw May leaving late one night in a car with two young guys. She didn't have any luggage with her. And she hasn't seen her since.'

'Was there any sign of force?'

'They were on either side and both had an arm.'

'Then Byland's where she must be. They'll have taken her cash card.'

'I don't like to think what they'd do to get the code off her,' Hugh said.

'I'll go in,' Jason said.

'Hadn't you better call the police?'

'No. She'd end up charged with far worse than conspiracy to facilitate illegal entry, I'm sure of it. And in her own house. I must get in there,' he repeated.

'You're by yourself aren't you?' Hugh said.

'My way in only takes one at a time.'

'Good luck then. I won't ring again, the mobile might buzz at the wrong moment. Keep me posted.' Hugh rang off.

'Did he say anything about me?' Rosie asked.

'Nothing.'

'Then he's stringing you along.'

'Yes. But it makes no difference. My mother's there and I have to get her out. You stay here, Rosie, I'll be back tomorrow, I promise. I know what I'm doing. There's nothing to it. I know my way round that place with my eyes shut. It'll all go off smooth as you like.'

Rosie was staring at the pattern up on the carpeted ceiling. 'I've a bad feeling about it,' she said. 'And there's another thing I had to tell—' But Jason was already at the door.

Chapter Three

THE RAVENGLASS DRIVER wasn't all that surprised to see Hugh round the offices before any else had yet turned up. Everyone knew the reason. The governor wasn't happy in his home life. It was that mouthy secretary who'd put it on the street. She didn't care for being treated like she wasn't there so she got back by listening in, and it seemed that creep Seker had been checking out Mrs Hugh Ricardo. It was the brother on the beach she was having it off with. Jason. The one in no hurry. After just a year. Seker dished the dirt to Hugh and Hugh didn't go home any more in the evenings.

'Morning Mr Ricardo.'

'Morning.'

'If you've got a minute—'

'Yes?'

'That matter we were talking about—'

'Yes?'

'That pal of mine at Seker's, Tony – he's still worried about the cargoes.'

'Tell him he needn't be. Charlie Seker and I had a meeting. He's on the level with his refugees – they're genuine cases. He looks after them, gets their situation regularised. It's straight up.'

How many other ways was he going to say it? 'All of them?'

'All of them. Now, if you don't mind, I know it's early hours but there's work to do round here.'

So that was it. Seker had it sewn up. Butt out of my business, friend Ricardo, and I'll keep you wised up on something you ought to know about. That would be the message. It was up to Tony what to do. Did he want his job, or did he want the law? Face it, the law isn't exactly the international trucker's best friend, one way and another.

The first shot came soon after six. And a few minutes later a couple more in quick succession from the far end of the wood. After that there was sporadic firing in different quarters, between long intervals of silence as the light slowly faded. It had been another very hot day.

'That's how it's done,' Jason said. 'In the evening the wood-cock sit tighter. Any other time you can't get near them. You work in to the centre.'

'It's disgusting,' Beral said.

'They're hard to hit.'

'They don't hit back, do they? It's murdering innocent defenceless animals. And I bet it's the females catch it.'

'You belt up, lamebrain,' Nick said. 'Go on,' he told Jason.

'With the full moon, they'll carry on late. It's when most of the accidents happen.'

'Any luck,' Beral muttered. No one paid attention. She was practising her rights, stuck in the company of three men.

'And when they stop, they've gone inside for a few drinks. They'll have their dinner about an hour later. That's when to go for it.'

'Then we must light the barbecue straight away,' Alex said. 'It's no good going for it on an empty stomach. Hunger slows the reactions.'

'There's loads of time,' Jason said.

'Get the barbecue lit. You heard,' Nick told Beral. He seemed to have acquired a lot of consideration for Alex during the day. Perhaps Alex had hinted he might buy a sculpture.

'Here's what we'll do,' Jason said. When he'd laid out his plan of diversionary tactics he produced the wire cutters he'd bought in Manchester. 'State of the art. I'll be in in a flash while you draw off the rottweilers.'

'What I don't understand, maybe none of my business, is, what exactly are you going for?' Nick said. 'When you're inside? And how d'you get into the house, come to that?'

'There's a way. Tell you later. There's someone there I have to get out.'

'Would it be a member of the family?'

'Yes.'

Nick nodded at Beral, who had suspended work on the barbecue to listen. 'What we thought,' he said.

At some moment or other, Beral would surface from a trance and guess the truth. It was the sort of right guess that a girl like Beral – downtrodden and spaced out – might make. Jason smiled at her. It was funny, but with her as the only female in the party you were bound to get to feel a bit fond. She didn't smile back.

'Now listen,' he said. 'We don't know how many they are but I'd say three. Maybe one other. Their evening's been screwed up. They see you drive away without lights, they check the wire where you were and find it intact. They bring the dogs back and get on with it.'

'Are you saying it's some kind of concentration camp in there?' Nick asked.

'To tell you the truth—'

'Run it past us,' Nick said.

'—I don't know. If it's on the level I'll talk my way out.'

'You're breaking and entering a home, even if it's all falling down. Not just a home, a residence.' Nick raised a clenched fist. 'They'll call the chief constable. And he'll come.'

Jason saw no escape. 'Byland belongs to my mother,' he said.

'Now we're getting it,' Nick said. He looked excited and disapproving. Here was some sort of pile-up in the capitalist class, plus a window on the world where commissions get off the ground.

'If it's your mum and you want to rescue her, that's nice,' Beral said. 'But just because they don't want the law, why don't you?'

'Because his mum's involved, that's why,' Nick said. 'She's probably in it up to here and it's gone wrong. There's what it's all about.'

Best to leave it in the air. 'If you find your mother, how are you going to get her away?' Alex asked. 'Supposing she wants to come?'

Jason turned to him. 'Give me an hour and take the van in where I've cut the wire. Follow the track. Blow the horn till someone shows up.'

'And then?'

'I'll be along there with you,' Nick said.

'What about me?' Beral asked.

'You can always lock the caravan and drive around. And don't forget the baby,' Nick told her.

'And here's the mobile phone,' Jason said. 'But promise not to call the Lancs Constabulary unless we're not back by – about ten in the morning. Not before.'

'She don't know about promises,' Nick said. 'I wouldn't leave that with her if I was you. She'll bell everyone she's ever met.

Starting with that sister of hers in San Francisco.'

'That's all right,' Jason said. 'There's spare batteries.' Beral grabbed the mobile and disappeared into the caravan.

'She'll be happy now till tomorrow. Red hot it'll be when you get it back. Don't say I didn't warn you,' Nick said. Actually he looked pleased about Beral getting this treat. Jason thought Nick was secretly much nicer to her than he pretended to be. 'Looks like we'll have to barbecue our own dinner.'

'We're at the front of the house blowing the klaxon,' Alex said. 'One or more of them come out. What then? I think there are holes in your plan.'

'I may be out there to meet you. If not, it's down to you.' Alex assumed a dead expression as if asked for money. 'Say you need to phone a doctor for the baby. Pile it on. Then ask for Charlie. Give your name. That'll bring him.'

'I'm getting to really look forward to this. Where's the wine?' Nick said.

When he brought it Jason said, 'Nothing can go wrong if everyone remembers the timing.' No one answered. 'You're with me?'

'Cheers to that,' Nick said, holding out a tumbler. 'And give us that way into the building just in case.'

The moonlight was so strong you'd be a moving shadow, sighted a hundred yards off. Jason followed a path older than the track, probably prehistoric from when the wood was a huge encampment with ditches and mounds. No one ever dug it up to look for pottery or arrowheads or coins. And now the defences were razor wire, up-to-the-minute invention from hell. Cutting it had felt good, like crushing scorpions. Nick and Alex were making a massive noise which even from here could be heard above the bellowing of dogs and distant shouts of the

183

men after them. Nick would be enjoying himself, half-drunk and hoping for a bit of bother, relief from the strain of being a first cause all day long – every stroke on the stone a commit-ment with no going back. Like inventing man and woman on day one with botchery and vices.

Jason knew the plan left plenty of room for trouble. Alex's private agenda, for one thing, was an unknown quantity. He hadn't given enough thought to that. What was Alex's idea, once confronted with Charlie? He doubted if Alex had thought it through either. He wanted to get the bitterness of years off his chest. With Alex, it would be all words. He hated Charlie and he'd never had the chance to say. That was bad. He wanted to tell Charlie how he'd given the name Charles Seker to the office of the French police running a dossier on paedophile video buyers worldwide. Would he come all this way just to do that? Jason felt pretty sure it was what Alex's project amounted to. At a turn in the path the building loomed like a heavier shadow through the trees, no lights showing. When May was young there'd been parties of her friends escaped from London, and if you kept your eyes open you learned pretty well all you needed to know, to start you off, on the relations of the sexes. In those days every light blazed through the night. This back side of the house was a plain block on three floors and an attic, all the Gothic went on round the front. Folly at Byland was skin-deep. On this side the only madness was the ice-house, conceived for an Italian climate. Now the dogs' barking stopped, so they'd been called in and were on the way back. The ice-house was beyond that wall, to reach it he had to pass the gate in full moonlight. On the edge of the clearing Jason drew breath, ran across the cobbles and vaulted over. Not a sound, not a light. Voices still far off in the wood. Then an owl again, surfing the night waves. They must have had ideas, those sheep farmers, to go building a covered ice pit. Jason could remember when a refrigerator was first introduced to Byland. No one said anything then about pensioning off the ice-house. It was forgotten by all, except him. The oak door would last for ever. Jason closed it as well as he could behind him and started feeling his way, bent double among the debris of straw and wicker trays.

Nothing had gone wrong yet. The passage came out inside a cupboard in the larder, and he stood there now in blackness. This was where the woodcock, if they'd killed any, would be hanging. But probably they hadn't. Charlie's tales of prowess were all bullshit, like naming the number of other people's women you've had. It occurred to Jason that if Rosie tried to get him on the mobile she'd find the line engaged. He should have warned her. The blackness wasn't total, there was a thin line of light at the bottom of the cupboard door, more white than yellow. The moon through the larder window. And no sound.

He flashed his torch over the ceiling. No woodcock hung there. He's been right. Charlie's party was only banging away in the wood with hired guns to keep up with each other. Not a single pellet had as much as ruffled a feather. Jason liked the woodcock and their ghostly flight and was glad. He went round the wall and through the old kitchen, reading contours in the dark like a bat in a barn. The only staircase to the top spiralled from here. Jason started up, sticking close to the inside newel and watching for the moonlight. With luck, he'd see before he could be seen.

A woman's raised voice from somewhere above, cut short. A footstep on a stone floor down below. Then silence again. The silence was surprising. Then the clock struck, in the hall. It couldn't have been wound up for years. That suggested May must be here. She had a horror of a stopped clock as if it was

185

her own heart. Eleven was later than he'd thought, he'd lost a slice of time, an hour had got away. When he reached the next shaft of moonlight he checked his watch. Eleven was right. Maybe they were all in bed except the woman with the raised voice in the attic. If everything at Byland had an innocent explanation, she could be a Portuguese brought from London to dogsbody for the party. But Jason didn't believe it. He was past the landing at the second floor. If it hadn't been for the woman's voice you'd say the place was deserted.

The key to May's bedroom door was on the outside. So if she was there, she was locked up. He slipped in, closing it behind him. There was no moonlight. When he tried the light switch nothing happened. 'It's me, Jason,' he said in a low voice. Suppose she was in bed with Brian? 'I'm going to shine a torch and find a light that works,' he said more loudly. The silence was like a drugged sleep. He knew where the bed stood and aimed the torch to one side where there used to be a desk with a lamp. She scribbled her letters there in a large, irresponsible hand, letters full of easy, fleeting emotions. The lamp didn't work either. The wiring was antique; maybe the whole system had blown and the steps he'd heard was someone searching for a fusebox in a strange house in the dark. He turned his torch on the bed. It was empty, covered with a dust sheet.

So why were the curtains drawn, and the key on the wrong side? The room had one big window above the crown of trees with the hill beyond. He pulled back the curtains and moonlight flooded in, showing the furniture, the carpet, a couple of pictures, all without colour as on a silver screen. There was no sign anywhere of clothes, no mess on the dressing table, not a book in sight. He opened the wardrobe and saw only a few things left from a visit long ago, and on the floor, part of May's collection of hundreds of pairs of shoes, superannuated like

Byland – actually, all her shoes became superannuated a few days after she bought them. If she wasn't here, where was she? Jason pulled the dust sheet off the bed. Folded blankets. Possibilities lined up in his imagination. She could be held in some other room; she could be drugged in a hotel, in Blackburn, for example; she could have been done away with, an inconvenient patron whose funds were running too low to be any more use and whose only importance was that she knew too much. The worst of these seemed to him the likeliest, and the most absurd. That sort of thing didn't happen to people like her, so bursting with the life force at its most selfish. And what about Brian? He would have to be put away too. A massacre. It wasn't thinkable. Hugh's information was wrong. Cash withdrawals? Some mistake. Jason stood in the window, looking down at the fringe of grass, the unweeded gravel in front of the house, then the curve of the hill in the distance and above it the stars showing up sharp through dry air now that the moon was low on the other horizon. He was on a wild-goose chase. He'd made a clown of himself.

He noticed an ash-tray smell. But May never smoked. It was hot too, and Jason opened a window. At the same moment he heard a metallic sound behind him and as he turned, the light hanging from the centre of the ceiling came on. Someone must have found the fuse box. On a table near the bed was the ash tray: he'd seen Brian smoking; maybe they were here after all. But the bed was unused, so that didn't work. Jason thought he had no gift for snooping, doing something was what came naturally to him. He went over to the door. It was locked. He switched off his deductive powers at once. All this was some kind of balls-up. He and Hugh had both been mistaken in thinking May was here. The door was kept locked because this room wasn't used, someone had checked up and turned the key.

He banged loudly. He would say he'd forgotten something last time. Just a bad moment to pass through. This was, after all, his mother's house. He put his ear to the door but heard no footsteps. He returned to the window and leaned out. The attic was behind a parapet of bogus battlements just above him. If he stood on the ledge he might reach. Could he pull himself up? He climbed out, holding the central mullion. When he straightened up he found he could grasp the parapet at arms' length. It should be about within his—

'Come back offa that, buster,' said a voice behind him. 'It's a long way down and Mr Charlie Seker wants you in just the one piece for now.' Jason felt a grip on his ankle.

He crouched, slid his hands down the mullion, and jumped to the floor. The movement gave no chance to kick where a kick would score. Jason saw that Raoul held a gun in his fist.

'We were expecting you, shithead,' Raoul said.

'I can see.'

Raoul was wearing boots like an SS man, and standing in the doorway was another one, in jeans, who Jason had seen with Charlie in the Nauticlub. In this light he looked about seventeen. 'I was right to lock the door, wasn't I, Raoul?' he asked.

'You did the only thing, babe,' Raoul said. Jason looked hard at Raoul's gun. Was it real? Raoul raised it to point at his chest, on the side of the heart. Was it loaded? 'Don't fuck up,' Raoul said. Speaking low-budget lines didn't make him less dangerous if it was.

'Where's Charlie? I want to see him,' Jason said.

'On his way. Sit in that chair and put your hands in front of you, palms upward. That's right. Now you stay here with Johnnie and mind yourself.' Raoul gave Johnnie the gun. 'If he moves his hands or gets up, blast his kneecap,' he said.

'I'll do that,' Johnnie said, sounding as if it wasn't one of the skills he'd learned at public school. 'Will you be long?' Raoul didn't answer. He shut the door behind him and locked it. After a good interval Jason let his head begin to fall slowly forward, his palms upward and open as ordered. Johnnie was probably afraid of him, which might make him careless with the trigger. Jason didn't want any harm to come to either of them. If he kept quiet, sooner or later the boy would say something, and anything he said was bound to throw light on what was going on here.

'Do you smoke?'

'No,' Jason said.

'D'you mind if I do?'

'The ash tray's on the window sill.'

Johnnie laughed. 'I'm not that thick,' he said. 'I go behind and you jump on me.' He put a cigarette in his mouth and fumbled about trying to light it with one hand.

'Haven't I seen you at the Nauticlub?' Jason asked.

'That's right.' Johnnie drew himself up a bit and expanded his chest. 'I aim to increase my muscle volume to match my height. I was a weed when I started.'

'I wouldn't let it worry you,' Jason said. 'So there's you and Raoul and Charlie. Did you manage to hit any woodcock?'

'I didn't go out. I had to wait here, in case—'

'In case I showed up?'

'Among other things, yes. And you did.'

'What about the others? Did they get any?'

'Not Raoul or Mac. I think Mr Seker maybe did. He said so anyway.'

'They left you in charge by yourself?'

'I didn't mind. I didn't want to go shooting.' Johnnie seemed to remember something. 'Don't ask so many questions,' he said.

'If you've got any more you can ask Mr Seker. Then you'll see the sort of answers you get.'

This meant there were four of them here, including Mac, whoever he might be. And they'd brought no girls, apparently. If they had, Johnnie would have let it slip out that he'd been on his own with them. He wasn't at an age to keep mum about the presence of girls. So there was just the woman in the attic, and that didn't count as a presence. Still, the fact that she or they were here could explain why no other women had been brought. Unless May was still to be discovered. No. May was somewhere else and he'd been . . . he turned away from where the thought led. 'Does old Raoul always talk like that?' he asked. 'Like he only just learned the words?'

Johnnie sniggered. 'It's the books he reads,' he said.

'Raoul reads books?'

'American ones.'

'Muscle volumes,' Jason said, and Johnnie sniggered again. Maybe he didn't like Raoul much. He was an easy man to take against. 'In prison you tend to lose muscle for want of exercise. Raoul should look out.'

'You have to be pretty dumb to get caught,' Johnnie said. 'So I suppose he will, some day. No offence to you though.'

'It depends what you're doing. And who you think you can trust. That's where women often come in.'

Johnnie glanced at the ceiling and adjusted the aim of his gun. 'I expect so,' he mumbled, and shifted his weight from one foot to the other.

'Is that Charlie?' Jason said, and Johnnie turned towards the door. How easy it would be – a knock at the base of the neck and a knee between the legs. But gratuitous. When Alex turned up, sudden surprise would do more than a bit of violence now.

Johnnie turned back. 'Did you hear something?'

'Perhaps it was from upstairs.'

'There's nothing upstairs.'

'There's an attic with four rooms.'

'I haven't been up there,' Johnnie said. Unlike girls of the same age, very young men are no good at lying. Johnnie might not have been to the attic, but he knew what was in it.

'I think it'd be worth you having a look,' Jason said. And at that moment there was a voice the other side of the door and the sound of the key turning.

Raoul came in first, with a bottle of whisky, water, and a couple of glasses. Charlie followed him. 'Hallo there, Jason. I'd love to know how you got in,' he said. He sounded in excellent humour as if it was only in the country that he could relax, like a busy actor.

'I was just passing,' Jason said.

'Quite right to call. Have a whisky. Pour it, Raoul.'

As there were two glasses, Raoul didn't look pleased about this. He poured a large dose for Charlie and a small one for Jason. 'Water, Charlie?' Charlie nodded. 'You?'

'No.' As far as Jason could see, nothing else had been slipped into the glass. He raised it.

'Looking at you, motherfucker,' Raoul murmured.

'*Santé*,' said Charlie. Jason pretended to take a mouthful. It was years since he drank a whisky and he hated the smell. French whisky had circulated undercover in the Baumettes – Barons and Earls, it was called on the label. 'You haven't told me how you actually penetrated the building.'

'Raoul must have left the kitchen door open when you went out after woodcock,' Jason said. 'That's how I found it. I just walked in. I hear you got one, by the way. Well done.'

'Two, actually. A brace, you say. Every land its folklore. In Hungary we think in hundreds. You came on foot?'

'You know there's a game larder to hang them?'

Charlie made an impatient gesture. 'That's where they are, naturally.' So he hadn't got any. 'You must have cut the wire.'

'Ugly stuff, your razor wire. May wouldn't like it. Are you sure the lease lets you do that?'

'The lease is about to be superseded by a purchase. What I do here will no longer concern May, or you.'

'Or Hugh?'

'Or Hugh. Well now, Jason. Did you leave something behind? Another fetish? This is your last chance.'

'Will the wire be electrified next time?'

'There'll be a pitbull or two,' Charlie said.

Jason thought he heard the sound of a vehicle labouring through the wood. Charlie didn't seem to notice, but Raoul jerked his head that way. Was Charlie a bit deaf? Of course, the long hair masked a hearing aid. 'Actually, Charlie,' Jason raised his voice, 'I came to see May. I thought she might be here. Do you know where she is?'

'Isn't she in London? I saw her a few days ago.'

'She left St George's Square without telling anyone she was going.'

'So that's why you're in this room. Well she certainly isn't here, as you can see. And I've no idea where she is.' Jason believed him. Like Johnnie, Charlie wasn't good at lies. He'd probably never thought lying was a skill, just usual intercourse. So the skill hadn't been honed. When he lied about the woodcock Jason knew at once. This time it was the truth. Therefore whatever Charlie's scam, even if May knew, she was only an accessory at a distance.

'Charlie—' Raoul said.

'Wait. I'm speaking. Now I know why you came, Jason, nothing stops you leaving. Don't try and come back. Raoul will

192

drive you down to Preston tonight in the Land Rover. You hear that, Raoul? There's a hotel near the station never closes, perhaps you know it. The first train to London is five thirty in the morning. Be grateful and board it. We can part friends, no harm done. No toenails drawn.' Charlie laughed good-naturedly.

Surely any hearing aid must pick up the noise now, the van with revving engine labouring along the last bit of track and then round the side. To make sure, the horn began to sound, as arranged. Charlie stood up. 'What in Christ's holy name is that?' he said.

Chapter Four

JOHNNIE WAS RELIEVED on guard by Mac, a much rougher proposition. He wore a cotton singlet and his arms were tattooed with designs which blew up impressively when he flexed them. It was clear at once there would be no conversation.

'You need something bad, like go to the toilet, you make a sign this way with your hand. I don't want no mess on the floor. But it better be real good. No games. The mouth, you keep it good and shut,' he said. From his voice, it was impossible to know where he came from or where he'd been. It was a voice with no characteristics other than meaning business. You couldn't even tell if English was his first language. He was dark-skinned and had lost most of his hair early on. He looked as if he took a lot of carefully planned exercise, in front of a mirror. He might be South African, Jason thought. A South African of mixed race who'd chucked the skin of his accent, that could be it.

'I do want to go to the toilet. Bad,' Jason said.

'I said you make a signal.' Perhaps Mac had served some time in the army. There was nothing to lose by making the signal, so

Jason made one. 'You walk in front and you don't try anything.'
Jason led the way to the staircase and down to the bathroom
floor. 'Leave the door open. You need to shit, you shit bang
there in front of me, like it or not,' Mac said.

All Jason actually wanted was a quick look along the stairs,
both ways. Standing with his back to the open door he urinated
as long and loud as he could. He didn't want Mac any more
suspicious than he was. Then he shook and buttoned himself up
slowly. Through the window he could see part of the van roof
down in the forecourt. The van was pointed in the direction it
came from, the track going round the back. Now he heard the
engine start up, then the van moved slowly forward, turned the
corner of the building by the time he'd flushed the lavatory.
What was going on? There was no noise of voices, though from
the bedroom they'd been audible, up and down like the sound
of dogs barking in a wind. Had Raoul or Johnnie been ordered
to drive the van away? If so, why? The firing of a shotgun, one
barrel after the other, seemed to rule that out. A warning not to
come back. It also showed that the handgun held by Mac was
probably the only one here. That was worth knowing because it
looked as if Alex and Nick hadn't got past first base. Charlie's
nerve had held and they'd been ordered off. Now the dogs were
loose again, bellowing away into the wood.

'Talk about shake a salad, you finished and got it back in yet?'
Mac said. 'So move it.'

As he reached the landing with Mac a few steps behind
him, Jason saw a bare foot disappear up the turn of the stair
ahead and heard the sigh of a skirt moving against a leg, or
on itself. So he had neighbours who were either not shut in
or, more likely, knew a way past locked doors. It was a
cheering thought.

When they were settled again, Mac took out a crumpled pack

of American cigarettes and lit one. 'You smoke?' he asked, pushing the pack back in his jeans. Jason shook his head. If Mac wanted to get in touch he was going to have to work at it more than that. In the silence, Jason tried to listen for sounds beyond the ceiling. It seemed there was something that might be whispers. But it could be just the breathing of old masonry. However, he put his money on female whispering. He moved his feet and cleared his throat. 'Yeah?' said Mac. Jason reached to the table near him, raised the glass of whisky he hadn't touched, and offered it. 'Plus, you don't drink, man?'

'Only wine,' Jason said.

Mac took the glass, sniffed the whisky, and drank a sip. His way of doing this – caution, look of commitment – told Jason that Mac was a drinker who would undergo a change after the second glass. Luckily, the whisky bottle was still here. Johnnie had picked it up from the floor, looked at Jason, and Jason motioned with his head at the wardrobe. That's where it was now. Mac sighed and looked at the glass. 'Some real poke there,' he said.

'No water.'

'Is that right?' Mac took another sip, bigger this time. He seemed to settle further into himself. You could see the whisky ignite behind his eyes, on a slow fuse. Jason made the signal for requirements. 'What you want?' Mac sounded irritable. He wasn't even into his second drink and here this wanker already wanted something.

'The bottle's in that cupboard.'

'Is that right.' Mac drained the glass and went over to the cupboard.

'I'll join you,' Jason said.

'You should be so lucky, you join me. There's the one glass, just.' After thought, Mac handed Jason the glass, half filled it with whisky, and sat down again slowly with the bottle between his knees. 'Prosit,' he said, and raised the bottle.

'Prosit.'

There was a sound of footsteps on the stair and Mac rose with the swiftness of the trained drinker and put the bottle in the cupboard so that by the time the door opened he was back in his chair, observing his tattoos as he flexed them one after the other. Charlie came into the room, alone this time. 'Raoul won't be driving you down to the Station Hotel,' he said. 'You'll be our guest for the night.' He touched Mac on the shoulder, and Mac vacated his chair. Charlie sat down. 'Frankly, you're an unwelcome one. I find you beginning to be a nuisance. I've just had the visit of some friends of yours – I suppose they're your friends, or I don't see why they're here. One of them a person you mentioned a week ago. And I've sent them away. Byland is not open to the public. You will be removed tomorrow. Is that whisky? Mac, take the glass.'

'Removed?' Jason said.

'A truck is on its way from London and you'll travel in it to Brussels, then Marseille. You will be asleep. The rest will be for the judge. When you're found, you'll be carrying a quantity of so-called *stupéfiants*. In fact you'll be round them. The authorities will have to purge you. I think as a source of nuisance you'll dry up for a long time.'

'From here to Marseille – quite a sleep,' Jason said.

Charlie smiled. 'Insomnia won't be your problem. And meanwhile Mac takes good care of you.'

'You mean I have to spend the night up here?' Mac said. His eye wandered to the wardrobe.

Charlie looked at his watch. 'It's twelve thirty. Johnnie relieves you at four. Tomorrow will be an easy day once the truck's on the Brussels run. We can enjoy ourselves again.'

'So Raoul's the one gets the good night's rest like usual,' Mac said.

'Raoul's out with the dogs. I doubt he'll get any rest at all.'

'Is that right,' Mac said. He sounded pleased about Raoul's mission. Maybe he didn't like dogs.

Charlie rose slowly from his chair like a man with legs weak for his height. Exercise programmes were for underlings, not the brains behind the outfit. He turned to the door, hesitated, and took the key from the lock. 'Just to be on the safe side,' he said, turning back to Mac, 'I'll lock you in.'

'What if he needs the toilet again? What you told him could give a fellow the Rangoon runs.'

'In this sort of house every bedroom has a chamber pot. You know what that is? It's probably in the wardrobe.'

'Okay, I'll find it,' Mac said hurriedly.

On his way out Charlie hesitated again. 'By the way, I hear your brother's planning a family for after you've gone.'

Beral had just finished talking for the second time to her sister in San Francisco when the mobile buzzed in her hand. 'Yes?' she said, then looked at it suspiciously like it had a will of its own and meant to punish her for liberties taken.

'Who is that?' a woman's voice asked.

'Me, Beral.'

'Oh, Beral, hullo. I've heard about you.' The voice sounded to Beral composed, confident, a woman with a nice house and a good marriage. And a pair of credit cards.

'Who from?'

'Is Jason there please?'

'No.'

'Where is he?'

Beral said, 'I'm not supposed to give information,' using a

voice she'd heard many times on television and round the Social Security.

'I'm his friend.'

You mean you fuck each other, Beral thought but didn't say. And if that's what you mean, why don't you say it? I would. Nick and I fuck each other, I'd say, night and day. We quarrel and fuck, fuck and quarrel. It's the way to live. Not saying "I'm his friend". Friendship doesn't come into it. Friendship's for bum-boys and dykes. 'That's nice,' she said instead.

'I'm worried. I don't know what's happening. I think he may be running into trouble.'

Beral asked, 'What sort of trouble?' She'd seen so much, such a variety, such a continuity of trouble that the word held less fear for her than it would for this lady on the other end of the satellite.

'Where's he gone?'

'They all went into the wood. They're looking for Jason's mum.' As soon as she said it, Beral realised how stupid it was. Of course they were after something much more important than Jason's mum. Beral didn't expect her baby to grow up into a man who would go out rescuing his mum, even if he knew who she was, by then. Men were interested in . . . oh, bigger-deal things than that. 'But I expect that's not the real reason.' She relit her spliff, drew it in like turning the lights back on.

'Have they left you alone?'

'No one's ever alone with a mobile phone,' Beral said. She didn't feel responsible for anything or anyone. Her sister had told her that's how it was, if you were really aware. And the mobile was one half of the ticket to get you there.

'Did you know that's my mobile you're using?' asked the voice.

'Jason said it was all right.'

'It is all right. But I need to know what they told you.'

'They said, don't do nothing sooner than the morning,' Beral said. 'They don't want the law round here.'

'I'll find a car and come at once,' the woman said. 'Some-where near Clitheroe is it? When I get there, I'll call again.' She was composed all right, getting up in the middle of the night to hire a car. Beral wondered how many thousand a year it took to be truly, always, aware like that and the thing that went with it – being able to say when you'd stake yourself out and when you wouldn't. A lot, probably. Out of sight, anyway.

Beral said, 'If it's engaged, keep trying.' She felt quite pleased with herself. She was learning. Now, let's see, who hadn't she belled yet?

While she was still thinking, there was a noise outside. Beral wasn't afraid, but she didn't want the dogs to start up and go and wake the baby. It was a good baby, the substances it breathed in the enclosed space of the caravan kept it quiet a lot of the time, and she wanted it to stay that way. She opened the door a few inches and peered out. The only sound from the dogs was a pleased groaning and snuffling. That meant it must be Nick. But where was the van? 'Nick?' she called.

'Come out here,' he said.

'Where's that fat bloke?' Beral asked. 'I heard shots. What's happened?'

'He's okay, he's in the van, by the wood. How many days has Bella been on heat?'

'About ten. A bit more.'

'When did you last see blood?'

'Day before yesterday.' What was Nick getting at? What did Bella's period have to do with anything? Beral didn't ask, because Nick didn't like a lot of questions. In fact most of the time he didn't like any questions at all. He thought they were a

201

way of making him wait for whatever it was he wanted.

'That's fine. She's ready to go wandering. Now listen while I tell you what to do.' She was to put Bella in the car, then drive down to the wood with the windows open. When she got there, she was to walk Bella up and down, in and out, for as long as it took the dogs inside to get wind of her and come belting up the track. There were three of them, all male, and they were out loose tonight, for obvious reasons. When she saw them coming, get back in the car, let Bella go off up the hill with the dogs following, and wait for the poor bitch to come home. A few hours, probably. 'Is the baby . . . you know, asleep?' Nick went.

Beral said, 'He won't wake up for a long time.'

'Right.'

'What are you going to do?'

'We're going back in. Jason's locked up there and we're going to try and get him out.'

'His woman rang.'

'What for?'

'She's on her way.'

Nick said, 'That's all we need, another Ricardo galloping about in the wood in the dark.'

'She isn't his wife. She says she's his friend.'

'She's his brother's wife, is how I read it.'

'The fat guy said so?'

'As good as.'

'Jesus,' Beral said. Nick had a brother, but she'd never dared think about him, not that way. Not out loud.

The plan with the dogs worked smooth as a dream. When they'd all disappeared up the hill there was a voice calling them from far inside the wood. After a bit, it stopped. The bloke had had enough of running around in the dark and probably gone back to bed. Nick and Alex started off along the track not long after, moving so quietly Beral heard almost nothing. She was to wait up for the girlfriend, and stop her trying anything on her own. Beral looked forward to a talk. She might learn quite a bit more off of her.

There was a light tapping on the door, so faint it must be done with finger tips. Mac wasn't asleep, but most of the whisky had gone and his head sagged forward from time to time as if it was a tiring weight to carry around, so late at night. But considering what he'd drunk, the gun-holding hand stayed remarkably steady. The tapping was repeated, then stopped. Jason watched the lock. The tapper had probably just noticed the key on the outside. Then the same sound began again. Whoever it was had worked out it would be dangerous to unlock the door without getting an answer.

'Someone wants in,' Jason said, hardly above a murmur. A startled drunk is the worst kind. Mac rose at once and crossed quietly to the door, keeping his head turned towards Jason and the gun still on him.

'Yes?' he said, his face close to the panel. Jason didn't hear anything but Mac seemed to be listening. 'Come on,' he said, and when nothing happened, he gave a couple of harder taps on the wood and then on the lock. After a moment, Jason heard the key turn. Mac was holding the handle and pulled the door open sharply. There was a woman standing in the opening with a child behind her. Mac sized them up with one glance before turning back to keep his eye on Jason, then signalled them in. He took the key from the lock, shut the door, and locked it on the inside. 'Yes?'

The woman spoke a few words in her language, presumably Romanian, and indicated the child, pushing her forward for inspection. It was a girl, probably a bit older than her size suggested. She wore a thin cotton dress and the form of her breasts was visible under it, pressing up to the light. Jason wondered what she wore apart from the dress. It was obvious what this girl was here for. She looked frightened but dumb before the inevitable. The woman was still speaking fast in a sing-song tone, like repeating a refrain; then she took hold of the child's dress at the shoulder and pulled it away from her arm, tugging it roughly down towards the waist. Jason's question was answered. The girl wore nothing underneath. Her skin was dark like Mac's, and the exposed breast small, with a brown nipple large in proportion. Mac only took his eyes off Jason for a second or two, to size up the deal. What did he give that woman in return for the child? Money? Drink? Food? If the attic was a prison, then the usual laws ran. Drugs, maybe? A return in kind later on – if that was what she needed?

'That's a child,' Jason said.

'Zip it. You can have a go after, if that's what's eating you.' Mac pushed the girl towards May's bed. He went round the far side so he still faced Jason and the woman near the door. The only sign of the whisky inside him was an unfocused look to his eyes and a faint glaze over them like something in a pastry shop. He leaned towards the girl and ripped the remains of the dress off her; she lay over the side of the bed without being told. 'No one moves,' Mac said, opening his jeans and keeping the gun steadily trained on Jason. 'Other than me. Have yourself an eyeful.' Not surprisingly, Mac seemed to be in trouble getting it up. He tried working at himself, then put two knuckles inside the girl's mouth to hold it open and entered there, keeping still for a minute as if taking his blood pressure. That seemed to do the trick, after a bit. Using his free hand he parted her legs, raised the knees, then stooped forward with his weight supported on one arm, the other still holding the gun.

204

The girl gave out a cry like a small animal and began to struggle under him. Mac had to lower his other arm to grip her harder.

The woman moved forward fast as if she was on skates under her long skirt, until she was beside Jason's chair. From behind her, like a conjurer, she produced a stone the size of a pineapple. She must have hung it there like a baby in a carrier. Jason took it from her. Mac's eyes were straining from his head, the pastry glaze thickened so he looked near to death, all awareness concentrated. Jason stepped quickly up behind him.

At the last moment, Mac moved his hand to the gun, twisting the upper part of his body half round. Jason had no time to argue the rights and wrongs. The gun was loaded and Mac had yet to come. Any second now. Jason raised the stone pineapple above his head and brought it down. There was a yielding thud, a sound like a car hitting an animal on the road. Mac lurched sideways, half off, with one leg doubled up and lay there without moving. Blood began to run on the back of his head; not profusely, if he'd had more hair you wouldn't have seen it. As it was, it made a bright stain on a scalp that looked vulnerable now the body it belonged to lay so still. The woman came forward to pull the girl free, and they started chattering at once in whispers like monkeys spotting a leopard.

Jason stooped to inspect Mac's bloody head. It was a mess. Where you'd expect a bump, there was a lacerated concavity. Mac's eyes were open and he gave off a strong smell of sweat and whisky. He took the gun from Mac's hand and felt for his pulse. It seemed as still as the rest of him. He turned the body and put his ear to the chest, above the heart. Nothing. He'd hit too hard. Harder than he'd meant, but how do you judge the force of what you mean, the right force for a blow like that? Jason examined the stone. Not a hair – Mac didn't have many – not a speck of blood or skin. A perfect weapon if you wiped the fingerprints off it. Jason did so with his shirt tail. For the first time, you've killed someone. He'd never liked killing woodcock, but they were in zigzag flight. This victim couldn't defend himself. The only way to see it was to remember the child. Jason put the gun in his pocket and turned to the woman. Communication was going to be a problem. Were there other women in the attic? He pointed upwards and tried French.

'*Vous êtes plusieurs, là-haut?*' The French produced no result. The faces were blank. The girl was still naked, as if waiting to see what other possibilities there were in the situation. Jason had read a news item about child prostitutes living in Romanian sewers. Maybe it was quite a long time ago she'd been a virgin. Maybe he'd been wound up. If so it was a smart performance. He had a go at Italian. '*C'è ne sono . . . altre donne?*' It was the best he could manage. They turned away from him as if he was deep in the Romanian countryside and gabbling in double Dutch. They were conferring together and it struck Jason that the girl took the lead. She must be the one with the ideas. He picked her dress off the bed and held it out. It would be too easy to let himself be wound up again. The child – if she was a child in any sense – was beautiful. Perhaps they didn't realise the danger in delay. You can get so hardened to danger it loses ordinary meaning and then means nothing, like you don't know you're breathing till it's too late to notice you aren't. He pushed the dress into the girl's hand.

The woman laughed. 'Same gentleman,' she said.

'You understand English?'

'Three, five word.'

He pointed at the ceiling again. 'More women?'

'Woman, yes.'

'Go and get them.' Jason made gestures, finishing with a

finger to his lips for silence. 'Out quick. I know a way.' He pointed towards the hill, across the trees. He could have the lot of them through the ice-house and in the wood in ten minutes – only the stairs to worry about. If there was trouble with the dogs, well, he had the only handgun on the place. He was sure the woman took it in but she stood there looking obstinate and saying nothing. She was working something out. Then she whispered again to the girl. They both looked at the remains of Mac on the bed, and the woman leaned over him and opened his eyelids wide. The girl took the door key from his back pocket. They seemed to agree what to do next while the girl did up her dress. Then they went to the door and disappeared up the stairs. Jason took the key, locked up and waited on the landing. There was a body to think of. He took a look at the name on the gun. A Browning. Hardly state of the art.

There were bedrooms on the floor below, then the living quarters, then the straight flight to the hall. The offices were a dozen steps down the spiral. Charlie was probably in one of the bedrooms. Raoul might be in the house, he might still be outside with the shotgun. Jason believed there was nothing to fear from Johnnie: he was a pliable character and more or less a juvenile. What Johnnie needed was to be got away from the others before any charges could be made to stick on him. But that wasn't Jason's problem. The women were, and they seemed in no hurry. He could hear their rustling movements, their whispers, their coming and going. Maybe they were collecting belongings, if any. Women like that could have their all in a few gold chains. Were there gold mines in Romania? He wondered if they were refugees who'd paid to be smuggled into England, or just the catch of a Bucharest press-gang. What was sure, they didn't want to be here at Byland fenced in with razor wire. Now at last there were footsteps, coming down.

The girl was the first to appear. Behind her were a bunch of women and a couple of young girls, younger than her or anyway less precocious. And last, the woman Jason already knew. A lot of females to get through an ice-house and a wood in the middle of the night in good order. With no common language. Jason stood in front of them and made signs for silence. They were watching him, but he could see on their faces an undeclared agenda of their own. Not a mutiny, just a course on different readings. He led the way down, beckoning with the Browning.

It was at the level of the bathrooms they began their noise. High-pitched, rapid and in unison. They were halted behind him, watching. The place was chosen. Everyone else in the house must be lower down, and could be seen coming. And he was in front, with the gun. This, then, was their agenda. They wanted to be found now they had an armed protector, and not just fade into the night. And they'd had plenty of time to know the habits of the personnel. Nothing Jason could do was going to silence them. They'd seen him killing Mac, and he didn't know yet what was best to do about that. Till he did, the women had him over a barrel, and they knew it. He went on down, keeping close in to the newel since anyone entering the staircase must come from the outer side. He could sense the girl following just behind him, the women further up, their noise louder, amplified in the drum of the stair.

So when Charlie appeared in the first-floor archway he was looking upwards, hearing before he saw. 'Hands back of the head, Charlie,' Jason said. Charlie was in blue pyjamas that made him look somehow innocent, as if he'd had them for Christmas. He raised his arms. The expression of his eyes wasn't just panic. Jason noticed for the first time that they were perfectly round. In there with the panic was, for a moment, a

208

look of relief, almost as if he'd hoped for what was coming to him. Then it vanished.

'Where's Mac?'

'Flaked out.'

'Drunk?'

Jason saw no need to answer. Charlie was a prisoner now like him. The girl slipped round behind Charlie, then turned him. She carried something plaited in her hand, made from strips of sheet or towel, and signalled with it to Jason. 'Lower your hands behind you,' Jason said. The girl tied Charlie's wrists together, taking a lot of trouble over knots which she tightened with rapid wiry arms.

'Raoul!' Charlie screamed, 'Raoul! Find Raoul!'

The girl turned back laughing. It must be what she wanted. The women pressed down as Jason saw Charlie move across like a rat from the spiral to the main stair. Raoul could be on it with his shotgun. 'Come back,' Jason shouted, but Charlie kept going. There was no time. He aimed at the wall to Charlie's left. The noise came back from the stone all round, echoing up and down. The women's voices were stilled.

'Don't shoot, they're mad,' Charlie shouted.

'Turn and come here.' A small bloodstain was spreading on Charlie's ankle below the pyjamas. 'Stand against the wall.'

'I'm wounded,' Charlie said. He looked amazed. Violence in the free world was to give, not receive. His whole appearance was changed. But in the silence he'd heard a step on the main stair, and so had Jason. Must be Raoul. You could read it on Charlie's face.

But it was Johnnie. He had one sock on, the other in his hand, he was half awake, and he wasn't carrying a shotgun. With the Browning, Jason waved him to the wall. 'Keep still.' Johnnie seemed glad as well as scared. He turned his head to look at the women, and the obvious reassurance grew. Jason decided to take a risk. 'You want a chance to be clear of this without ending up in court?' he said.

'Yes.'

'Go and put that spare sock in Seker's mouth from behind. Make sure he keeps quiet.' Johnnie did this with alacrity. Jason looked at the women. They seemed to have a good grasp of the situation. He remembered what Alex had said about ferocious. They were motionless and silent, watching like him towards the stairs. And watching him. Then the girl in front lifted her hand and pointed down. Not a sound reached Jason but he put his faith in her and pressed back against the wall. After a moment a slithering noise came up, say a man moving about in thick socks. Raoul had sacrificed his SS boots.

Chapter Five

IT WAS SUNDAY so Hugh was mucking out the aviary. Usually a labour of love. But the pink doves hadn't been fed for days and they were agitated and noisy. Their noise irritated his shredded nerves. The more they went on the more shredded he felt. And seeing him, they redoubled the noise.

London was ghostville in the heat of today. He'd have been glad of even May's presence in St George's Square; her contempt would be better than the void. A quarrel in the air-conditioned kitchen would be an improvement on silence. But he had no idea where she was. She'd scarpered and until she needed more money, even the lawyer didn't know her whereabouts. 'Your good mother has taken my advice and made a tactical withdrawal. I'm liaising with her bank,' he'd said on the telephone in his precise voice. Hugh could picture the fleshy mouth indecently touching up each word as it slipped out of cover. Especially liaising. He made it sound like something you did with twelve year-old girls.

Hugh hadn't been up to the bedroom. Certain odours came at him down the stairs from that region as he entered the house – lethally sweet as the whiff of corruption. A woman's absence.

He went into the kitchen and got a whisky, though it was ten in the morning. Then he added some more. He could hear the doves complaining, nagging, from here. They were supposed to be peaceful, reconciling, and all they did was demand respect for their habits. He went and fed them, the whisky spilling on the floor of the aviary so he had to fill his glass again to the brim as a reward.

Jason was no drinker. After the first he lost interest. Hugh had aimed at that power of detachment but missed. After his first, he tended to lose count. It was one of the differences. In adolescence he'd watched Jason, already a man, back off into sobriety while he took to the sauce when the inside problems got the better of him. Hugh looked up the green planks of the staircase to the bedroom door, then out at the aviary. He didn't need any books to tell him that a man must enter and possess or die out. His trouble denied him that vital moment of free entry and possession. He jacked off into the void and the void claimed him for its own. The birds were happy now, rocking back and forth as they pecked the seed. Hugh sat in the leather sofa with his whisky.

Looking up from his glass he caught his own eye in the mirror hanging on the opposite wall. He'd forgotten the mirror was there. It belonged to Rosie and didn't go with the rest of the furniture. It was gilt and fancy. It was too good for the surroundings. He studied his face staring back at him – grey, the watching eyes black and hateful. He hadn't shaved since Friday night and he looked like a hit-man, a latino with his black hair that never looked quite dry, a hit-man working for himself. That's how he felt. But with no target. The ones he owed it to were out of shot.

He was here for a shower and clean shirts. He refilled his glass and took it upstairs. The door of the room where Jason had slept was half open. Hugh pushed it back and went in. Had she come to him in here? Or did Jason go to her in their room overlooking the conservatory, the aviary, the garden? At Byland he and Jason used to share a room, when May's friends came. Jason filled him in on what they were all up to, in the other rooms, and explained how it was done. Naturally, Hugh knew already but pretended not to because it was exciting to hear the detail in Jason's husky voice, just broken. In those days it felt to Hugh like they shared everything. And always would. The word – always – meant something, then. Still ahead. He slammed the door behind him. Get out of the house and not come back. Contact the agent tomorrow. From the foot of the stairs he threw his empty glass out into the conservatory where it smashed, throwing up a shower of splinters that caught the sunlight for a second and scattered over the Spanish tiles that had cost such a lot of money. To please Rosie.

Let the doves go. Drive them out. They must fend for themselves now. He opened the conservatory doors wide, entered the aviary and picked up the shovel he'd been using for the droppings. Then urged them towards the exit. There were six of them, they'd spent their lives in safety and comfort and they didn't want to go. He would get one near the door and freedom, and see it dash itself in despair against the glass and fly back inside. One by one he drove them out into the garden where they dispersed in a frightened, disorganised way towards the neighbouring roofs. There was a single obstinate bird left, turning and turning in a corner with incapable wings and cries of alarm. Alone, like him. He made one more try. The bird huddled against the wire, frozen now, knowing him, as he approached with the shovel raised. After the third blow it looked dead, broken, but not dead enough. Still all of a piece, still alone. Annul that isolation and completeness. He threw the shovel aside, leaned down and gathered the warm feathered remnant to tear it apart in his hands – wings, head, legs – breast – and hurl it all out into the garden. Aloneness, once it was severed and scattered like that, was nearly abolished.

The woman said she was in a call box in Clitheroe. 'It's Rosie. Did I wake you up?' Beral reckoned she was being sarcastic. If she was in a call box, she'd probably been trying to get through for ages. Beral had some cousins in Australia. It's good to keep in touch and there'd been a lot to catch up on. 'Don't worry about the phone bill. It goes to my husband.' So she'd only been joking after all. Beral laughed to show she recognised this, though it seemed to her Rosie was doing him enough dirt already without an astronomical phone bill. Still, that was their problem.

'You got there quick,' Beral said.

'How do I find where you are?'

Beral didn't have an overall view of the route in her head, like reading a map. All she could do was visualise the journey in detail – every sign, gradient and turning – as if she was making it herself. Rosie listened in silence. Beral thought there was something a bit superior about the way she didn't repeat any of the directions after her, but maybe it would be unaware to do that. 'The last bit isn't easy, it's just a track, but I don't suppose you'll meet anyone. If you do, you want my opinion, don't stop.'

'Thanks a lot, Beral. I'll be with you in about twenty minutes. Can you leave a light on?'

'I'll put the gas lamp in the caravan window.'

'Happy phoning. It's on Hugh.'

Beral wondered how he'd earned all the shit that was being thrown at him. He must be a bit of a limp-dick or he'd do something about it. You wouldn't try anything like that with Nick. Not twice, anyway. Not one and a half times. When she saw the car lights approaching, Beral unlocked the caravan door and went out on to the step. She wanted to see this Rosie walking over the grass. The big surprise was that Rosie seemed about her own age. She'd thought of her as a lot older. And she was dark. Very dark, in this light, as if she came from Turkey, or Egypt, or somewhere like that. Anyhow, down that way. Beral always envied dark women from distant lands. She believed that men were secretly in awe of them, not like the blondish or mousy specimens such as herself, there to be kicked around. A dark woman had a bit of the witch about her. Of course Turks and Egyptians probably kicked them around all right. And closer to, she was a good looker. Very sleek. So she had something of everything, you could say. 'Hallo,' Beral said.

Rosie was stopped a couple of yards away, in the gaslight from the window. The first sign of dawn was showing over the low line of hills to Beral's left, and though the moon was down, it was still near enough the horizon for the night to not be dark at all. 'Hi, Beral.' They stood looking at each other. Beral knew that Rosie was trying to weigh up what she was worth. 'I picked up a poor old bitch on the road. She looked lost. I've got her in the car.'

'That'll be Bella,' Beral said. 'She's on heat.'

'Is she? Well now I expect she's good and pregnant. Puffing and panting away.'

'Poor Bella,' Beral said. 'Actually, she was pregnant already. Nick said to let her out and enjoy herself. Did you see any dogs?'

'One. He looked completely done for. You know.'

'Are you hungry?' Beral asked, because she was hungry herself, and thirsty; her throat was dry from talking to Australia.

'A cup of coffee would be good.'

'You can come in the caravan if you want,' Beral said.

Rosie looked at her as if she didn't at first spot this as an invitation. 'Don't you want to get Bella out of the car?' she said.

'Oh, yes. Then we'll go in.'

Bella was obviously happy to be back, in a guilty sort of way. She looked as if she feared that the general opinion of her would nose-dive, and that this was deserved. Some people say animals know nothing about guilt, only fear. Beral's observation was different. Bitches, especially, were very liable to guilt, and quick to rub it in to any other dog caught doing wrong.

Rosie was looking at the baby. You could see she didn't have any of her own and didn't much want one. It could have been something from outer space, by her expression. Beral knew the feeling. 'Lovely baby,' Rosie said, and turned away.

'He's a heavy sleeper. What're you going to do?' Beral asked, handing the coffee.

'I'm not sure,' Rosie said. 'You wouldn't have a shot of whisky to go in this? I've got the shivers.'

It seemed to Beral that Rosie had no serious idea what she should do. Beral approved that. A bloke would lash out in all directions without thinking about it, usually causing some poor cow to come off worst. She produced the whisky bottle, which had been their only resource until Jason arrived with his cartons of wine, flowing ever since. Beral hated whisky. 'You want my opinion, I wouldn't go in that wood,' she said. 'There are guys there you wouldn't ever want to meet.'

'Where's your . . . where's Nick?'

'Oh Nick – he goes in everywhere head-first. Except carving stone. He doesn't like a quiet life.' Beral wondered if Rosie was sympathetic to the cause of disadvantaged women. Probably not. She'd never been at a disadvantage herself. Look at her clothes. And if she was pissed off with her husband, she fucked his brother. Such a simple life. But then what would you do after Jason? To Beral he seemed about as high as you could go. She hadn't thought about it before, but now she did. A sailor. Know his way round the compass. She'd seen him looking at her like he was off a desert island. 'He went into the wood after Jason with the fat guy – Alex.'

'Is Alex the Frenchman?'

Thinking about Turkey and Egypt had cleared up Beral's vision of how Alex was. 'He's like one of those big pussies in a harem,' she said.

'Not much use in an emergency.'

'You can't ever be sure. There's less hanging there to lose.'

Rosie laughed, though it was no laughing matter. You neutralise the oppressors, the race dies out. Pleasure too. That's the problem. 'They've got guns in there?'

'Going off all the time.'

Rosie finished her coffee and stood up. 'What fools they all are,' she said. She wasn't talking to Beral; she said it like a sudden discovery, startled out of her. 'Dragging us in it after them like a poor bitch on the end of a rope.'

Beral agreed. What was she doing up here on this fucking moor, but being dragged along after Nick? She'd always thought it was just because she was too spineless or strung out. It was a bit of comfort to know that someone as sleek as that could have it happen to her too. Maybe a wimp was easier to live with; yet here was Rosie, who apparently had one of those at home, and she ups and does a runner with his brother. It should tell you something about women, but being one herself Beral didn't want to know. It would be a bore. Blame the bloke. 'Don't go into that wood,' she said.

'I must go in. It'll soon be getting light. I'll go then.' The wall and the opening in it were visible, two tones of grey different from the sky. 'Is that where the track goes to the house?'

'Yes. There's the van. Nick and Alex went back in on foot.' From over the wood an owl called. Probably telling the other owls it was about to roll over and drop off. Then came the sound of a shot, muffled, like echoing back on itself. 'That's indoors, I reckon. It sounds different from when they're shooting at birds,' Beral said.

'That wasn't a shotgun.' Oh yes, Rosie was the kind of woman who knew all the sounds. Like the tweedy breeders Beral saw swarming over the moors in Range Rovers since the middle of August, afternoons she was trying to talk Nick into a condom. The difference was, Rosie looked frightened. She seemed a lot less cool than before, and she needed help. Beral knew the best way for delivering that.

'Don't go yet. Being alone with the baby – it spooks you after a bit. D'you smoke?'

'If you mean what I think you mean, no. On the other hand another bit of whisky in a coffee, it's yes.'

'All one,' Beral said. There was such a thing as passive inhaling which could relax a person, too. She lit up while the kettle was on. She didn't think Rosie would be going all that soon. By the time the sound of a second shot came along, she was quite mellow.

'Put it on the floor and no one gets hurt!' Jason shouted it, aiming for surprise. As he expected, Raoul came up the spiral on the inside so his left temple and the top of his head were visible before he had a chance to see what lay round the turn. Jason should have waited a second longer. The head disappeared. He fired twice into the empty space. This was getting easier. Trigger happiness. There was a crash of stone splinters, a cry, and the sound of metal clattering downward. Jason counted the steps as he went, moving cautiously. He was on the tenth when Nick appeared from below like a jinn out of a bottle. He had hold of Raoul by one arm behind his back, Raoul's other hand was on his face with blood running on the knuckles. 'Where's the shotgun?' Jason asked.

'Alex'll pick it up,' Nick said. 'I had a job squeezing him through that tunnel, I tell you.' He was obviously enjoying himself enormously. He looked up at the women on the steps above and took them all in at a comprehensive glance – age, height, radius. He could probably draw them from memory the day after tomorrow. 'So that's what it's all about,' he said. 'A talent factory.' The women were consulting again with plenty of excited gesture and what sounded like argument. But that was misreading their signs. They knew exactly what they wanted. Three of them, headed by the girl, came fast down the stairs. They attacked Raoul like hornets on a fallen fig. His hand was pulled away from his face, showing a bloody mess round the eye, and fastened with another plaited strip behind his back. Now he was doubled over and gasping for air. Part of a score had been paid off with the jerk of a knee. Jason had a feeling it was only an instalment.

All the same, the situation was odd. He was the one with the gun, yet these women were taking charge. Victims' rights, as in any revolution. Also, they'd witnessed the end of Mac. He ought to assert himself but they wouldn't understand him. And naturally they weren't afraid. He was their saviour, with blood on his hands. 'Alex! Where are you?' he shouted down the stair.

There was a slow heaving from below. Alex must be saving his breath. When at last he called something up in their language, all the women seemed to answer at once. Here was a

219

new factor Jason hadn't thought through – an interpreter has a
free hand. He can make alliances you know nothing about. He's
in control and trust is all you have to go on. When Alex came
puffing into view with the shotgun he went straight up to Raoul
and felt around in his pockets, removing cartridges and trans-
ferring them to his own. 'You found your mother?'

'She isn't here. I don't think she was.'

'You been stitched up,' Nick said. He inspected Johnnie.
'Who's this? Don't look heavy as villains go.'

'Johnnie. He wanted to get out while the going was good.'

'They fired up our arses from the front door,' Nick said.

'That was Raoul. Not me,' said Johnnie.

'We'll give you credit,' Nick said, 'but I wouldn't let them get
to me on a dark night from now on, if I was you.'

'I won't,' said Johnnie. 'I only came because they said there
were going to be girls. But this lot – they're not even here of
their own . . . not guests, not paid either.'

'Shut up now, there are more important things,' Jason said.
He turned to Alex. 'We need to know how they were brought
here and if there are any others anywhere.'

Alex went up the four steps separating him from Charlie.
'Rather a mistake throwing me out into the night, Charlie,' he
said. 'With so much to talk about. Now here we are, down to
gestures.' He raised the shotgun so the muzzle rested on
Charlie's Adam's apple. 'Only a joke. Now I'll go and have a
conversation with these ladies. Did you ever learn Romanian? I
thought not. See you later.' On the next step he had an
afterthought. 'Female conversation – you'll miss that where
you're going.'

Nick had been thinking. 'There was a dark guy, thin on top.
Tattoos. Where's he?'

'Shut upstairs,' Jason said.

'Not joining the party?'

'Not very likely.' Jason could see problems building up. This was Lancashire, the law of silence didn't run here. He shook his head at Nick.

'Resting, is he?' Nick said. He was having too much of a good time to keep his wits about him; eyes dilated, unnaturally restless and bright.

'Nodded off,' Jason said.

'Maybe I should nip up for a butcher's. He might come round.'

Jason shook his head. '*Niet.*'

'*Niet?*'

'No need.'

'Ever?'

Jason shook his head again. Nick looked at him with a new respect, he thought. Murderer's due. Still, the problem of Mac's remains, remained. This was May's house. A decomposing Mac on her mattress, he must be spirited away. Something to think about.

Alex was in consultation. Every now and then he seemed to trip on Romanian idiom but the women swept him along. Mostly, he listened. At one point, the woman who'd been in the bedroom waved in Jason's direction, and Alex looked at him, blankly. The Balkan witnesses were filling him in. He was in sole charge of delivering their story, as much or as little as he chose. He was indispensable.

'Can I let go of Mr Seker now?' Johnnie asked.

'Yes. Stand in the archway so no one runs for it.'

'I won't try,' Raoul said. Blood was still trickling down his cheek and on to his neck, and his right eye was closed up. His American accent was forgotten. 'Catch the little cocksucker another time.'

Charlie had chewed and spat out Johnnie's sock. 'Keep quiet, Raoul,' he said.

'I only—'

'Shut your mouth.' Charlie wasn't a fool. He was watching Alex and the women as if he knew Jason was sidelined, even with the gun in his fist. Waiting for the women. Everyone waiting for the women; victims, emigrants, misfits. Like all of them here, one way or the other. But the women most of all.

Jason was thinking too. He couldn't claim he'd bashed Mac with the stone in self-defence. The blow was to the back of the head. Possibly the girl wasn't even a minor, and even if she was, are you within your rights to crush the man's skull? Mac's remains must be wiped from the face of the earth. If it wasn't for that, they could clear out of here, leaving Charlie and Raoul for someone to find. Still turning the problem over, Jason noticed Charlie move his head. Of course. It was getting light and he was expecting a truck.

'You,' Jason told Johnnie, 'go down and watch the drive. Whoever turns up, keep him talking.' But a single shout from up here would give the alert. Proper gags were needed. 'First find a towel and a pair of scissors. Fast.' Now Alex was explaining something, Romanian coming more easily. That's the gift of tongues. If you have it, you hardly need to learn, you're plugged in. Jason called up to him. 'I want to know, Alex.' Alex stared down at him, through him, as if he hadn't heard. Johnnie, earning his remission, was back in a flash with the scissors and towel. How do you tie on a gag that works? Something inside the mouth like a wedge in a door. When the women saw what he was at they sent one of the children for a bar of soap. Jason waved her away but she paid no attention. How could a sewer child respect a man afraid to shoot children? 'Go on down,' he told Johnnie. 'Shout if—' the sentence got lost in the tense silence around.

Instead of giving the Browning to Nick, Jason stooped and put it between his feet, then held the towel in one hand with the scissors in the other and cut the strips like a tailor.

'This is in your own interests, Jason,' Alex said. It was nearly an apology, he was white and shaky but in earnest. The girl darted forward, lifted the Browning and backed off. Now Alex came towards him until he and the girl were side by side. 'Give me those strips,' he said.

'What's got into you?'

'Give them here.' Jason obeyed and looked away.

How it was done, he never knew. He heard Nick say, 'That's heavy-duty.'

'Keep back,' Alex said. Otherwise there was no sound, only the friction of bodies in uneven conflict. When it stopped, Jason turned. Charlie and Raoul were gagged and the child who'd brought the bar of soap was lost again in the group.

'They puke, they'll choke to death,' Nick said. The girl was watching him, just out of reach with the gun aimed at his chest. Jason had no doubt she'd pull the trigger, scattering shot joyfully like on a fairground stall. At that range she was bound to hit somebody. She shifted the aim to Jason, then back.

Alex waved the shotgun at Charlie and Raoul, helpless now as people who must either vomit or breathe. 'Sit.' He turned to Jason. 'These are only the women who've got too old or sick. The children are the next to go out. Six or seven of them pass here every week. They don't stay long and they're not seen again. Some were the family of those women. It's the youngest they go for in your industrial towns.'

'It's your public, you sell to it,' Jason said.

'My merchandise is synthetic.'

'Where do you think the consumer began?'

'Crawling about the floor,' Alex said, and there was no arguing with that.

'Do they know where the girls go? What town?' Jason asked.

Alex put the question to the women nearest to him. They shook their heads. 'They come in trucks and they leave in trucks. That's all they know.'

'Well, these two shitheads must know all right,' Nick said.

'Or the one downstairs,' Alex suggested.

'No. He only just arrived.' The telephone rang in the hall below. 'Say who it is,' Jason shouted. Everyone listened while Johnnie's voice could be heard indistinctly speaking a few words, then he appeared at the head of the stairs.

'It's a driver out at the gates. He wants to know what to do.'

'Alone?'

'Yes. He's afraid of the dogs.'

'Take his number and tell him to wait,' Jason said.

'He wants to speak to Raoul.'

'Say Raoul's out with the dogs on patrol. He'll come and unchain the gate when he gets the message.'

'What message?'

'The message you're going straight out to give him when you can find him, for Christ's sake. That's what you say.'

'Sorry,' Johnnie said, and disappeared downstairs. If he'd been a bit brighter, he probably wouldn't be here in the first place. Jason looked at Nick.

'Means well,' Nick said.

'Nothing stops us undoing those gags now. The driver won't come,' Jason said. Charlie was rocking and heaving and some kind of liquid was running on his face. 'You don't want a couple of corpses.'

'A couple more,' Alex said.

'Let's undo the fucking gags while they're still alive,' Nick said, and stepped suddenly forward.

'Wait,' Jason said. Alex hesitated. A shotgun fired in an enclosed space with a lot of people around is a massacre. Left to himself, he would have agreed about the gags, Jason believed. He would still be the armed interpreter. But he wasn't left to himself. While he hesitated the girl fired the Browning in Nick's general direction. Nick had moved, and she was firing at anything that moved. The recoil nearly knocked her over but she recovered. The bullet missed and struck somewhere behind. At the same moment the women came down in a mob with one mind and surrounded Charlie and Raoul. Now Charlie was upright in the midst of them; holding him, pressed close to each other, the women moved down the stair. Raoul was left where he was. He didn't look well. His face was grey and his eyes, wide open, had only an expression of surprise. Jason stepped over and leaned down. There was a hole in Raoul's shirt, just above the heart, and a patch of blood, slowly spreading.

'He was the lucky one,' Nick said as Charlie's convoy went out of sight.

Chapter Six

Rosie had asked her not to let her doze off. But Beral dozed off herself, and in the end it was the baby woke her. It was broad daylight, another clear sky, not a breath of wind. It was going to be roasting again. She gave the baby something to suck and opened the caravan window, quietly. There were birds here she liked to see – plovers and larks rising straight out of the turf and hovering above you higher and higher in the sky like the Holy Ghost. Beral was raised a Catholic and every now and then got an echo from childhood like that. It didn't bring back faith, just a kind of longing which didn't do you any good at all. Nick said if he ever caught her going in a church by herself he'd denounce her to the police as an Irish terrorist. When he went into churches it was for the stone carvings, he said. 'Art is God, God's crap,' he said, and she had no reason to think he was wrong. The creation you can believe in is making something out of nothing under your eyes, such as a shapeless block of stone off the hillside.

'Oh my Christ,' Rosie said, sitting up straight. 'Where've I been?' She looked alarmed, her wide, smooth, tan brow all ruffled like the surface of one of those windy lakes.

'We both needed a zizz,' Beral said undoing her shirt. 'I'm going to feed him.'

'I think you should change the nappy first.'

'I'll take him outside.'

'Don't bother. I must go myself.'

'Use the chemical if you like.'

It seemed Rosie didn't like. 'I need a breath of air,' she said.

'Behind the trees then. Help yourself,' Beral said. She still felt quite happy, even though the baby had begun the long day's demands. She always felt quite happy for a time after a high, like some people at their best with a hangover. Out of sight. It might have something to do with the fact that Nick always started work early in the morning. She circulated round Nick like a moon but she was quite glad when he was too busy to think about her. Some women were the opposite. They wanted to be thought about all the time. But then they didn't live with Nick. Any time Nick gave his mind to you, it was to bend you to his will.

Rosie was back. 'We'd better call the police,' she said. 'Anything can have happened. I must go in there. Let's get them on the mobile.' She looked over her shoulder at the wood. She didn't seem all that keen about it.

'Jason said don't call them before twelve and then only if there's no sign of life.' This wasn't strictly true but Beral didn't think Nick wanted those scuffers poking round the place unless absolutely necessary. She knew he'd turn up some time soon. He was like the weather up here – hard, plenty of it and never missing for long. Now she guessed that Rosie was about to ask her to come along with her, and she was against the idea. When blokes start throwing punches or pulling triggers, you stay out of the way. A woman like Rosie wouldn't know that. They'd only seen triggers pulled on man's feathered friends. 'Go

228

ahead,' Beral said. The baby was yelling, louder than usual, purple in the face and elsewhere. 'Rosie . . . could you just come and look at him and say what you think? I think the foreskin's too tight. He ought to be circumcised. No one even knows what it's for. Look. It's bursting, poor little bugger.'

It worked. Rosie hurried off towards her car with hardly a backward glance. As Beral thought, she was a woman who might like a dick in a special case but not the thing in general, certainly not hung on a baby. It's all according. 'Wait,' Beral shouted. 'We'll come with you.' Poor cow, she looked so terrified. Holding the baby to her breast, Beral ran down the track after the car.

'Hand it over,' Jason said.

'I haven't finished with it,' Alex said, holding on to the shotgun and starting to lurch downstairs. He was already at the turn when he stopped and drew himself back into the wall. 'Go in front, both of you.' This wasn't the same old parasite, living on chocolates and thumbing mail orders. Jason and Nick obeyed. The women's voices, still moving away, were coming from the kitchen quarters. 'Follow them.'

'If we don't rescue that guy in time they'll shred him, starting with his private parts,' Nick said. Yes. Alex could let the women do his work for him while he looked on. Jason turned. Alex was shaking and supporting himself by the stone newel as he came down. But he was watching them. When they reached the cobbled yard it was daylight, the sun still behind the trees. The women were on the fringe of the wood. Charlie's head, moving clumsily, showed above theirs. One of them had an iron bar. Another carried a stone.

They halted fifty yards from the buildings, sunlight now up in the leaf canopy. They encircled Charlie, turning about him and holding him upright as if he'd choked to death already on his vomit. The stones and bar might not be needed.

'Stop here,' Alex said.

'You're not into murder with witnesses,' Jason said. Alex considered him, weighing possibilities. It could have been a mistake to say about witnesses. Those women were capable of anything and only Alex could communicate with them.

'Don't move,' he said.

They were examining something on the ground. Blood was running with the froth from behind Charlie's gag, he must have bitten his tongue. Jason took hold of Nick's arm. He'd brought Nick here and he didn't want to return him maimed to Beral. 'Wait a bit,' he said. 'That's the trap to the old septic tank.'

'Full—?'

'With this lot, overflowing.'

'And a body – it'd just blow—?'

'It's not the first place you'd look for one.' Alex was watching as the trap came up. He breathed deeply. Then he turned. He was smiling as if he'd swallowed an ortolan. 'Do nothing stupid,' he said.

'I've an idea,' Jason said.

'Save it.'

The women were already pressing Charlie down, hands on his head and shoulders. 'Before it's too late,' Jason shouted, and they turned to look at him.

'What is it? They won't wait,' Alex said.

'Charlie's the one to say where to find the girls. While he's alive. It's the only hope.'

Alex was thinking. He'd stopped shaking, it was action that made him shake, not thought. If the women ungagged Charlie, they could still tear him to pieces after and he could let them get on with it. That's how he'd see it. They were impatient,

230

there were signs of agitation. 'Stay here, I'll try. If either of you move, at your own risk.' A long negotiation followed, everyone speaking at once. Charlie was visible from time to time, curled on the ground. His face looked blue in the dappled sunlight under the branches.

'Hurry up,' Jason shouted.

It looked as if a conclusion was reached. The girl came over and planted herself in front of Jason and Nick. She was waving the gun about and enjoying herself a lot. The Browning was a toy and she knew how to work it. She'd already scored. She said something in Romanian, and there was no need to translate. Alex was leaning over Charlie like a hedgehog inspecting an insect. He nodded his head a couple of times. Now they pulled Charlie to his feet, holding him close by arms and legs. Someone undid the gag.

'Water,' Jason shouted again, and the girl jabbed the Browning at his face above her. Soon one of the women went off in the direction of the kitchen yard and returned with a bowl. Charlie's colour improved, it went from blue to white and vomit ran down his chin and neck. But he was alive. The bowl was held up to him. He drank like a dog. Then his legs gave way.

'Neat, that,' Nick said. 'With your hands tied behind you, if you fall, your head hits the ground. His didn't. He's not stupid.'

'It won't get him far,' Jason said.

'Shucher gob,' the girl said. She must have learned the expression from Mac. She seemed to have an idea. She laughed, showing little even teeth sharp as scissors, then stuck the barrel of the gun in Jason's crutch, looking up at him. She prodded, probing to find the place.

'Jason, come down here,' Alex called, and added something in Romanian for the girl. She withdrew the gun with regret, then moved it to the same part of Nick.

'She could let go any time. Play it cool,' Jason said.

'Cool play good for balls,' Nick said.

'Shucher gob,' the girl said again, joining in.

'Feel in my breast pocket,' Alex said. The air smelt of sick and sweat. 'There's a notebook.' He leaned over Charlie again. 'Take your time, it's your only chance. All the addresses.'

Jason hadn't seen a tortured man before. He squatted next to Charlie's head. Charlie wasn't likely to have much voice left. He looked forty years older than half an hour ago. Jason didn't feel sorry for him, only shaken up. 'When you're ready,' he said.

It was a whisper that came out. The vocal chords must be raw. It hurt to hear it. 'Hands . . . Jesus' sake.'

Jason shook his head. 'Sorry.' Was he sorry because of May? Of where Charlie's hands had been? Did that make a circle – mouth to tail? 'Talk, then they'll undo you.' Hopefully. Even for a man like that, the septic tank's no way to go.

The whispering began again. 'Girls' hostel, Chapel Street—'

'Hostel?'

'And Bradford . . . Paul's Square . . . Tonight Videos—' the whispered, perverse directory continued. If a young female knows nothing different, what then? Do the beasts of the field? 'Sheffield . . . Haymarket—' Jason wrote it all down. Charlie had a remarkable memory, unless he was inventing.

'Phone numbers?' They came out too precisely for invention. The memory was photographic. 'Sure that's all?'

'Yes.'

Jason closed the notebook and stood up. 'They could untie the poor bastard, he won't go anywhere,' he said to Alex.

Alex spoke to the woman nearest to him, motioning with the shotgun. Sounds of protest arose, but he motioned again and the woman knelt behind Charlie and fiddled with the bands on

232

his wrists. The knots were too tight for her. 'Help her,' Alex said. When the girl saw this she came hurrying down, driving Nick in front of her. Alex spoke to her calmly and she stood for a moment watching Jason work, an obstinate expression on her face and in her eyes. Then she began to talk to the women around, in a loud, fast monotone.

'What's she saying?' Jason asked.

'It's a dialect I don't know.'

'Ask her, then.'

'She wouldn't tell me.' Charlie's wrists were free. Jason watched his face as the blood came back into his hands, and Charlie watched the hands. He didn't complain or flinch. There must be a moment when any change is for the better. New pain for old. Nor did he try to get up, but sat doubled over on the ground, breathing like a punctured bellows and wiping his mouth on his sleeve. He didn't look relieved or grateful, just concentrated on being half alive.

But the terms of the bargain hadn't been realistic. They didn't take enough account of Balkan furies. The women were silent now, watching. They'd settled something, or the girl had settled it for them. It was her they were watching.

'Look out!' Jason said. Nick dodged sideways like a crab but Alex didn't have the advantage. Now blood was running from his hand and the shotgun was on the ground. The breech was smashed. The shotgun was written off. Only the Browning was left. Jason took Alex's hand and had a look. 'Nothing much,' he said.

'Nothing much?' Alex's voice was shrill. 'I'll bleed to death. Crazy little bitch. It hurts.'

'You earned it,' Jason said. Alex was moving his fingers experimentally. 'Tie it up with those strips of towel.'

'You're a hard friend, Jason.'

Charlie had no more information to take with him into the septic tank. It was only a few paces off. There were no cries, no struggle. Jason looked at Alex. His hand was taking all his attention and he was past caring about vengeance. Now the women were stooping, silent as nuns at prayer. In a moment they'd have Charlie in.

But like the snapping of a limb over your head, a sound came from the wood. All heads turned, action froze. The noise was approaching. Not loud enough for the truck which hopefully was still at the gates. Jason had a project for that truck. A car, then, bumping along the track. The girl came up behind them. She understood about hostage moves.

The women were the first to get it. Charlie's head and shoulders were still above the trap, his hands clutching at the dry earth around the opening. One of the women stamped on each in turn while another put her foot, in its split high-heeled boot, into his open mouth as a last cry came out of it, and pushed down. Charlie was gone and by the time the car reached the clearing, the manhole cover was back in place. Everyone standing around, one way or another, was accessory. Even Nick. Who would ever believe that he couldn't have got the better of an adolescent girl with a handgun she could barely hold steady?

Two dogs were running ahead of the car, the third following. The girl was the last to run forward. When she got there the car was halted behind an oak, the dogs panting round it.

'Can you make out what—?' Jason said.

'It's Beral,' Nick said, his voice full of admiration. 'She's got Bella there. And the baby. Little sod, stuck on her tit like a limpet. But I don't know the one at the wheel.' A thought struck him and he jumped forward. 'Drive away, bugger off, crazy women here,' he shouted. He could have saved himself the trouble. The women were crowding about the car, smiling and laughing, waggling their fingers at the baby and Beral and making gestures at the mouth and breast. Charlie and the septic tank were forgotten, old history now. Just another Balkan incident. Beral wound down the window and smiled in a new way, showing the baby to the world, Bella's muzzle shoving past her shoulder. For the refugees, murder was shelved. And it wasn't just Beral and the baby they were crowding round. They gazed at the driver like an icon. They'd been held down a long time in a lousy male universe. One of them touched her hair.

'She's something else, that one, for a gendarme,' Nick said.

'No. That's Rosie.' There she was and it seemed quite natural.

'Wow. Tough on your brother.'

'Not much luck for anyone,' Jason said.

'Other than horizontal. As and when.'

'All right.' Nick was evidently someone who liked to chat about this and that when an emergency was still on. He lived above it, his attention went where it wanted and he followed. 'Sprint back to the house and fetch Johnnie,' Jason told him.

'Yeah, right, if you say.' He hesitated. 'Which one are you worrying about?'

As Nick went, Rosie and Beral were getting out of the car. Between women there's a ganging up in presence of a baby, long anterior to efforts such as the pyramids or the ark. These women here, with no common language, stood around them like the first band of sisters. Going cautiously and holding Alex just above the elbow, tight so he'd feel it, Jason approached.

The nearer he got, the more he wanted to wrap Rosie up and take her away from Byland, London, and Ravenglass down to the last hook and sinker. Then he corrected himself. A woman is not a commodity. He felt a drop in spirits. But only for a moment because there are ways round. Correctness isn't the only move. As soon as she saw him she came running the few yards between them, dark hair flying about, red catching the sun through the leaves.

'We heard a lot of shooting,' she said, and put her arms round his neck. There was a slight smell of burnt hay. 'Is anyone hurt?' she asked.

'Alex got a flesh wound in his hand.'

'Let me see.' Rosie took Alex's hand and examined it closely. 'That's quite deep. When did you last have an anti-tetanus? You should get to a doctor.'

'He's all right. There's things to do first,' Jason said.

'Tetanus?' Alex said. He sounded more interested than alarmed.

'Where's the nearest cold tap?' Rosie asked.

Before Jason could answer, Nick arrived at the double, Johnnie beside him. 'Don't let Bella out of the car,' Nick shouted.

'Go to the gates and get that driver and his van up to the house,' Jason told Johnnie. 'Tell him to stay in his truck. We won't be long. Women and children first.' Beral's baby, sated now, let go its grip on her nipple and gazed drunkenly about with its mouth open. The nipple, moist and deserted, looked to Jason as chewed up as a discarded lover. It was quite a thought – a nourished, full-up baby could grow into a businessman like Charlie and end in a septic tank. 'Say there's dangerous dogs loose.'

'Where's Mr Seker? I don't see him,' Johnnie said.

'Joined the other Sekers in the sky,' Nick said, looking up at the brassy blue, 'but don't tell the driver.'

'I get it.'

'Well I don't,' Rosie said. 'Who's that girl? What's going on here?' Rosie wasn't supposed to be at Byland, her presence

236

raised problems to which Jason saw, for the moment, no solution. Like the remains of Mac and Raoul. But he was glad she was, because – oh well, he was just glad. He got his own message, looking at her, with her cap and hair all over the place. But she was soon going to see him in a new light, when she heard. A thug after all, put behind bars by the judge in Marseille where they know about thugs.

'I'm sorting it out,' Jason said. Nick and Rosie watched him, waiting. 'I want you to take Beral and the baby back to the caravan. I won't be long. A couple of things to clear up.'

'That's a hopeless idea,' Nick said. 'The minute the baby drives off, those women go batshit again.'

'I'm not going anywhere. Anyway, what are they? What have they done?' Rosie asked. She looked around her and across the yard at the house. 'Where *is* Charlie?'

There was no other way out. The lid must be kept tight shut on the septic tank. 'They haven't done anything. They're fired up. Some of their kids have been taken. For now, we've got a couple of bodies to shift,' Jason said.

'Bodies?' Rosie looked at him even harder. He could see her taking it on board and stowing it away. Her big dark eyes winding him round in their Cornish climate. Judging him, perhaps. He wasn't used to that. He didn't allow even May, with her prerogatives, to judge him. 'You can count on me if you need me,' she said. 'What's happened to the children?'

'I know where they are,' Jason said, putting the notebook in an inside pocket. 'It's down to me. No one else.'

Alex had been talking with the women. He was coming back, holding the girl by the hand. She looked like a child again – well, almost. 'Does he know their language?' Rosie asked.

'Enough,' Jason said.

'That girl's been abused.'

'She isn't the only one.'

'What arseholes most men are,' Rosie said.

'Mankind, you mean,' Jason said.

'No I don't. I wasn't including you.'

'She's called Tinka,' Alex said. 'Rather nice. They sent her to ask about the missing girls. You saved them and Tinka's their delegate. It's a republic of Balkan women.' Alex seemed to find the situation amusing. He held his wounded hand up against his chest like a medal he'd won. 'They won't let go of you. That's what happens to saviours. And I think we'd better find something to tell them, quick.' Tinka was looking up at him, her hand still wrapped in his podgy one like a bomb in a parcel. 'You've seen how they are.'

Now Tinka stared at Jason, and from him to Rosie and back again. He hadn't noticed before: the brown of her eyes was so light it was almost yellow. She knew too much not to try and use it – even the pineapple that finished off Mac so neatly, she could identify that. And accuse Jason of anything she cared to think up. The thought made him insecure. Presumption of innocence has a way of getting suspended, where there's so much rape around.

He took the notebook out and held it up. 'Tell them it's finished. They've had their time.'

'They're women.'

'Okay, but they must do what I say. I'm the one who can find the others. Where's that gun?'

Alex turned to Tinka. Her yellow eyes went green while he explained. Then she put her hand under her cotton shirt, fished around, and produced the Browning.

Jason took it. He looked at Tinka to see how she was. She was okay, cheerful. Surrendering a weapon's a male thing. This

Tinka would never be defeated so long as her powers lasted. A long time, a wide net.

'We must split up,' he said. Here was a wood full of odds and ends with different agendas. He didn't have the habit of ordering people about but it had to be done. 'Nick, get them out of here as fast as you can. Out to your camp through the wood. Alex, go with them and say we're working on it. Say it'll work. I know the way. Rosie, take the car with Beral and the baby. You're the beacon.'

Nick nodded in the direction of the septic tank, looked back at Jason, and raised his eyebrows.

'Kiss of life?' Jason said.

Nick shook his head. 'I'll hit the road,' he said, 'and never come back no more no more.'

'Where'll you be?' Rosie asked.

'Get in the car and drive it,' Jason said. She didn't look pleased.

'What d'you plan to do with that thing?'

Jason looked at the Browning in his hand. 'Lose it.' He could hear the truck approaching. 'Get going, quick, all of you.' Rosie turned the car round with Beral and the baby in it while the rest of them started off up the track. Then she stopped, got out and came back.

'Take care,' she said. 'You may be needed. What I was going to tell you at Manchester – I think I'm pregnant.'

Because he didn't know whether to believe her or not, Jason laughed; Rosie went back to the car and he felt bad about it afterwards in case it was the truth. He hadn't shown a mature reaction. Come to think of it, Rosie hadn't said anything about a father. Perhaps that was a mitigating circumstance. No, it wasn't. You could only say that mutual obsession leaves no room for mature reaction, and hope to do better, some time.

Jason turned quickly and went back to the manhole cover on the septic tank. How had those women got it off? It weighed a ton. It must have been like a religious fervour in them, moving mountains. He had it to one side. The stink made you angry yet you accepted it like part of yourself. The liquid was thick and black as mud. Just below the surface was something which could be a mass, or just a change in the consistency of the contents. A septic tank is not an inert body. It lives, the chemistry stirs, whatever you add. Jason chucked the Browning in and it disappeared at once. One day this would all be a problem for someone, probably Hugh, but by then he would be far away. Now the truck's engine cut out; there was silence from the other side of the building. Johnnie was running round to meet him, lifting his knees up at each pace as if in training. Trying to make a good impression. True, he had ground to make up.

'That bloke won't stir out of his cab. The dogs turned up,' he said. 'What next?'

'We find out if he has a crate.'

'He has. And he wanted to know should he turn the freezer up or down.'

Jason hadn't thought of that. 'Up,' he said. 'Tie the dogs up and help him get the crate inside. Then let them go when he's back in the cab so he stays there.' Everything was better spelled out. 'I'll wait for you round the turn of the stairs.'

'Got it,' said Johnnie. Willing, he definitely was. 'See you.'

They took the blankets off May's bed to wipe up the stains and cover the bodies of Mac and Raoul, and carried them down to the hall. Neither body had stiffened yet, and once their eyelids were closed they looked deeply sedated, though cold for such a hot day. 'Could you stand either of them?' Jason asked as they crammed the two sleepers into the crate meant for one.

'Mac wasn't as bloody awful as Raoul,' Johnnie said. 'But he was pretty grim all the same.'

'It's meant to be me in that box.'

'You're a large-minded man, Mr Ricardo,' Johnnie said.

'It's Jason. Mr Ricardo's my brother.' Jason went out of sight while Johnnie and the driver carried the crate to the truck.

'It's a fucking weight,' he heard the driver say.

'He was a big man,' Johnnie said.

'Bigger they are the longer they take to freeze. Same as capons. I'd better turn the thermostat up more.'

He didn't bother shutting the gates. Anyone was free to go in and camp and poach woodcock. The dogs were locked up and Nick would sort that out. He'd call the RSPCA and report night-long howling. The best thing May could do was flog the whole thing, lock stock and barrel. It would make a picturesque bed and breakfast, or club for the gilded youth of Preston and Bradford.

It was late at night by the time he got them on the road. If you once start giving orders you have to go on. People expect it. They stand around with their mouths open and their hands hanging loose. You wouldn't even get them to vote. 'Johnnie, take the women to London in the Volkswagen. Take them to Charlie's place off the City Road. That house.'

'I haven't got a key.'

'Knock down the door then.'

'Sorry.' Johnnie turned to Tinka who was looking his way. 'Understand? Anything?' Tinka smiled, a street smile. Easy, willing prey, Johnnie. 'Where can I find you?' he asked.

'What do you want to find me for?'

'I think they'll crucify me in the City Road if—'

'If they don't get their children back from your boss's brothels. Tonight, I'll be at this hotel in Manchester. Alex, you come with Rosie and me to Manchester in her car. We'll put you off at the airport.'

'Where am I supposed to sleep?'

'Catch up on it on the drive. You'll be back in chocolate land in a few hours.'

'And us?' Nick asked. 'By the way, your friend, he's wacko. Mental. And I mean he really should keep on taking the tablets. Not just the chocolate ones.' He sounded a bit sad.

'What about your carving?'

'Not another motherfucking syllable.'

'He may come back to you.'

'It won't kill me if he doesn't.'

'Keep in touch,' Jason said.

'Oh sure,' Nick said. 'I'll e-mail you. My caravan to your prison.' Alex must have told him about that, while they watched the carving grow. A little delinquency on the side wouldn't seem much, to a struggling artist.

Thank God in the hotel room there was a mini-bar, everything else in the town being tight shut. 'Whisky or brandy?' Jason asked.

'There's a half-bottle of champagne in there,' Rosie said. 'Nothing special, but it's the only thing at two in the morning.'

'Are you really pregnant, Rosie?'

'What d'you mean, really?'

'Are you?'

'I should have started ten days ago.'

'Then you can't be sure.'

Rosie looked shocked, as if he'd passed her in the street without recognising her. Jason opened the champagne and poured it into the two glasses provided within the room like a bible. 'All I meant—'

'You meant it's a heavy responsibility for a young lad of forty or so, single with no income.'

Rosie's knee was irresistible, smooth, lifted like that, however difficult she was being. Jason leaned down to it— 'I can get an income,' he said. 'And while I'm thinking about it, it's been a long day.'

Chapter Seven

EVENTS AND SUCH weren't working out that brilliantly. If anything goes wrong on a small island you soon know about it. And so does pretty well everyone else. It started downhill when May discovered a drink called Strega – the witch – and since then she'd undergone something of a personality change. For one thing, unlike some, she'd only ever liked certain games when sober and now she so seldom was that the erotic side of the idyll was pretty well seized up. The entire population of Ischia seemed to be aware of this, and Brian thought people looked at him mockingly when they saw May, face flushed and eyes glazed, sailing erratically along the narrow streets, between the oleanders. Another cock-drop of an Englishman who can't keep his woman happy, their expression seemed to say. Yet he'd always been attentive, had loads of stamina, and considered himself adept at timing. It was unjust, and he'd begun to hate Ischia and everybody on it. Not May herself, of course. All down to the Strega.

It was the day she found him, on coming round from her two-hours siesta, at grips in the garden of the villa with Ignazio from the *spiaggia degli Inglesi* that she said she wanted to go

245

home to St George's Square. 'You're my toyboy and I don't lend things. They're never as good when you get them back. If you get them back.'

'You haven't been yourself recently,' Brian said.

'Well if you were being yourself just now with that fisherman, I preferred you when you weren't. Anyway, London's the only place where there's room to be as many selves as you feel like. No one knows.'

She drank no Strega that night and they crossed to Naples next day and booked in at the Vesuvio. 'I'd better find out from Hugh what news,' she said, her voice a bit shaky. 'I mean if it's safe. Perhaps I should have a drink first.'

'No way,' Brian said, authority restored now that he was clear of that bloody island, its witchcraft and deceits.

She had quite a long talk with Hugh who was at the office. 'He says he sleeps there. He says there's nothing to worry about. Charlie's a hundred per cent on the right side, he says.'

'That means the same side as Hugh.'

'Hugh's never done a risky thing in his life. Not like Jason. That's why he's so boring. Hugh's a completely honest man.'

'Didn't he ask where you'd been?'

'No. He was very tactful. I think he's very considerate, really, poor Hugh. I've never been fair to him. It's Jason who's thoughtless and unkind to his mother. Now I really must have a glass of wine, at least. Ring the bell, Brian.' Brian thought that might just be all right.

'Send down for a great big hotel breakfast,' Rosie said.

'It's four o'clock in the afternoon.'

'Go on, try.' Jason took it as a good sign.

'Good appetite?'

'Ravenous.'

'What'd you like?'

'Scrambled eggs.' As soon as he'd done it, she sat up. 'Beral's still got my mobile,' she said.

'Then give her a buzz.'

'Saying what?'

'Why not tell her to keep it, while it works? That thing's made a big difference in Beral's life.'

'Perhaps I will.' She had to look up her own number in her diary, then watched him when she'd tapped it out. 'Better put something on. Is that you, Beral?' She moved the mobile away from her head for Jason to hear.

'Who is this, please?'

'Me, Rosie.'

'Oh, hi Rosie. There was a voice mail for you.'

'What d'you mean?'

'Your husband, I think. Hugh Ricardo, very nosy guy.'

'What did he want?'

'I think he wanted to know what happened to Jason.'

'What did you say?'

'I asked Nick. Nick said, say Jason's emigrated. He seemed happy with that.'

'He didn't ask for me?'

'Why? Does he know about everything? Aren't you scared?'

'Hang on to the mobile, Beral, and use it as much as you like till he has it cut off. Which won't be long. Get updates from the far side of the world while you can.'

'Cheers, Rosie.'

'Take care Beral.'

Rosie was looking as if she felt sorry for him. 'Too bad,' she said.

'About what?'

'You and Hugh, those years of manly trust.'

247

'Too bad about him and you, come to that.'

'Don't apologise,' she said. 'There's the breakfast. Do up your trousers.'

Not long after, the telephone rang. 'Yes?' Jason said.

'Johnnie here.'

'Everything all right?'

'Almost everything.' From his voice, Jason could tell that Johnnie was hungry for excitement. He was afraid of life going boring on him.

'You got them safely into Charlie's house?'

'Oh yes. They're hanging their washing from the windows. Knickers and that. A couple of them are up on the roof.'

'Doing what, on the roof?'

'My guess, looking for a way out. They want to find their kids. Hysterical about it, from what I can make out.'

'Get them down.'

'Easier said than done.'

'There's one of them understands a bit of English. Say I'm on my way. I'll save their girls for them.' Posturing as a hero.

But Johnnie asked for nothing better. 'Look forward to seeing you,' he said. Obviously, his outpost was a lonely one. 'By the way, Tinka sends love.'

'Did she know the word?'

'I've been explaining. Hardly slept,' Johnnie said.

'Keep it up.'

'No problem, mate.' Johnnie had come on in the last twenty-four hours.

Jason tried Alex's Paris number, to check he was out of the jurisdiction and unlikely to do more harm. Also because he didn't know when he might need Alex again. Even a saviour doesn't live on air. The answerer recited in four languages, before Jason hung up, that Mr Békassy was speaking on another line. So Alex was holed up. Lying low. Maybe he was still in London. Jason tried the Paddington hotel. No, his friend hadn't returned and wasn't expected.

He explained to Rosie. 'I must move it to London. Those women . . . you know, if they once go loose and start talking with an interpreter—'

'What can you do about it?'

'Find my mother. She wanted refugees. She has them.'

'And what am I supposed to do?'

'I think,' Jason said cautiously, 'just while I sort it out – it might be best if you went to your sister.'

Rosie's crown of hair seemed to him to turn redder while he spoke, but she said nothing.

He went first to Charlie's place. Tinka opened the door. She was wearing lipstick, a big mistake, aesthetically. All the same you could see that, cleaned up, she was a bit of a winner. Jason felt a regrettable pang of lust. He'd left Rosie late and been on the road most of the night in the van. 'Johnnie?' he said.

'Johnnie shower,' said Tinka. She bared her teeth. 'Shower big dick.'

'Never mind dick. Fetch Johnnie.' He signalled up the stairs.

Tinka put out a hand and ran it over the swelling behind his zip. 'Come on. Tinka come on,' she said, and led the way. Any resettlement agency was in for a problem, Jason thought, following. Luckily or not, Johnnie appeared at the head of the stairs in his towel.

'You got here quick,' he said, looking at them suspiciously. 'Tinka. Wash Johnnie pants socks.' He waved towards the room behind him. 'Pronto pronto,' he added.

'That's good, you got them organised,' Jason said.

'It was the only way.'

Jason nodded agreement. Being disorganised is a major problem, whatever generation you come from. He should know. Later on, Johnnie would surely wind up in the City where youth dies early. Let him be a pasha in the few moments till then. 'Don't let them loose in the street,' he said. 'It's important. You'd be in the shit.'

'I don't mind as long as I can keep her,' Johnnie said. 'For a bit at least.'

'You wouldn't.' What can you say to obsession? Even a surface one. His own was too much with the tides behind it. 'You know she'd be housed and deported.'

'Right. No one leaves the building till further notice, not for anything.'

'They'll say they need things from the chemist. Or the doctor's.'

'I'll go, locking the door behind me,' Johnnie said.

'And food. Got any money?'

'Hadn't thought of that.'

'Here then.' Jason handed over a couple of twenties. 'I don't know how long I'll be. I need heavy back-up and they all need homes. Don't give them drink, they'd go up the walls.'

Next, he rang Deakin & Deakin. 'You know me by name,' he said hopefully. 'Jason Ricardo.'

'Oh yes?' the solicitor said.

'May Ricardo's my mother.'

'I'm aware of that.' He sounded as if Jason was bad news whatever he had to say. And there, he was righter than he knew.

'I want to find her.'

'Mrs Ricardo doesn't confide her whereabouts to me on a daily or weekly basis.'

'How d'you mean, on a basis?' Jason asked. He felt he'd heard the phrase once too often.

250

'I mean every day or every week.'

'Do you know where she is?'

'No.'

'Then I'll report her missing at the Pimlico Police Station. You'll have to confirm it. I hear there's been a break-in at her house up in Lancashire. I'll report that at the same time.'

'Actually, Mrs Ricardo did telephone me yesterday – I think it was yesterday – from Naples. In Italy. She gave no address.'

'What did she say?'

'She's returning.'

'When?'

'Overnight.'

It was like a tax office, anywhere. Information was withheld on principle if it could be. Or else Hugh had been getting at this man. That could be different. 'Over which night?'

'The night of the day she rang,' the solicitor said.

'Yes. The basis is diurnal, of course. What else did she ring you for?'

'I am not—'

'Don't say it. At liberty to divulge.' Jason hung up. What a twat. Hugh must have something on him. But then so did he.

In St George's Square, the sun was breaking through. Everything glistened, leaves, bark, sky. Once again, London on Thames looked like where you'd like to be if it wasn't for all the sorry fuck-ups. Jason wondered what had become of Sandy. Usually, for women like Sandy, it's downhill all the way. That was why she was so angry about the mishap. He hoped she'd struck lucky, somewhere. When he rang the doorbell nothing followed. After five minutes he walked on to the Embankment to the first telephone. There used to be a code for when May was lying low. You let it ring three times, then hung up; then

251

twice; then once. After that, she answered if she felt like it. He tried it now.

'We know who this has to be,' Brian's voice said. There were no secrets from him. 'Where are you?'

'On the Embankment.'

'I'll come down.'

'Like shit off a shovel if you know what's good for you,' Jason said.

Brian appeared at the door wearing an Italian-looking jacket with four white buttons, all of them fastened like a straitjacket. Jason stepped up and took hold of it by the lapels, pushing Brian backwards into the hall and against the rail of the staircase. 'Where have you been?'

'Your mother wanted a little holiday.'

'At Naples?'

'Ischia.'

'Now you're back there's work to do if you don't want a lot of serious grief.'

'How brutal you are, Jason. Unhand me.' Was it an AC/DC joke? Must be. Jason pushed him towards the lift.

He didn't kiss his mother this time. She was at the piano and he let her pull her hands away before he shut the lid of the keyboard with a bang. 'Finito all the buggering about,' he said.

'Jason. I'm your mother.'

'Like your solicitor says whom you rang yesterday, I'm aware of it.'

'You shouldn't speak to me like that. You're a delinquent.'

'It's in the blood.'

'The Ricardo blood,' May said. Which way would she go? It seemed she hadn't decided yet. Laughter, rage, tears? Her eyes wandered to the door of the dining room where the bottles were, on the sideboard.

'Ravenglass blood. You've got yourself in a lot of trouble, mother.' She smiled. After all, mother's a title, in a way.

'What have you done with Charlie?' she asked.

Jason never remembered not to be surprised the next time round by these flashes of sideways thinking. 'How d'you know I've done anything with him?'

Now she laughed. 'I've only to look at you, you great booby.'

It was infuriating how she won an advantage as soon as she was obviously and provably in the wrong. If only she'd had a daughter as well as him and Hugh it wouldn't have happened like that. A daughter would have made her human. Now he must keep his temper, at least till she lost hers – and even then. 'I've liquidated part of the Charlie problem to protect you, but not all. You need a lawyer.'

'I haven't done anything wrong.' Odd how this tall, deliciously scented woman could make herself sound like a little girl. If she happened to be your mother, there you were caught in the generation trap.

'You have to do something now. And Deakin must help you. Ring him. Tell him to come at once. Here. Otherwise Deakin & Deakin will go the same way as the firm I read about in the paper – Emanuel and Miller. I'll see to it myself.'

'You're a hard son to have, Jason.'

'Be grateful.' It was no time for excuses. 'Go on.'

May sighed, and went into the dining room from where he heard the clink of glass and then her voice on the telephone, cajoling and commanding. When she came back she said, 'He'll be here in fifteen minutes.' She sat at her piano with her hands in her lap. 'What is it you want me to do?'

Jason pulled the notebook from his pocket. 'I've got addresses here where Seker placed some of your refugees into child prostitution. You and the lawyer must go north and find them. Today. Discreetly, without the police. Otherwise you'll all be in it.'

'Charlie did a thing like that?'

'Not a thing *like* that. That's what he did. And I don't want to hear how little you knew about it. I've decided you didn't know anything, otherwise—'

'Otherwise you couldn't live with it.'

'Yes. And right now there's about a dozen women and girls at Seker's place off the City Road. They need situations, and fast. Brian worked for Charlie, didn't he?'

'Yes, poor boy.'

'Well, he gets his arse down the City Road and looks up Charlie's files for addresses. The personnel's disbanded. Those girls must be placed in straight coffee bars or families. When the children arrive from the industrial towns, we'll see. Or you will. You must salvage the Ravenglass name, whatever is costs. It's rescue work. For you and them. You must do it.'

'That's a lot of musts.'

'There are ruder ways of putting it.'

'Hugh's kinder to me than you, really. I was saying so to Brian yesterday. Or the day before.' Her eye wandered to the dining-room door. Her thought, obviously, to the sideboard.

Jason could feel his temper beginning to crack under the strain, like an old plank bridge. There was a void below it. 'Isn't it kind of me to set up real refugee work for you to do all on your own? Like you've always wanted? Without Charlie to push you out of the way?'

'What's happened at Byland?'

'The house is empty. You can have it back. The lease fell in,' Jason said. It was another responsibility she should never have shuffled off.

May looked over at Brian. 'Charlie was going to buy it and take it off my hands. Brian was arranging it.'

'Is that right? Price? Mark-up, those details?'

'Of course.'

In one way, this information was a bit of luck. It meant anger could be displaced from May to Brian. Less stressful, that. Less guilt by association. 'Well it's a minus for Brian. Poor boy.' Jason looked over at him. He seemed a bit shrunken. 'Choose better company, mother,' Jason said. And an idea came to him. Brian hadn't turned out as harmless as he'd believed he was. Now might be the time to replace him.

'I needed the money,' May said pitifully, angrily.

'Money? Money's for Hugh.'

'You've come back to me in a very bitter state of mind, Jason. I don't like to see it. You must be unhappy.'

'I am unhappy.'

'Brian – Jason's unhappy. Please fetch a bottle of that lovely soft wine from Pau.' Brian was looking unhappy too, and went without making any objection. 'What are you unhappy about? Tell your mother.'

'A private thing. A decision to make.'

She considered him for quite a long time in silence. He knew he shouldn't have said that. She was setting her intuition on him like a mob of terriers on a holed-up fox. 'I know what it is. You've quarrelled with Hugh. That always made you unhappy. You always thought you had too many advantages. And now you've used it somehow. I think I know how. It's like the stags, it's natural. But it makes you unhappy. It spoils your fine idea of yourself.'

That did it. She'd gone too far. Damn mothers, they should do their primary job and vanish. When he answered Jason's voice rose so much that Brian, reappearing with the wine, dropped a glass. 'It's my fine idea of you that's been spoiled. You don't think. You don't look five minutes ahead. You're like a woman about to kill herself later this afternoon. You let everything go – yourself, the ideas you had from grandfather Ravenglass we heard so much about. And now the refugees. They're like too much trouble because none of them are May Ravenglass herself. The widow Ricardo.'

May turned on the piano stool, upright as ever, with the full glass of golden wine from the vineyards of Pau and held it up like a toast. 'So your father's really and truly dead?'

'What d'you think? What does intuition say?'

'It says, tell Cain to take Abel's wife unto him and be happy if they can. Intuition speaks in borrowed voices and not always the same.' Jason hoped she wouldn't wreck it with mystery. Lateral thinking was enough. And she was edging her way back into the strong position, as always. That was because she wasn't afraid of him. Whatever she did, she knew she could count on him. He'd protected her over the prostituted children, he would protect her, somehow, against Hugh the day her money ran out. Jason would never see her lose rank. 'Now I'll rush off with Brian to the City Road and take care of those girls.' She swallowed some wine to celebrate herself and put the glass down. 'Come along Brian. No time for you to hang around drinking now. Don't forget your reading glasses, you'll need them.'

A bell in the passage began to ring and continued ringing as if rain had reached into the bellpush and made a short circuit. It was loud and urgent and you wanted to turn off its life-support system as quickly as possible. 'The door,' Jason said.

'Wicked, isn't it,' Brian said.

'Aren't you going?'

'See out of the window first,' May said. Apart from the great studio light above, there was one small opening in the outside wall of this room, and from it you could watch the steps from the street in a magnifying mirror carefully placed and screwed to the frame. Jason had done it in the days when he took pride in odd jobs for this dramatic mother who could do little or nothing for herself. Except manipulate her way through the world.

Brian peered out. 'It looks like Mr Deakin. He's got a hat on. A Panama with a stripy band. Nice. Some club he belongs to perhaps.'

'He's in disguise. He's frightened out of his wits. Go and let him in, Brian,' May said. When Brian left, she didn't help herself to another drink. 'Leave Deakin to me. You can trust your mother, Jason, those children and girls have a better friend in me than they know. He's a lawyer with a lot to lose and he knows his way round. Give me the addresses.'

Jason handed over the notebook. 'Don't waste any time,' he said. 'Ring first and put the fear of God into the pimps.'

Brian had left the door open and the lift could be heard on its way up. May stood with one hand on the piano and the notebook in the other. 'You've got to face Hugh some time. It's better,' she said. 'Don't ever turn your back on him.'

'Is it better? Better than what?'

'You were thinking of running away?'

'I don't know.'

'In that case I can't imagine what she sees in you.' It was the right sort of corrective, immediate as a turn of the wheel. He felt glad she was finally good for something. 'You thought you'd never really love any woman. Bed was enough for you. It must be the colour of her hair.' May was laughing at him; she'd walked all over him. But it was a serious laugh. There were voices on the landing. 'I'm impartial,' she said, 'but I wouldn't want you wrecking a woman's life now you've found one at last. And not just an easy fuck.'

He'd never heard her say the word before. Well, it was her birthright, let alone way of life. All the same you didn't expect her to bring it out, that word from the shadow of the act. 'I don't run,' he said.

'Your father did.'

'That's what you say. Maybe you drove him.'

'Maybe I did. I'm a spoiled woman.' Another thing he'd never heard her own up to before. Perhaps on Ischia she'd got a clearer view of herself. He softened towards her.

'Dear May—' the legal adviser was saying as he came in from the hall, holding his Panama in front of him at crutch-level like a shield.

It seemed to Jason she was viewing the lawyer sardonically. Perhaps he hadn't come up to scratch when he had the chance. Going to bed with May Ravenglass was a privilege not accorded a second time if the first didn't score. She was a summit not for the climber out of condition. Good and fresh, they must be. Johnnie, for example. And after him? There's no after, no before, for a Ravenglass. That's the rule of the sea. With just one exception. The before and after between brothers. To be settled, paid for, on one side or the other.

'Willie,' she said, and left a pause. 'I shouldn't have made you come. We must all go straight back to Lincoln's Inn. Then the City Road. Do you know it? It doesn't matter, Brian will drive us in the Rover.' She looked at the first address in the notebook. 'And to Sheffield.'

'Sheffield? Tomorrow? Perhaps the day after when I've had time to—'

'Today,' May said. 'You can buy a toothbrush when we get there. And give that absurd hat to Brian. You're much too old

258

for it. Wait for me in the lift.'

She took Jason by the arm and drew him behind the grand piano. 'I know you'll be gone. What shall I do?'

'You'll meet a young friend of mine in the house off City Road,' Jason said. 'He's someone who needs a bit of guidance, but he could be useful. I'll be back.'

'But not free any more,' May said, a bit sad. 'But it had to be. She was made for you. And you for her. Don't forget your mother, however far you go.'

'I'm not likely to,' Jason said.

'You and me, we're people who have to do what we want. I know it hurts others. There are laws and laws. And lawyers as long as you can pay. *Avanti.*'

'See you, maybe,' Brian said quite cheerfully, down on the pavement by the Rover. His spirits had risen and he had the Deakin & Deakin Panama with the club band on his head. Johnnie was going to seem like fresh stock just in, compared to him.

'Maybe,' Jason said. Brian got into the driver's seat, all leather before the veneer of the dashboard, and the Rover drew off along the Embankment, passing near the steps where Jason had first known a woman on the inside. You thought, at the time, you were getting the goods, the lot, because it felt so . . . total, so simple; but it turned out there were many, many more convolutions than you'd seen then. He crossed to the telephone box and rang the hotel in Manchester. She wasn't there any more. Watching the brown tide run eastward, he tried her sister's number. It didn't answer. Neither did Alex. Jason was where he needed to be, for now. On his own.

Chapter Eight

'TWO YEARS, ONE with remission. And fifteen thousand francs. How long has the individual served?'

'Ten months.'

'Have you fifteen thousand francs, Ricardo?'

'No, *Monsieur le juge.*' The young judge looked put out. Initiative was called for when he would probably rather be messing about on his boat in the Vieux Port, this lovely January afternoon. Jason sympathised. The judge inspected the papers in front of him again.

'This ship of yours—'

'It isn't my ship, *Monsieur le juge.*'

'The company is a family company.'

'I have no share in it.'

'No matter. You are the Master.'

'Yes.'

'The ship is an encumbrance to the Port Authority. It says so here. It takes space which could be more profitably used. It's overrun with rats. It's rusting to pieces. It's in the way.'

'It's still a good ship,' Jason said.

The judge smiled. 'I'm not here to listen to your opinion of the ship. I'm here to sentence you and, if possible, satisfy the Port Authority.' Jason shut up. 'What has happened to the Moroccans?' the judge asked, leaning towards his clerk.

'You ordered them deported, *Monsieur le juge*, only last month.'

'Oh yes,' the judge said. He turned back to Jason. 'That's not so easy with a citizen of the European Union. And it would leave the ship where it is. The Port Authority would not appreciate that.' He seemed to be dithering. He must be very inexperienced. New to the job of judging.

'With fifteen thousand francs I could take it out to sea,' Jason said.

'Silence,' said the judge. Everyone sat or stood quietly while he thought about it. 'Where would you take it?'

'I can get a credit on a Maltese company to fuel and sail to Malta.'

'Why would this company give you credit?'

'The ship sails under the Maltese flag.'

'I expect it does. But why the credit?'

'The company exports Maltese artefacts. It's cheaper by sea.'

The judge shrugged. Artefacts from Malta were outside his province. 'What do you need fifteen thousand francs for, then?'

'To take on a couple of hands, *Monsieur le juge*.'

'In that case apply to your family company.'

'With respect, I'll be serving the rest of my sentence a long way from a telephone.'

The judge moved his feet noisily about the wooden floor under his chair, then cleared his throat. 'I have decided that nothing would be gained by sending you back to prison. What little space they have is needed for more urgent cases. As in the Port. You are therefore discharged.' He leaned down to the clerk again. 'Have I power to order the ship to leave?'

'Subject to appeal, you have.'

'Who's going to appeal? I order the ship to sail within twenty-eight days and your discharge is conditional on obeying the order.'

'The fine,' the clerk said in a loud whisper.

'Deferred *sine die*,' the judge said, closing the dossier.

'The court will rise,' announced the clerk. Obviously, the harbour master and the judge were part of one and the same clan.

It had to be somewhere between Sicily and Malta, near enough the whirlpool of Charybdis to colour the story, not so far from the limit of Maltese waters that he'd get picked up by the wrong coastguards. Malta was where he needed to be, the only rock in the sea where he was sure of raising the wind while the insurance business went through. Which could be a long time. Hugh would make the claim and Lloyd's send out assessors, i.e. investigators, while he lay low in Valetta and stuck to his story. He'd told no one yet. Going it alone.

One certainty was Hugh refunding the Maltese company what they advanced, because of the deposit Ravenglass put down to sail under the Maltese flag. He was welcome to the rest. It was like ransom money, in a way. And the ship must be insured for about half a million, not that they'd cough up that much if ever he admitted there were leaks in the ballast, disastrous when the half gale got up.

There was a heavy swell now, and no moon. Already a huge oil slick on the water, reflecting the beam of the torch like a signal in a black mirror. The hired Italian hands, well paid to disappear, were in the other boat and heading for Sicily, being nearer. The *Kendal*'s watery grave was about three hundred yards away in the dark, the lifeboat's engine had fired at last and the radio message would bring out the guards within an hour or so. Jason felt no grief. He'd loved the *Kendal* like a birthplace but it was the love of a lonely man. Now his interior life was halved and his feeling for the ship was a figure receding along the track to death for one of them. He had a bottle of red wine and drank from the neck. He'd decided to stay at the Testaferrata Palace where there was a heated swimming pool. They'd like that all right, and by mid-March the air's already warm. Ravenglass would pay. His watertight evidence to the assessors was indispensable.

Right here and now, it was bloody freezing and the air stank of oil. He swallowed some more wine. Once safe in the Testaferrata Palace they could think about what was next to be done. The last night he spent there, wasn't it with that Egyptian, a Copt with huge pale blue despairing eyes? She was circumcised, it came as a shock. Jason finished the bottle and flung it out to float on the oily surface.

All the island lights were yellow, giving off a foggy glow southward over the sea. It was a big relief when the yellow glow turned to a sprinkle of pinpoints, rising and sinking with the swell. A helicopter with a powerful beam circled round, dipped, returned to base. Twenty minutes later Jason heard the roar of the coastguard launches. Both his passports were in an oilskin wallet in his inside pocket. In a sense he was coming home. One of his identities was making landfall.

The Testaferrata turned out a bit of a delusion, at first. He was held for ten days in close custody as the guest of some ministry and questioned again and again about the circumstances of the sinking. On the second day he asked for writing materials.

'Excuse me. What for?'

'I must let my mother know I'm safe.'

'Ah . . . yes. Your *mamma*—' Jason was given one sheet of paper and one envelope. 'Your letter to your *mamma* will carry the stamp of the Maltese government.'

Back in Marseille, Jason hadn't thought this operation right through. Drunk with relief was how he'd been after walking out of the court a fairly free man. Here in Malta he was looking down a perspective of middle years with no financial sunshine lighting it up. And Alex, once a standby, was too unreliable. He no longer answered messages left on his answerer, whether friendly or threatening. He wasn't going to be any help on the economic front unless Jason went to Paris. And not even then, if his nerve had gone.

Jason settled down in the deckchair provided in his cell and began a letter to Deakin & Deakin.

Dear Sir,

You will already know from Ravenglass that the SS *Kendal*, under my command, was lost off the Sicilian coast in a westerly gale last Tuesday. I am at the disposal of the port authority in Malta while the circumstances of the loss are clarified, pending the arrival of the Lloyd's assessor, to which I look forward.

I assume you are handling such an important claim, on the company and my mother's behalf. And naturally I hope it will go through successfully, and would deplore— (he liked 'deplore') —if any error of memory of mine impeded it— (he liked 'impede', too).

I have been employed at sea by the Ravenglass Line for the last twenty years, having obtained Master's Certificate in the time of my late grandfather. The activity of the company is now mainly ashore and I expect no offer of further employment.

I am willing to accept due redundancy terms equal to one fifth the net value of the insurance claim on my ship, paid to my account at the Banco Valetta in this town. (I will open the account on hearing from you.)

An equal fifth to be paid to my mother's private account at the bank she names. The balance for the company.

I believe my mother, as owner of the Ravenglass Line and claimant, will instruct you to agree to this arrangement. Please reassure her of my safety. I look forward to fully cooperating with the assessor from London.

Yrs etc.

PS I shall be staying at the Testaferrata Palace Hotel as soon as released.

Jason addressed the envelope to May with 'For the attention of Deakin' in brackets. That should get her interested.

A week later, the Lloyd's assessor arrived and Jason was let out under police control.

'Do you people have an arrangement with the Maltese authorities?' he asked the assessor, name of Blake.

'Lloyd's has a long arm,' Blake said. 'Where will you be staying?'

'The Testaferrata Palace.'

'Sounds good. I'll go there too.'

So they sat side by side on the edge of the swimming pool, had their meals at adjoining tables, slept in rooms on the same floor. A police car waited in the street and Jason didn't call his contact for money. On the third morning, the director of the hotel asked him into his office.

'This is not a cheap hotel, Mr Ricardo, and you've paid no deposit. May I know when you expect to do so?'

'I'll see about it right away,' Jason said. Blake, as he expected, was waiting for him in the painted hall, a space decorated with frescoes showing the assumption of Cardinal Testaferrata into heaven in 1702. 'I may move,' Jason said.

'I don't think you should. The claim's at the doubtful stage.'

'I may have to.'

'Why?'

'The hotel wants a deposit.'

'I see,' Blake said. He must know he was cornered. His underwriters weren't going to love him if he lost Jason, the only witness who might yet help them slip off the hook. Not that he was going to do that, however many drinks Blake stood him of an evening in hopes of tripping him up. 'How much?'

'Five hundred. It can come off the claim, I expect.' Jason returned to the director's office and handed over three, a generous gesture, he thought. Then he went to the bar and asked for a telephone to be brought. You can get that sort of service at the Testaferrata.

'Deakin & Deakin?'

'Can I help you?'

'Yes. Pass me the senior partner. This is Jason Ricardo.' He didn't have to wait long. 'I expected a letter from you.'

'Where are you?' the legal adviser asked.

'In the bar of the Testaferrata.'

'Has an assessor arrived from Lloyd's?'

'Certainly. Didn't they tell you?'

'Lloyd's are secretive. This means your brother Hugh will be coming out too. He'll give you the answer you expect.'

'No. I want it from your office. Undertaking now, settlement when I've done my stuff.'

'I see. Where is the assessor?'

'In the bar of the Testaferrata.'

'The undertaking will be in the next post. I'll fax a copy at once. What's the number at this Testyferarta?'

Blake came over to the bar from his table in the corner. 'Nice work, if you can get it,' he said. Evidently no fool.

'I think my brother will be here in a day or so.' That would be what Blake was waiting for. His own slice of carve-up.

On the rim of the pool with his feet in the water, Jason thought about Rosie. Blake was going slowly up and down like the elderly ladies at the Nauticlub. Another place where Charlie would be missed. In the Baumettes, Rosie had hardly entered his mind. Some kind of defensive mechanism, presumably. Now she was hardly ever out of it. Her image drew closer, shutting out more of everything else. Yet he'd done nothing. He got into the pool and thrashed about angrily. If Blake came any closer than that, he'd drown the sod. Blake waved from the far end. Jason didn't wave back.

'What about a pre-lunch drink or two?' Blake said, strolling up. 'On me.' He was overweight in his Bermuda shorts.

'Don't you ever take time off even to get a seeing-to?'

'Not on the job.'

So the call to Rosie, if he could find her, must wait till they were all tucked up in bed.

'My sister doesn't use that name any more.'

'I don't blame her. What name does she use?'

'Our name. Ross.'

'Rosie Ross. I like it.'

'Oh you do, do you,' the sister said. The conversation wasn't too brilliant so far.

'Is she there, please?'

'Who do I say?'

'Tell her Jason Ross. No relation.'

'You know it's half past ten?'

'I'm sorry.'

'I'll see if she's asleep. She may not want to come. She's off men.'

The sister was away for quite a time, then Jason heard Rosie's voice at last. 'Where are you?' she said. At least she wanted to know.

'I'm in Malta. I only got away about ten days ago.'

'You escaped?'

'They let me off.'

'Ten days. Plenty of time to ring sooner than this.'

'I wasn't a hundred per cent free. I'll explain later.'

'Yes?'

'It's March. It's marvellous here in March. Bikini weather almost.'

'For a woman six months pregnant?'

He'd forgotten. That day in Manchester he'd thought it was all right. Because of the big breakfast. What a fool. 'I love you Rosie, I think you know that,' he said.

'I suppose if you thought it, you didn't feel it necessary to communicate the fact. If it is one.'

'I'll look after you all the rest of your life,' he promised in a futile, atavistic way. 'Just come to Malta. We'll sort it all out here. You know I love you,' he said again.

'I'll sleep on it. Ring me in the morning,' Rosie said and hung up.

Hugh appeared at the Testaferrata early next day while Jason was swimming. He must have come in on a night flight. Jason got out of the water in a hurry. Seeing Hugh unexpectedly set up an instant audit in his mind. Whatever Hugh might have

269

tried to do to him at Byland didn't scrub out what he'd definitely done to Hugh. Well, May had said that some day he must be faced. Better for all, she'd said. This was it. And he had no doubt she'd found a good moment to say the matching truth to Hugh. That's what she did, always had done – stir it up, under cover of matriarchal counsel. Jason didn't resent it. It was her nature, and he approved of her nature.

'You're looking for me?' Jason asked.

'No.' Hugh stared at him with eyes diminished by grief and hatred. 'Where's that Lloyd's assessor?'

'On his way, I should think.' Jason went into the changing room. Later, he caught sight of Hugh and Blake climbing the grand stair. It didn't take much working out, and worked out, it looked good. By tomorrow Blake would be gone, Hugh would leave tonight, in a day or two Ravenglass would be richer by the amount agreed less Blake's personal price and the redeeming two fifths. The ransom was as good as paid. Jason would be independent, and free.

Not quite yet though. If Hugh was to be faced it had to be on his terms; otherwise it wouldn't really be facing him at all. It would be ducking out, doing a fade. Anyway, Jason believed Hugh would come to him, not the other way round. So he must wait. Because Hugh would want to know about Rosie. About her desires now that Jason was free. That's what would be torturing Hugh, Jason felt it as if they came from one embryo. He crossed the bar and went down the flight of steps, out on to the terrace overlooking the harbour and the glittering water of the Maltese Strait. The terrace was in shadow, the sun not yet up above the buildings behind, and there was no one about. Jason walked forward and leaned on the balustrade with the water lapping at the foot of the wall below.

A sound made him turn. Hugh was on the steps. He'd been

right. Hugh was seeking him out. They watched each other with the inside knowledge you only have of a sibling – each seeing through the other's defences. Reading the audit. They both looked away at the same time. 'Where is she?' Hugh asked.

'I don't know.' Why the lie? A sort of shame, perhaps. That was not facing up, it was putting on hold.

'Don't you? Were you thinking of ditching her? Well I can tell you. She's with her sister.'

'Look Hugh . . . I think—'

Hugh was staring over his head at a warship at anchor outside the harbour. His thought had moved on. He looked as though what they'd just been saying had nothing to do with him. 'I've ordered a car to go out to Hagar Qim. I always wanted to see it,' he said.

'Hagar Qim?' It rang a bell, unidentified. Some baroque village? A castle? A fireworks factory?

'The Bronze Age temple. I've been reading it up.' Hugh was speaking conversationally, as if he was split in two and this was the mellow side, entirely ignorant of the other. 'Suppose you come along too?'

Jason decided at once this was the thing to do. 'Okay.'

'Like going to Long Meg and her daughters,' Hugh said as he got into the back of the car. Jason had to think for a moment to work out what he meant. Had they ever been to some cathouse called that? He didn't think so, he'd always kept his distance from Hugh, there. Decently separate. Until Rosie. No, of course – what Hugh meant was a stone circle in the hills about fifteen miles from Byland.

'Seamen can go anywhere,' Jason said. 'Malta – Lisbon – Ravenglass – in a hollowed-out log, it's nothing.' Strange they could still laugh together at a simple joke with echoes. Maybe

Hagar Qim had that among its powers. What was the date? 20th March. The Spring equinox. Perhaps Hagar Qim was a temple dedicated to the equinox, not the solstice.

Jason noticed that the police car had disappeared. Blake must be already bought and he'd been on the telephone to the authorities. Quick work. It wasn't even nine yet. The whole island seemed asleep. Looked like a holiday. The car wandered round built-up lanes and dusty roads and then down among vines towards the south coast. Jason remembered now what he knew about Hagar Qim. You saw it from the sea, standing near the edge of the cliff, honey-coloured stone rings and horseshoes askew in the ground, like bad teeth in a skeleton. 'You must walk the rest,' the driver said. 'Down that path. You want I wait?'

'Yes,' Hugh said.

A landscape dotted with Barbary figs and oleanders; a closed bar near the entrance to the monument. No one about here either. A chill wind off the sea and no heat yet in the sun. They must all be in church. The temple consisting of a series of rooms, layout in the form of an ace of clubs on the cliff top. Some of the stones pierced with a hole at the height of your ear. 'Those were for announcing the oracles through,' Hugh said. 'Priests speaking with the voices of gods.'

'This is a devout island,' Jason said. He felt almost at ease, neither of them quitting neutral ground. The only noise was gulls circling the cliff and the offshore water breaking against rocks below the surface.

'Where did the *Kendal* go down?' Hugh asked, looking out over the sea.

'To the north. Other side.'

'Deakin told me the arrangement agreed with you.'

'We won't talk about it. It's between him and May and me.'

'You cleaned up there as well,' Hugh said. 'You came out of prison a parasite and screwed everything up for everyone else.'

'Not for Rosie.' It was said. Hugh went white the way he used to, and Jason walked forward to the edge where he could see the water breaking on the rocks below. It was a reminder that he wasn't a seaman any more. So what was he?

'We'd better get back,' Hugh said behind him. His voice sounded calm. Jason turned to look. Hugh hadn't followed him, he was standing on the same spot, rigid as one of the stones.

'In a minute.' It was as if, in this religious place, the home of oracles, Jason wanted to pray to the sea for guidance – about what he should become when he got the redundancy money, perhaps. The Maltese Strait is a deep bottomless blue as if the centre of the earth it washes over was bluer than the sky. The cliff was at his feet, the noise of the breaking water gentle, far down. Jason gazed into the blue for inspiration. He'd faced Hugh now, in a way, as much as he was going to. The audit would stay out of balance to the end of their lives and there was nothing more to be done about it. He'd taken May's advice. Part of it. What was the other part? 'Don't turn your back on him.' Jason swung round and leaped aside in the same movement, stumbled and fell on the ground a couple of yards from the edge.

Hugh had approached without a sound and was standing half crouched, hands close together, palms outward at chest level as though to catch something in flight. Or send it flying.

'Don't think of it,' Jason said from the ground, and got up, moving away. He felt lighter. He felt relief past measuring. The audit was looking cleaner. 'Go back and find yourself another woman, Hugh. One who reckons you more. Or stick to the professionals. They're not so unlike. Only if it's love, then it's everything.'

'So put her on the streets when you have her for your own.
It's where I got her,' Hugh said. He had an expression Jason
remembered from childhood defeats – a map of humiliation,
between a sneer and a laugh. 'Turn professional yourself. Set
up. Invest your redundancy in poncing.' He turned and strode
away fast towards where they'd left the car. Jason followed at
the same pace because it was a long walk from Hagar Qim to
the Testaferrata and there wasn't another living soul in sight.

He took a taxi to Luqa airport where Rosie was due on the
flight at twelve thirty. The island had woken up, the sky was
like blue glass and the air was warm. Sportsmen behind stone
walls fired low at migrating birds too exhausted to rise. It must
be some saint's day because church bells were ringing in every
village they went through, bells ringing in any order, jangling,
yelling at the sky as though to crack the glass.

Blake no longer followed him around, so he'd had to look for
him. 'Has my brother left the hotel?'

'He's gone to a bank. He'll be on his way when we've
finalised the details.' That meant Hugh was fetching an advance
on Blake's kickback. So the two of them could part good
friends.

'You leave today?'

'He's fixing a flight at the same time.'

He arrived early at Luqa, and waited outside in the sunshine.
Tension mounting. Anticipation mixed. Suppose, face to face,
they no longer felt the same, like one essence, two genders?
Suppose she'd rethought him in absence and found him want-
ing? Not much more than a common bandit? The sun was hot.
Jason unbuttoned the sleeves of his flowery new shirt and rolled
them up. From inside the airport building, an announcement.
The flight from Gatwick had landed.

274

★ ★ ★

She looked good, sumptuous. She was wearing a long knitted coat of many colours, swelling before her like a patched sail. Her face was a bit fuller and had a healthy tone from living in the country instead of the North End Road. Her hair was all over the place and altogether she looked as if she'd just got off a horse after a canter round the shire, or somewhere. Jason wondered if she'd been having too good times while he was in prison not thinking of her. When she saw him she gave a big smile, dispelling cloudy afterthoughts like the March sun.

Holding her, he was aware of the other, the new presence shoving against him, shoving him out of the way. Breaking it up. Near the main doors he stopped and held her again, for a long time. Later on he would have to share.

'You're a shit, but I'm thinking of forgiving you,' she said. He knew she was wet. 'Why did they let you out?'

'I hadn't done anything much.'

'Make sure you never do nothing much again.'

'Don't worry.'

'So what's in Malta?' She was holding on tight to his free hand. 'We need a lot of calm and no nasty surprises, me and the god forbid you forgot.'

'Malta's a port of call to anywhere . . . a launch pad . . . it's a starting point.'

'Make up your mind,' Rosie said.

There was a queue for taxis, and while they stood in it there was time to think about the bed in the grandiose Testaferrata bedroom. Trouble was, that had to be postponed. 'To the Testaferrata Palace please, but round the island first. *Avanti.* We'll take a look at Mdina. There's nowhere like it.'

'We're staying in a palace?'

'You'll see.' Jason turned to her beside him on the back seat.

275

'Do you know what time that plane goes back to London?'

'Yes, I do, actually. They turn round in ninety minutes. Refuel and empty the sanitation.'

'That should about do it,' Jason said.

But it didn't. When they drew up in the forecourt of the Testaferrata, Hugh was standing with Blake on the top step. They were staring at the sky, bare and blue from one horizon to the other. Their London eyes spread wide to drink up the last of that nude March blue.

'Drive round the harbour,' Jason said, leaning forward to block the window. But it was too late.

'Hugh's there,' Rosie said, her hand on the door.

'Stay in the car.'

'I have other job waiting. You must get down here. And pay me,' the driver said.

'You knew,' Rosie said.

'Just a minute,' Jason said.

'No just a minutes please,' the driver said. 'Bloody Englishman. Out now. "Go round the island." I arrive Southampton – "*Avanti*, go round the island" – what you think happen? I tell you. Boot up arse. You owe me fifty bloody English pound.'

'Fair enough.' Jason patted him on the shoulder. 'You're right. Englishman plenty to learn.' He took both Rosie's hands and held them against his chest. 'But everything's all right. We'll make out. Nothing to be afraid of.'

'You didn't say. You knew and you didn't say anything.' Rosie opened the door on her side and stood on the crumbling golden gravel. When Jason finished paying he ran up the steps after her. Hugh was watching. He looked down to take in Rosie's shape and his expression changed. He took a pace forward, eyes wide now.

276

'Mine?'

'No, not yours,' Rosie said. 'How could it? Sorry.'

'His?'

'Must be.'

'Still in the family then,' Hugh said. 'Don't ever give it a brother.' Blake was behind him with his bag. 'Remember and ask before you get into bed if he's had a blood test recently. He's been ten months inside. That's a couple of hundred emissions. How many on his own? Ask.' He strode down the steps like a blind man on the run, between Jason and Rosie, knocking both of them to one side. Blake followed.

'Thanks for the help, Mr Ricardo,' he said. 'I'd need a serious premium to underwrite your life. Anyhow the claim goes through. Ravenglass will be looking at the money in a week. Best of luck to you all three.' He lowered his voice. 'A very fair exchange. Cheers.'

'What did that man mean?' Rosie asked.

It was a question to put off answering. Jason fetched Rosie's luggage and went to the reception desk. 'This is Mrs Ricardo. Where's our new room?'

'I'm supposed to share with you? What room was Hugh in?'

When they got upstairs, Jason opened the window on to the balcony. The sea and sky, same coin two sides, spun over and over to the Sicilian horizon. On the far limit a blister of blue rock pushed up above the water. One of those volcanoes, for sure.

'What did he mean? I want to know.'

'He meant the claim on the *Kendal*.'

Rosie said nothing for a minute but still watched. Jason felt like an open book, bent back. 'You sank her?'

'She did sink.'

'I never want to hear another lie, Jason.' Sooner or later they

277

always say it. The trouble is, you can be in love with someone as never before and not know them well enough to be sure it's safe to tell the truth.

'So I let her sink.'

'Why?'

'She needed the rest.'

'For the insurance? For Hugh?'

'For Ravenglass.'

'You mean Hugh. You bought me. You thought it was all right to do that.'

Jason went out on to the balcony. The whole Roman world lay there, coasts all round the compass, out of sight though so narrow in the global scale. 'You look right here,' he said. She was on the balcony too now. Her anger seemed a small thing against all this. Still, it was hers and not his to dismiss. He ran his fingers through her untidy hair and spread it out behind like a fan. She looked a bit absurd like that, but she didn't know. Absurd and alarming and fertile like one of those figures in the archeological museum here. He heard chanting from further along the street, mostly children. A procession for the saint of the day. 'I did it for us too.'

'I don't feel right. Too many churches.'

'There's a good maternity hospital.'

'How d'you know?'

'Because I asked, of course.'

'You're lying.'

'Honest.'

'I like the stone,' Rosie said. 'Honey. It looks soft.' She might be coming round. 'You don't think Hugh'll jump out of a window?'

'No. He's got the insurance award to keep his feet on the ground. That was the point.' He felt a passionate pity for

Hugh, like a child dying of something painful, a child already dead; but he didn't feel remorse any more. Hagar Qim had cured that.

She looked at him. 'Was it?'

Jason toughed it out. 'Oh yes.'

'Then how did you mean, you did it for us too?'

Jason saw he was dealing here with someone pretty sharp. Just as well. She would keep an eye on him, and the redundancy money. He explained about that. 'I made sure my mother got a straightener as well.'

Rosie laughed with what sounded like big relief. 'Oh if you're still worrying about her—' she said. 'So we're all in the same lifeboat.' She had one hand on her belly, and put the other to the back of Jason's neck and held on hard, like tying up to a capstan. 'It won't be ships any more, will it?'

'Ships, they're finished. They had a long run, nothing's for ever.'

'So this is where we begin.' She stared out at the domes and cranes and towers and the sea beyond. 'But I don't want you redundant.'

'We'll invest,' Jason said.

'Will we? What in?' Sideways on, they looked at each other, searching for an answer. 'I hardly know you, really,' Rosie said.

'But in a way better than you've ever known anyone else. Same for me.'

'One way isn't many.'

Jason thought she meant could she trust him? How far, for how long? Blind trust to be withdrawn any time a person sees the light is probably overrated anyway. He'd have to work on it. He turned, took the hand she had on her belly and raised it out of his way – so it was not just their eyes meeting, merging; but the whole system at once.